RAVEN'S SHADE

Lyrics quoted from the song I Go Like the Raven are (C) David Robert Carter (BMI) admin. by Tracy Grammer Music and are used with permission.

Interior design by Kamila Miller kzmiller.com

ISBN: 9798707796708

First print edition 2021

This is a work of fiction. Any resemblance to real people, living or dead, is purely coincidental.

RAVEN'S SHADE

SHAWNA REPPERT

Author's Note

Readers from the Pacific Northwest and in particular Portland will find the setting quite familiar. The Blue Moon and the Barley Mill are real pubs owned by McMenamins and both Fireside Port and Terminator Stout are among the offerings. (I particularly recommend the port.)

Of course, there are differences. The Ravenscroft house in the Nob Hill district of Portland does not exist since the Ravenscroft family as I have written them do not exist. (There are other Ravenscrofts, certainly. One is a hatter in the UK, and one was a collector of folk ballads in the manner of Childe, though not as well known. To the best of the knowledge there is no relation.)

The song Tony is singing along to is I Go Like the Raven (© David Robert Carter (BMI) admin. by Tracy Grammer Music. David Carter is sadly no longer with us, but his music lives on. He was an amazing singer and song writer and I strongly recommend you check out the albums he released with Tracy Grammer as well as Tracy's solo work. (As an aside, they used to live and perform in Oregon and still have a strong following here.))

Wilhelm's Mausoleum, which gets a brief mention in the book, is a real place. It is historic and full of beautiful stained glass and statuary. They have occasional open houses with tours, and I highly recommend you take advantage if you are in the area. The sexton Simon Reeves, however, is a fictional character of my own invention.

The town of Devil's Crossing and the butte known as Devil's Boneyard are fictional locations loosely based on the geography and small towns in the high desert regions of the Pacific Northwest. Likewise, the particular petroglyphs mentioned in the book do not exist. This was a deliberate choice as I did not want to appropriate or misrepresent the culture of any existing tribe.

There are, however, ancient petroglyphs in the Pacific Northwest. The most famous of these is She Who Watches in the Columbia Hills Historical State Park, Washington. Though I have yet to have the privilege of being in her presence, my experiences with the other petroglyphs in the park inspired, in part, this book.

I mean only the greatest respect to those who brought the petroglyphs into being and to their living descendants.

Dedication:

To the memory of the late Mary Rosenblum. More than just an editor, she was a mentor, a coach, a supporter and a friend. My writing would not be what it is today without her. I hope always to do her proud.

And, as always, to all the people who believed in me even at those times when I didn't believe in myself. These are as much your books as they are mine.

In Memoriam

For Eddie Osborn, reader and an early and constant supporter. The world is diminished by your loss.

One

Raven should have been suspicious the moment that his wife's work partner asked to meet up even though Cassandra was not herself home from work. In fact, as the conversation unfolded, he began to suspect that the timing was deliberate. And yet he found himself sitting at the Blue Moon, sipping a glass of Fireside Port, watching Rafe make abstract designs in the condensation on his pint of Terminator Stout. On the table by Rafe's elbow was a manila folder of the type Cassandra often used to bring home files for the cases that she was working on.

"You're the only one that I can ask," Rafe wheedled. "You know I wouldn't ask otherwise. When have I ever asked you for a favor before?"

Raven sat back against the wooden backrest of their window booth and closed his eyes. The warm, salty scent of the house-made fries that Rafe had ordered rose up from the basket between them. Raven had never developed the fondness for pub food that Cassandra and her colleagues shared, but the scent was appetizing.

Raven took a sip of the strong, sweet port as he contemplated Rafe's request. In the back part of the pub, pool balls clacked gently.

In truth, he could never recall Rafe *ever* asking for a favor. Their acquaintance had gotten off to a rocky start—Rafe had attempted to frame Raven for a crime that would have seen him locked behind magic-dampening fields for the rest of his natural life. But in the intervening years, Rafe had become a solid friend to Raven and Cassandra both through good times and bad. Raven felt better knowing Rafe had Cassandra's back no matter how dangerous things got at work. Hell, the man had even babysat Ransley when they were truly strapped for a sitter.

The waitress stopped by their table to ask if there was something else they needed, though they were barely halfway through their drinks. The way her eyes passed over Rafe betrayed the reason for her attentiveness. Rafe, like most Guardian International Investigations agents, took fitness seriously and it showed in both his frame and his carriage. Combined with his stylishly disheveled black hair and roguish grin, the man caught his share of attention from both men and women.

Once, Rafe would have noticed the waitress' appreciation. Pre-Cam, it would have won her a flirtatious grin, if not an invitation to dinner. Raven hadn't suspected that he would miss the old Rafe. He liked the man Rafe had become when he had been with Cam even better. Rafe had already begun learning to see shades of gray that fell between black and white before he had met Cam, but Cam had changed him further still. Rafe had become softer, somehow. Not in any way that would interfere with his job. But he had been more willing to see the good in people, more ready to see the value in giving people second chances. Those changes had not gone away with Cam's death, but Rafe had become more somber. Less spirited. Stuck to business instead of lightening the mood with his dark humor. Raven missed that, even if Rafe's jokes had often been at Raven's expense.

Raven was not the man he would have been without Cassandra, and his life was infinitely better for it. He had wanted that same happy ending for Rafe and Cam, but that fairy tale had been cut short by a madman's knife. Raven could only hope Rafe would someday find someone—not to replace Cam, as Cam was irreplaceable—but someone to be to Rafe what Cam would have been in the fullness of time.

"I may consult with GII from time to time," Raven said. They both knew that Guardian International Investigations called him in whenever it found itself dealing with magic more complicated, powerful, or dark than it could handle on its own. "But you know I'm no trained investigator. And the more time I spend working with GII, or even the local Guardians, the more I respect what that means."

Rafe chuckled. "Never thought I'd hear you admit it." He toasted Raven with the microbrew in his hand before taking a swig. "But seriously, I think you've picked up more than you realize. I'm not asking you to do much. Just go up there and poke around a bit. Just a few days. If you find anything of interest, you can turn it over to the local Guardians and be on your merry way."

Rafe was probably betting on the possibility that if he found anything of interest, he'd be too intrigued to leave it alone.

Raven selected one of the soft pretzel sticks from his own appetizer and swiped it through the cheese fondue. "What is your interest in all this?" he hedged.

Rafe blushed, the flush evident even over his golden-tan complexion. "There's a guy I know who asked me to look into it."

"Wait, so you're asking me to look into this case because you have a personal stake in the outcome, or because you're doing a personal favor for a friend?"

"Um, a little bit of both?"

Raven raised both eyebrows and waited.

"So I met this guy."

"Go on."

Raven fought a smile. The more Rafe hesitated, the more Raven suspected there was more to the story. He enjoyed teasing the man, of course he did, but he was happy to see him take *some* interest in someone again. Cam wouldn't have wanted Rafe to stop living his own life just because Cam had died. He had been too kind and too in love with life to wish that for Rafe.

"I was—oh, God, this is going to sound weird, but I had gone out to put flowers on Cam's grave. It was a year ago last week that—" Rafe broke off and took a deep, steadying breath.

A year since Cam had been struck down by a killer with a grudge against Rafe's and Cassandra's boss at GII. Raven had nearly lost both Cassandra and their infant son to the same madman.

Rafe scrubbed his hands over his face as though washing away the memory, and Raven knew he was as trapped as a suspect in a sting. He would do whatever would help the man find a new shot at happiness. Gods help him. And Cassandra wasn't even here to talk him into it, so he couldn't blame her for it later.

"Start from the beginning." Raven sighed. "You may as well tell me everything."

Two weeks earlier.

The memorial, dedication, and ribbon-cutting ceremony had been excruciating. Rafe was glad that so many people remembered Cam—the man deserved to be remembered. He had been the finest human being Rafe had ever met, had changed Rafe's life so fundamentally that he knew he would never be the same man he was before, didn't *want* to be the man he was before. And this—a newer, bigger facility for the troubled kids that Cam had dedicated his life to helping, with a better gym and recreational facilities, private consulting rooms that were both better sound-proofed and more comfortable, and an animal-assisted therapy program. A few blocks away was a shelter for kids that had either run away or had been kicked out of their homes. By fall there would be an out-of-town equestrian program with a shuttle running between. How much of the funding came from the Ravenscroft Charitable Trust, Rafe could only guess, and Raven would never tell.

It was bittersweet, seeing Cam's family again for the first time since the funeral. Mrs. MacEwan had been the one to do the ribbon cutting, although she had first offered Rafe the honor. He declined, not because he didn't support the project with all his heart and soul. But he felt that the woman who had brought Cam into the world and raised him to be the man that he had been had far more claim than the man who had been his lover for less than a year. Lover, not husband. Rafe had just been waiting for an appropriate period of time to ask Cam to accept a ring to follow where Rafe's heart had already been given. A year seemed like the right time, in fact the absolute minimum. Now he wished he hadn't waited.

The speeches had all been made, the ribbon cut, and if Rafe had thought the worst of it was over, he was wrong. The MacEwans came to surround him like a warm blanket of strawberry-blond and auburn familial love, asking why he'd made himself a stranger and when was he coming over to dinner and no, they wouldn't take no for an answer.

"You're still part of the family, you know," Mrs. MacEwan had said, and that hurt worst of all. Because he had *wanted* to be part of this family, wanted there to be huge family gatherings where the rose-pale MacEwans and the golden-dark Ramirezes mingled like chess pieces that had declared a permanent peace in order to talk about grandchildren and football and the best dishes to bring to church potlucks. But that would never happen now. Oh, the families would still get on like puppies in a playpen, but it would be a shared grief, not a shared joy, that united them, and it would never be as he had dreamed.

Still he hugged her. "It's so good to see you, Mom MacEwan. I promise I'll be by for cake when that rascal Erin graduates from film school."

"That won't be long now, and I'll be sure to hold you to it." She kissed his cheek before dashing off to snatch a chubby fair-haired toddler in a Hello Kitty dress who was trying to stuff a handful of leaves into her mouth.

He had thought he had healed, moved on. But now he wondered if reminders of what he had shared with Cam, of all he had *wanted* to share in their futures, would ever fail to knock him flat.

He walked two blocks to a florist shop on the corner, one owned by a Craft person of literary bent. Rafe hadn't figured out yet if the man practiced shamanic magic, Wicca, or something else entirely, but he could feel that he was neither an Art practitioner nor a Mundane. Rafe bought from him a bouquet filled with rosemary (for remembrance, according to the proprietor, who quoted some line from some play that Raven would probably recognize instantly), sage (sweet-smelling and used for cleansing and consecrating, though Rafe declined to ask what exactly was supposed to be cleansed or consecrated) and a half-dozen blanketflowers. The name of the flower had probably come from the bright-colored Pendleton trade blankets, but Cam had liked them because they reminded him of tie-dye, and Rafe liked them because they reminded him of Cam.

With all the times he had been there, it took him less than a thought to teleport to Cam's graveside. He knelt and laid the flowers against the stone. "Hard to believe it's been a year," he said as he said as he straightened up. "I thought we'd have forever. I *meant* for it to be forever. Did you know I was looking for rings?" He sighed, half in fondness, half in sorrow. "Probably you did. Knowing you, you were just giving me the space to do things in my own time. I thought there was no hurry. Now I wish I'd gone down on one knee that morning after the very first night, right after we had that disagreement about forgiving youthful offenders involved in death magic, and you forced me to admit that you might have a point. By the way, that kid we were arguing about just turned nineteen. I wrote him a reference letter for Guardian Academy last week.

"Anyway, I should have asked you right then. Or if not then, then after I messaged you drunk after we lost too many good men and women taking down William and for some reason I thought that a crazy, bleeding-heart social worker was the only one who I could talk to. Well, I was right. You came over, got me sober, and held me until I fell asleep." He laughed softly, shaking his head. "You might have just been crazy enough to say yes, even though we'd just met.

"I think I knew, even then. It just seemed kinda crazy, you know? And by the time we'd been together long enough for me to trust it was real, well, I was just trying to find the right time. The right place, the right way. Did I buy the ring first? That's always how it goes in the movies. But then it seemed like you should have a say in picking out the rings. We'd have been wearing them for the rest of our lives." He paused to swallow, trying to rid himself of the lump in his throat. "And then, in an instant, I realized that none of that mattered, and then it was too late."

He put a hand on the rounded top of the tombstone, letting the cool solidity of the granite ground him. Granite, not marble. The MacEwans had been Portlanders from way back, and they knew that granite stood up to the Pacific Northwest rains where marble melted over time. The breeze picked up, ruffling his hair. He tried to imagine it was Cam's fingers combing through the short strands, tried to imagine Cam there with him, but he lacked the ability to lie to himself like that.

"You needn't bother. There's no one here to impress."

Rafe stood and turned in one movement at the words spoken behind him, startled to be disturbed in so private a moment and too confused by the words to immediately find the anger they deserved. "Excuse me?"

"You made your token show at the ribbon-cutting ceremony. You've demonstrated—for any that will believe you—that you Guardians aren't just waiting for the center's kids to screw up so you can lock the kids away for good. At least leave Cameron's graveside to those who knew him best." The man who spoke was about Cam's age, which made him only a little younger than Rafe. Shoulder-length hair, tightly curled, sun-bleached. Eyes ice-blue; cheekbones high and prominent; nose long, sloped, and slightly pointed; skin Nordic-pale. In different clothes, he might make an extra in that Vikings show one of his Mundane friends demanded that he watch. Not a warrior— he didn't have the bulk of someone who routinely swung a battle-ax. Maybe a villager, a potter or some sort of craftsman. Easy enough on the eyes that, in another time and place, Rafe might have considered trying to pick him up.

He was not anyone Cam had introduced him to, not even in passing. Cam had a lot of friends, but this interloper was not someone easily forgotten.

Rafe narrowed his eyes at the stranger. "Knew Cam well, did you?"

"Well enough to know he wasn't the type to consort with Guardians."

"Really. And where did you know him from?"

"Undergrad. We both did a psych undergrad at Reed. We were close as brothers, once. But he went on to PSU to get his Master's in social work and I dropped out and went backpacking through Europe. I've never been good at staying in touch. I eventually finished up my Bachelors and then took some time off to decide what I wanted to do with my life. I was on a retreat, hiking in Iceland when Cam was killed. I didn't hear about it until six months after. There was a letter from his mother in my held mail."

"I was in the waiting area down the hall from the operating room when he died." Rafe said.

"Oh." The stranger's voice softened a little, lost some of the challenge that had edged it. "He was working with one of your suspects?"

"He was my lover."

The man flushed bright pink with embarrassment. "Oh. Oh, I'm sorry. You must think me a total ass."

"You could say that." Rafe wasn't in the mood to mince words.

The stranger ran a hand through his unruly hair. "Oh, gods, Cam would give me hell for this if he were here."

Rafe couldn't help but smile a little. "Probably. But a very quiet, reasonable, supportive hell."

"That makes you feel worse than if he hauled off and ripped you a new one."

"So you did know Cam."

The look of bittersweet nostalgia that crossed the stranger's face caused a reluctant swell of fellow-feeling. "I did. And every time we met up, or even talked on the message crystal, it was like the months, the years since we last got together just vanished. But each time more and more time passed between, and I kept meaning to reach out, but something always came up, until three years had gone by and I was looking at a letter from his mother inviting me to his funeral and the postmark was six months old."

"Damn." Despite himself, Rafe felt a twinge of sympathy. He'd lost touch with a lot of his friends from Guardian Academy, and the last get-together had been the funeral of a promising lieutenant.

The stranger grimaced. "Nobody's fault but my own."

"Hey, Cam was never a fan of fault and shame." Though Rafe had never been a big believer in the idea of ghosts lingering to guide the living, he still had to blame his late lover's generous spirit for that one. Or maybe Cam had just influenced him that much in the time they were together.

The stranger gave a soft chuckle. "Thanks for that. Especially after what I said about Guardians at the beginning."

Rafe wasn't going to rub it in; the stranger did a good enough job of that all by himself. "I'm Rafe, by the way." He extended a hand.

"Name's Scott."

Cam's old friend had a good handshake—firm, but not the crushing grip of a man with too much to prove, the hand itself pleasantly warm but not sweaty, the skin callused. Rafe's wayward imagination instantly wondered what those hands would feel like in an entirely different context. Clearly it had been too long since he had gotten laid.

"Scott—?" Rafe prompted, though he had absolutely no idea why he would want the stranger's last name, or any other information about the man. True, he had been Cam's friend, but sounded like a bit of a fly-by-night and he clearly had a chip on his shoulder with law enforcement.

"Scott Mankin. Though if you plan on doing a background search, my full name's Percival Prescott Mankin."

"Percival Prescott?" Rafe repeated incredulously, before he had time to consider the rudeness of his response.

Scott laughed. "Yeah, if you think I'm a flake, you should have met my parents back in the day."

Caught off guard by the man's perceptiveness, Rafe stammered. "I never said—"

"You didn't have to." Scott seemed more amused than offended though. "My mom called me Percy when I was young, gods help me. I started introducing myself as Scott by the time I was in middle school."

Rafe grimaced in sympathy. "My parents named me Raphael Romeo Ramirez. Fortunately, I had older sisters with more sense, and so they started calling me Rafe before I even came home from the hospital."

And why had he confessed to that? He could think of few people outside his immediate family who knew his middle name, and he liked to keep it that way.

Scott laughed again. He had a nice laugh, deep and warm, and the skin at the corners of his eyes said that the crows' feet just beginning weren't all due to squinting into sunlight. It was very hard to dislike the man when he laughed.

"Look," Scott said after a moment. "Do you want to grab a beer or something? This isn't a come-on," he added quickly. "I'm not tacky enough to try to pick up a man at his lover's graveside. It's just, I'm not looking forward to sitting alone in my generic hotel room, staring at the generic art on the walls."

TWO

Raven saw Rafe shudder as though shaking himself back to the present. Raven was surprised at the level of vulnerability the man had shown him. He was more surprised still that he didn't find it more uncomfortable than he did. Oh, they had long moved past mutual distrust. Raven could count on Rafe to have his back in a magical firefight, and he knew Rafe would return the favor. Had, in fact, on more than one occasion.

But heartfelt talks were another thing entirely, for both of them. The day of Cam's memorial must have been really rough on him. This Scott was the first person, man or woman, that Rafe had shown interest in. Though nothing in Rafe's tale made the man sound particularly charming, to each his own. Just the fact that Scott caught Rafe's attention, got him thinking about something other than his grief and his work, made him worthy of Raven's assistance.

He sighed. "All right, tell me everything you know."

Rafe smiled in relief, though there was a touch of smugness, as well, as though he'd known all along that Raven would give in. "How much do you know about the Devil's Boneyard golf course?"

Raven shrugged. "Idiot from the East Coast with more money than sense trying to build a golf course in the middle of high desert."

Rafe nodded. "And trampling all over ranchers' and tribes' irrigation rights in the process. Not to mention destroying an environmentally sensitive area with a lot of cultural significance. They just discovered a cave with petroglyphs that had been forgotten since long before the Mariner landed. Petroglyphs believed to be older than even the oldest found in Mariner State."

Raven hid a smile. Cam had certainly left his mark. The old Rafe would never have given a thought to environmental concerns, let alone heritage preservation.

"Scott's been working at a place not too far from the Devil's Boneyard. Place called Second Chance Ranch. They run rehabilitation programs for troubled teens. Some of his kids were up in arms about the whole thing—not literally, but it was close. Anyway, Scott decided to use the whole thing as a springboard for teaching about civil disobedience, political activism, the pros and cons of various methods to promote one's cause within a democracy. Even had a lawyer friend come in to teach a unit on property law, land use restrictions, the whole gamut. Some of his older kids managed a coalition that united the local tribes and the local ranchers to work against the project—something that most politically experienced adults would never even dream of."

"Impressive." Why was Rafe telling him all this? If he was looking for a pledge of funds, he would have been more likely to go through Cassandra as the softer touch. Raven wouldn't be averse to writing a check, but he had a feeling that Rafe wanted something else.

"Magnum Lansing—that's the chief East Coast idiot—was found dead in the cave under the butte at Devil's Boneyard. The cave with all the petroglyphs. The coroner wasn't able to determine the exact method used, but the whole cave was so thick with dark magic that even the Mundane deputies who secured the scene could feel it. Devil's Crossing is so small that they don't have separate Mundane police and Guardian departments. They called out the sheriff, who's Art-trained. Guy's a part-timer who runs the only bar in town, place called Devil's Pitchfork." Rafe rolled his eyes at the name.

Raven shuddered, imagining a tacky sign with a stereotypical red devil in a cowboy hat, holding a pitchfork. Not exactly a cultural mecca Rafe was trying to send him to.

"So, this Craig Schmidt —that's the part-time sheriff—his leading theory is that one of the recent graduates from Second Chance is responsible." Rafe finished. "Morgan Jansen. Kid dipped his toes into dark magic once, but he had a clean record before and was a counselor's dream in the program. Bright kid, Scott said. Should have been in college, not doing time in juvie. Probably blew his whole future on that one mistake and he knew it, but he wasn't about to make the same mistake twice."

"To play devil's advocate—if you will forgive the pun—any investigator would be remiss if they didn't even look into the possibility. Stopping the golf course is a pretty strong motivation, and at the risk of sounding like a hypocrite, one can't discount entirely a history of dark magic."

Rafe shook his head, chuckling. "Who would have thought we'd come to this?"

"It does rather seem like a role reversal of the day we met, only without the shouting and the death threats."

"Look, I'm not saying for sure the kid is innocent," Rafe said. "I realize Scott is hardly an impartial source. But from what Scott said, the sheriff isn't even looking into other suspects. There's a whole lot of people out there who hated Lansing, for a whole lot of very valid reasons. And the sheriff has his own interest in the golf course controversy. He thinks that the resort will bring more business to the bar. Personally, I can't imagine those fancy golfer types slumming at a place like the Pitchfork. It's more likely that some of the local folk will start going to the nice, quiet restaurant and bar that the resort is holding up as a benefit to the community. But from what Scott says, the sheriff's the type to latch onto an idea and not let go for something as silly as logic."

"And you're afraid this tendency carries over to his investigative work." He refrained from pointing out Rafe's own history. The man had changed, and Raven could hardly ask people to overlook the mistakes of his own past and not grant the same grace to others.

Rafe grimaced. "I just would sleep better if someone I trusted looked things over. One thing I learned, getting involved with Cam and the Center, is that it's hard for a kid in with a reputation to get a fair shake, even with supposedly sealed juvenile records."

Raven gave an ironic smile. "You don't say." In his own case, his family name had been enough to damn him back in General

Academy. He hadn't even been practicing dark magic, at least not until well into his majority.

"So you'll go, then?"

Raven sighed deeply. "Maybe Sherlock can let the locals know I'm on my way."

"Locals aren't always terribly fond of GII," Rafe warned. "Not so sure that'd have them rolling out the red carpet."

The turf wars between local Guardians and Guardian International Investigations were every bit as legendary as those between Guardians and Mundane police. "Yes, but with her reputation for protecting her people, at least they won't be tempted to arrest me on trumped-up charges." Sherlock was clever, determined, and knew how to leverage her team's success rate into political capital. The recent public revelations of questionable associations of her youth may have left her reputation with a slight tarnish, but it diminished her influence not a bit.

"Here, look at these." Secure in his victory, Rafe pushed the folder across the table to Raven.

The first thing he saw when he opened the manila folder was black-and-white photographs of Magnum Lansing's corpse as it was found in the cave. The man had been fit in life; he was built like someone who had played football in his youth and still exercised occasionally, although the belly sneaking over his belt said he sat down to a good steak more regularly than he went to the gym. If the body had not splayed like someone frozen as they writhed in pain, the well-tailored suit might have hidden the extra pounds. Raven himself admired a well-cut jacket and well-fitted trousers, and Lansing certainly spared no expense in presenting a sharp image.

A lot of good it had done him. No amount of tailoring could distract from a face so contorted by fear and pain that it looked nearly inhuman. Raven's first thought went to soul-stealers; could even a small-town coroner miss such an obvious cause of death? But no. As he looked more closely at the photo, he realized that what he had taken for a puddle of water or even a shadow was a pool of blood, the red turned black by the grayscale image. Quite a lot of blood. Raven was familiar with how much blood the human body held and what it looked like spilled out onto a floor. If Magnum hadn't died of terror, he'd bled out. Probably from the mouth and nose, to judge by the streaks on his face, unless the body's position hid some sort of wound to the back. No soul-stealer caused that sort of blood loss. He could name a number of magically-enhanced poisons that might do it, but he couldn't imagine even the most incompetent coroner missing the toxins in the blood.

He flipped forward to look at the tox report. Yes, they'd run a full panel using both forensic magic and Mundane toxicology, and there was nothing remarkable in the blood, not even alcohol. And, gods, when had he started talking like a Guardian in his head? Cassandra and her friends were clearly a bad influence.

Raven itched to get out to that cave before the last vestiges of a magical signature faded. He'd have to get permission from the local law enforcement if the cave was still taped off as a crime scene. He sighed. Sherlock would never forgive him if he broke the law without a damned good reason, and he didn't think she counted impatience and inconvenience as a good reason.

"You're welcome to come to dinner," Raven said. "I know Cassandra would love it. You haven't been by in months." Not since they'd hired Tony Borzoff as a male nanny. (Raven refused to use the ridiculous modern slang, *manny.*)

"Will *he* be there?"

No, I thought I'd just leave Ransley all alone in his crib while I popped down to meet you. "Considering that he lives in my house and cares for my child, I should think so."

"Then thank you, no."

"I know you don't like him—"

"Look, I get that he saved Cassandra's life. I understand why you felt obligated to give him a hand up. Personally, the idea of him alone with Ransley makes me shudder, but I accept that being an honorary uncle doesn't give me a vote in your child-care decisions. Believe me, I sincerely hope that you're right and I'm wrong. But I refuse to sit down at the table with the man who threatened my life."

Raven didn't bother to point out that the threat had come years ago, and had been the empty bluster of a desperate young man in an emotionally fraught situation. That Tony had admitted that he'd been stupid and impetuous and had never had any intention of carrying through. That Tony had only turned to the manufacture of illegal magically enhanced pharmaceuticals because he'd been caught in a financial quagmire not of his own making, that he had served his time and was doing his best to turn his life around.

It was not a long walk back from the Blue Moon, not long enough for Raven to get those images in the folder out of his head. What kind of magic did that? Dark magic, obviously, but he'd never seen anything quite like what the pictures had shown him. Dark magic that even he didn't know. Frightening indeed. He entered the door to hear—was that that fiddle music? Tony was dancing around the parlor, bopping Ransley up and down to the music and singing along. *Shine the merlin moonbeam eye, set my dancing feet to fly, o'er the dark and dervish sky I go like the raven.*

What in the world?

He must've said something out loud. Tony turned around, snatched up a remote and pointed it at the stereo Cassandra had insisted that they needed. The music muted but did not stop. *When they hear my bowstring strings tightenin', angels gay, devils frightenin'. Come on fire and midnight lightning to the garden gancy.*

Garden gancy? What even was that? And what did the singer have against final *g* sounds?

"Oh, hi, boss," Tony grinned cheerfully. His feet had stopped, but he still bounced the baby up and down. "Dave Carter and Tracy Grammer. Heard them before?"

It took Raven a moment to realize that he was talking about the music.

"No, I don't suspect they're your kind of music." Tony grinned as he answered his own question. "Should give it a listen though. Carter was classically trained, believe it or not. Though on cello, not guitar. Tracy is the one on fiddle. Dave wrote all the lyrics."

Raven merely nodded. He was not going to be one of those heads of household who insisted that the help be seen but not heard. He refused to be anything like his father.

Besides Tony wasn't exactly a typical nanny, having been less than a semester away from a degree in magic/chemistry fusion when his arrest forever destroyed his hopes and dreams. Very much overqualified to be a household servant, but his criminal record meant no lab would ever hire him. But Raven had his own personal reasons for believing in second chances. Not to mention, with Tony living in the house, they had a ready consultant whenever GII had a scientific issue that needed to be dealt with. At least one that wasn't computer related; for that they had Chuckie, Cassandra's former partner and self-styled techno-mage.

"You're looking a little grim," Tony said. "Thought you were just going for lunch with Rafe. I know you guys snip at each other all the time, but I thought you enjoyed it."

"Yes. No. Lunch was fine. Rafe just wanted me to look into something for him."

"Something case related? Thought he'd go to Cass for that."

"Not official business. Just something he wants me to poke my long nose into."

He wasn't going to ruin anyone else's day with the knowledge of what happened down in Devil's Crossing.

Ransley, still on Tony's hip, gurgled loudly, smiling and waving a pudgy hand in the direction of the stereo speakers. His son, transitioning from infant to toddler, already started to exhibit preferences in music. He preferred Mozart to Brahms, although Little Bunny Foofoo remained his favorite. Raven just hoped the child didn't pick up Tony's tastes, but he'd read enough parenting guides to know he'd have to grin and bear it if he did. But surely playing Ransley more classical music would keep him on track.

"Oh, I talked to Cass on the crystal while you were out. She's stuck in Seattle chasing down a lead in that human trafficking case. Said to go ahead and have dinner without her. With luck, she'll be home late tonight. Otherwise she'll grab a room in a hotel up there."

Raven had hoped for a quiet night in with Cassandra, since he was going to be gone for a few days. Still, he had known what he was getting into when he married her, and he was proud of his wife and her work. This human trafficking case was particularly grim. The traffickers had, for reasons yet unknown, turned on their latest load of human cargo, slit their throats, and dumped their bodies in the Willamette River.

He was glad of Tony's company over dinner. Much as Raven loved his son, the one-year-old wasn't much of a conversationalist. Left alone with just Ransley, Raven spent entirely too much time worrying about all the mistakes he might make in raising a child to adulthood. Tony took his responsibilities seriously, but he never seemed to have the same types of worries. The younger man stepped into the role of caregiver with a cheerful, casual confidence Raven felt the least bit intimidated by, though he'd never admit it.

When Tony moved in, Raven hadn't imagined he'd have much in common with a tie-dye wearing folk music aficionado. But Tony had a brilliant mind and shared Raven's interest in magical innovation and experimentation. His background in magically-enhanced chemistry might be different than Raven's training in pure magic, but that just meant long discussions on comparative approaches.

When Raven had negotiated his pardon, the best he had hoped for was a quiet, solitary life in his ancestral house on the hill. Somehow, his life kept getting fuller and more complicated as he went along.

Raven woke as soon as the bedroom door opened. His past had made him a light sleeper, and the relative domesticity of his present life had not lessened the trait. Cassandra padded lightly across the polished wood floor. She must have removed her shoes downstairs in a vain attempt not to wake him. He smiled at the courtesy, even though it was useless. He continued his pretense at sleep until she had undressed and slid into bed, then rolled to face her.

"Hello, beloved," he said, voice deepened by the dregs of sleep.

She smiled and leaned in for a kiss. "How long have you been awake?"

"Since you came into the room." He pushed back a lock of her wildly curling hair before stealing another kiss.

In this light, her hair looked black as the night around them, as dark as his own. In sunlight or firelight her hair would glint here and there with auburn and flame-red, while his would remain the onyx-black of his Welsh ancestors.

"I had to call Rafe for some details I'd forgotten when I was wrapping up the case. I think I woke him."

"Good," Raven said without heat, a pretense of animosity for old times' sake.

Cassandra narrowed her eyes at him, meaning it exactly as much as he had meant the comment. "He said you were going down to someplace called Devil's Crossing to look into something for him."

"Yes. You don't mind, do you?" He belatedly realized that a good husband would have asked before making plans. He tried, he really did. He thought he was getting better.

"Of course not." Cassandra's tone said he was being silly. "After all the times I've gone dashing up and down the coast chasing a lead, and with little or no notice?"

He let out a breath he didn't know he was holding. Their marriage was anything but normal, but he doubted normal would have worked for them. He shifted himself closer to her naked warmth. She snuggled into his chest and he wrapped his arms around her.

"I'm still not sure this is a good idea," he said into her hair. "I'm only a consultant, not officially GII at all."

"And this isn't an official investigation," she mumbled sleepily into his chest. "You'll do fine."

The casual way she gave the assurance, as though she didn't have to think about it, gave him confidence.

"Not like you to doubt yourself," she said.

"Not like me to play detective."

"Hey, you've worked with the best." Cassandra looked up at him with a sassy grin. "I'm sure you've picked up a thing or two. Besides, it's—"

19

"Not an official investigation," he finished with her.

"You know, Ana says she still feels bad about not helping you more when you applied for the Guardian Academy after General Academy. You would have been an amazing Guardian. You could be an agent with GII, not just a consultant."

"She gave me a letter of recommendation. That's more than any of my other teachers would do. And she negotiated the terms of my pardon when I decided to turn away from William, despite my years of dark magic at William's right hand. I owe her my life."

Ana *could* have done more, though. She had smoothed the way for her nephew, despite his questionable academics and disciplinary record throughout General Academy. Raven's only sin at that time had been being born a Ravenscroft.

"If I had become a Guardian back then we wouldn't have had someone on the inside to stop William," he said. "The Three Communities could be on its knees to him. Things worked out for the best."

"But at what cost to you?"

"It's all in the past now," he said after a moment.

It wasn't, not really. He still had nightmares about the screams of those he killed at William's behest. But nothing he could do could ever change what he had done. Perhaps, if he lived long enough and worked hard enough, he could come close to balancing the scales. But this was not the topic he wanted either of them to be thinking about as they drifted to sleep."

"I'm glad you're home," he said. "I'm glad I had the chance to see you before I left."

"Mmm," she agreed. "I just wish I weren't so tired."

He kissed the top of her head. "Sleep. We have our whole lives ahead of us."

THREE

Raven had arranged to use the hostess of the AirBnB as an anchor to teleport. The rental included the entirety of a small cottage separate from the main house. Raven usually preferred the reliability of a commercial, five-star establishment, but this particular lodging came recommended by Cassandra's aunt Ana. One of Ana's old school friends, a Healer-turned-artist, rented the place out for additional income. Raven disliked using a stranger as a teleport anchor—it felt too intimate. But given that he had never been to the place before, his only alternative would be hiring a Mundane car and driver, and he preferred to avoid those fast-moving Mundane death traps whenever possible.

When he fully faded back into existence, he found himself in a clearing at the center of a sweet-smelling herb garden. He stood face-to-face with a woman of athletic build with pale, straight hair that hung nearly to her waist. She wore a gauzy, embroidered blouse of pale rose and a faded denim skirt with paint splotches down the front. Looking closer, he saw a bit of blue paint on the ends of her hair, as if she forgot to put her hair back before starting to work on a canvas.

"Hi, I'm Jasmine. And you must be Raven. Let me show you the cottage."

He followed her down a path of mosaic stepping stones to a small yellow house trimmed in robin's-egg blue. The interior of the cottage was done in finished pine and still smelled faintly of that wood. It had an open floor plan; no wall between the bedroom and the living area and only a short half-wall between the living area and the efficiency kitchen. The cathedral ceiling exposed the support beams that held up the roof. The hand-woven tapestries and soft knitted throws made the place cozy in a way that reminded him of Ana's own home. The place was clean, and the distance from both the main house and the road meant that it would be quiet as well.

Raven agreed that the cottage would do nicely for his purposes, and Jasmine keyed the wards to him so that he could feel secure and yet still teleport directly into the cottage if he chose.

He stared at the wall, or rather at the landscape painting that hung on the wall, a beautiful acrylic of a sunset behind the Devil's Boneyard done in gorgeous purples, oranges, and reds. The boldly scrawled signature on the bottom declared it the work of his host. Raven wondered if it was for sale. Cassandra would love it.

Raven introduced himself to the deputy at the reception desk for the Devil's Crossing P.D. and she led him back to an interview room. The moment they crossed the anti-magic ward the hair on the back of his neck stood up and his heart beat faster in a flight-or-fight response. It was something he should've expected; after all, any jail that held mages would have one. No mage liked anti-magic wards, but Raven's unease was specific and personal. He'd been held behind similar wards a time or two in his life, and those were some of the worst memories of his life. He reminded himself that he was there of his own free will. He could leave at any time. No one dared lay a hand on someone with his contacts without a damned good reason, even if he was not there representing Guardian International Investigations at this moment. He jumped in his chair when the door opened behind him, instantly annoyed at himself for his nerves.

"It gets to all of us, you know."

Raven spun the chair to see a man in a sheriff's uniform standing in the doorway behind him. He'd heard the footsteps in the hall, but subconsciously registered them as another deputy or clerk going about business.

"Beg pardon?" Before thinking Raven spoke in the cool, slightly arrogant tones that tended to set off every Guardian's triggers.

Cassandra called it the Bad Old Raven voice, and usually trod on his toes whenever he used it. He could practically hear her voice in his head. *Yes, no one's forgotten you used to be a dark mage and William's right hand. But forcing them to confront the fact isn't helping. Believe it or not, the good that you've done recently outweighs the past in most people's minds, even Guardians. And for the rest, why give them the satisfaction?*

If the stranger minded the tone, he didn't show it. Instead, he smiled and made a vague gesture meant to take in the room, or maybe the building as a whole. "The anti-magic wards. I think they spook everyone who uses magic. Art and Craft both. My skin still crawls every time I pass into the custody section of the building. Some of my deputies will literally trade for the worst shit patrol jobs rather than get stuck behind the wards for a shift."

Raven took the opportunity to study the man. His skin was leathery from sun exposure and so deep a tan that it was impossible to guess the original skin tones, though the red-blond of his hair suggested northern European somewhere in his ancestry. His eyes were a warm summer blue, and his shoulders broad. Put him in a flannel shirt and denim instead of a uniform, and he'd easily pass for a farmer or rancher, a friendly type, one Raven wouldn't hesitate to stop for directions if lost on some endless country road.

"I'm Sheriff Craig Schmidt. Call me Craig, everyone else does." He held out a hand to shake. "Sorry to keep you waiting. The school called, and I had to go remind my sister's youngest that, no matter what Captain America does in the movies, the proper response to seeing someone bullied is to go tell a teacher, not go beat up the bully. No matter how great the temptation. You have kids?"

"Just one. A little over a year old." Raven had only the vaguest idea of who Captain America was—he tended to stop listening when Chuckie or some of the other younger Guardians started to ramble on about popular culture—but he hoped that if other kids tried to bully little Ransley when he went to school, he'd have friends willing to defend him.

It said something about the man that he appreciated a nephew who defended others from bullies, whether or not he approved of the methods used. It made Raven more disposed to like this sheriff, when he'd arrived prepared to hate him.

"So how did Morgan's lawyer rope you into this?" Craig asked.

Raven stiffened. Friendly or no, Craig was, if not the enemy, then at least an adversary, and Raven's own lawyer had taught him well over the years. "I'm not at liberty to say."

If the evasion bothered Craig, he didn't show it. "Ah, of course. Just making conversation. The kid definitely had a good draw from the public defender's pool. Rita's one of the best. Fairly young, but sometimes that's an asset. Hasn't had time to become jaded. Smart as a whip, too. Doing a summer of pro bono before she ships out to a high-powered criminal defense firm in LA."

Raven smiled. "It almost sounds like you approve."

"Of course I approve." Craig's voice raised a notch, the first sign that there might be a temper beneath the genial nature. "I took this job because I believe in justice, not because I enjoy steamrolling over suspects without regard to guilt or innocence. In order for the adversarial court system to work, it needs good lawyers on both sides. Good lawyers for everyone, not just those that can afford it."

It took effort not to raise an eyebrow. Clearly Craig had more education than the average hick town sheriff. That sounded like a direct quote from a university lecture, possibly even a law school lecture.

Craig chuckled. "I guess whoever fed you your background information failed to mention that I was two-thirds into a law degree when my dad had a stroke and I had to come back home and take over the farm and the pub."

"I'm sorry," Raven said. "I didn't mean to assume—"

"That I was a dumb hick from the sticks who has a hard-on for busting kids?" The humor in his tone softened the harshness of his words. "Yeah, I get that a lot. Listen, how much did they tell you about the kid?"

"I know he dabbled in dark magic as a younger teen. I know that he did time in juvenile detention for manslaughter-by-magic. Not a stellar beginning, I'll warrant you. But I'd be the worst sort of hypocrite if I didn't believe in second chances."

"Understandable," Craig said equably. "But when someone blows that second chance, only a fool would offer them a third."

"If Morgan did, indeed, blow his second chance, then I agree with you. But I also have intimate experience with how easy it is to blame the nearest available dark mage, reformed or otherwise."

"Ah, the thing with the last Archmage. We got the APB."

Raven smiled. "Among other occasions. That was the one time things actually went as far as a warrant."

"Yet you stayed on the straight and narrow. Surrendered yourself to Guardians. You and I both know they'd never have taken you otherwise."

"I only surrendered after I knew I'd proven myself innocent of the charges levelled against me." Even then it had been very much against his instincts.

"Look, I know a bit more about your history than you might think." Craig looked down, the tip of his ears turning pink. "I try to keep up on my Continuing Education courses as much as I can. I know that Devil's Crossing Regional Guardians and Police might not be much compared to GII, or even the Portland Guardians Bureau, but I'd like to think we do the best we can with the resources at hand. Anyway, I took a course on dark mages, what makes them become what they are and how to prevent young people from going down that path. You, uh, were one of the examples I used for my research paper."

"Indeed." Raven drew himself up straighter, crossing his arms over his chest. "I never imagined myself the topic of an academic paper. My work, maybe, but not my person. And what conclusions did you come to?"

"That if you had a better support system, and someone to advocate for you when your application to Guardian Academy was rejected without due consideration, you might never have sworn to William."

Odd that a wound so old could still ache when prodded. Ruthlessly he shut down any thoughts of might-have-beens. "Nothing can excuse what I did."

"Not saying it's an excuse. Just a contributing factor."

"Is there a point to this, beyond dissecting my past?" Raven asked darkly. He wasn't here for this local Guardian to take him apart to see what made him work. "You almost sound like you should be working for the defense."

"My point is, Morgan doesn't have any of those excuses. Yeah, sure, he's adopted, but his parents raised him from infancy. They're good people."

"Oh?" Raven thought of Adam, and how the hell his stepparents put him through had practically pushed him into the arms of William and Bloody Eric.

Raven had utterly failed to save him. Another wound that reopened just as he thought it had finally healed.

"Not what you're thinking," Craig said.

Raven opened his mouth to protest that the sheriff had absolutely no idea what Raven was thinking, but Craig cut him off.

"I can see it in your face. The Jansens aren't like the families you hear about in the news that adopt a whole pack of kids to prove to their Church what righteous people they are and then beat the snot out of them. Sam and Lucy wanted a kid, but didn't want to contribute to the overpopulation problem by having one of their own. Back-to-Earthers, but not in any fanatical way. Drive a pick-up truck to haul feed and supplies, just like everyone else out here. They even have a satellite on the roof for TV, even though about half the folks around here don't bother, Mundanes excepted. Didn't want Morgan to feel isolated from the rest of the world, growing up out here in the middle of nowhere. Made sure that Morgan had the best laptop they could afford for school. Lucy raises and trains cutting horses, so when Morgan joined 4-H, he got the best little buckskin they had on the place, no matter that Lucy had to turn down an offer for her that would have paid the mortgage for six months. Yeah, they weren't ski-trips-to-Tahoe rich, but Morgan had everything he needed and a good bit he wanted, and he was *loved.*"

Ah, small towns, where everyone knew everyone else's business. Raven thanked the gods he was raising his son in Portland where neighbors for the most part kept a polite distance.

"Do you know how he ended up in Juvie?" Craig asked.

"Not the details. I know there was dark magic involved. I know it was deemed manslaughter, which means the death he caused was unintentional."

"Or at least that his lawyer was able to convince the jury that it

26

was. The local high school sponsors one scholarship a year. It's a pretty big deal. One of the city founders had made his money in the California gold rush, left a large endowment. The scholarship's not quite a full ride, but for some of these kids it's enough to make the difference between going to college or working at the feed store for the rest of their lives. There's a complicated formula for who gets it, a point system involving grades, SAT scores, community service. Extracurricular activities come in if there's a tie-breaker needed. By midway through senior year, there were two contenders neck-and-neck. Morgan and this other boy, Matthew Brock. Both with a 4.0, both at the 98th percentile on the SATs. Matthew volunteered every weekend at the local hospital; Morgan built houses with Habitat for Humanity.

"April came around. The scholarship committee would be making a decision in a few weeks and neither boy yet had a clear lead. It looked like it would be coming down to the state OHSET championship in the first week of May."

"O-set?" Raven stumbled over the unfamiliar word.

Craig smiled "O-H-S-E-T. Oregon High School Equestrian Team."

"The scholarship was coming down to—a horse show?" Raven tried, and failed to keep his incredulousness out of his voice.

"OHSET is a big deal in this town." Craig's voice rose as though Raven had insulted the Rhubarb Queen, or whatever they had out here. "Not as big as football, but it's gaining traction. Regardless, both Matthew and Morgan compete in OHSET. Morgan's damned good on a horse. Been riding his whole life, and he worked hard at it besides. And, as I mentioned, that little buckskin of his is nothing to sneeze at.

"Matthew was good, too, but overall he couldn't hold a candle to Morgan. I guess Morgan thought the scholarship was his, until Matthew's parents bought him a new horse. Two-time National Working Cow Horse Champion with an amateur rider. Started trailering out every weekend to some fancy-schmancy trainer to blow hundreds of dollars on lessons. OHSET's not supposed to be about whose parents can buy the best horse or pay the best trainer, but, well, horses are an expensive game."

"But if his parents could afford all that, why did Matthew even need the scholarship?" Raven asked.

"He didn't, as such. But it was a matter of pride."

Raven winced. His family name had kept him out of Guardian Academy when he was Morgan's age, and his rage had driven him to apprentice with the most infamous dark mage of their time. He had no idea what it would be like to be denied a dream for financial reasons, but it had to feel a lot the same.

The sheriff shrugged. "Hey, I'm not saying it's right. But it's not against the rules of the scholarship. There's no needs test. Anyway, we come to the last day of the competition. Morgan and Matthew are even on points, and both far ahead of any other competitor. It was all coming down to the last event."

The sheriff's voice took on the very slightly sing-song rhythm of a talented storyteller. Raven wondered if Craig tended his own bar. He would probably be good at it.

"The pattern called for a spin," the sheriff said. "That fancy horse of Matthew's did a spin worthy of the Quarter Horse Congress finals."

Raven could only make an educated guess as to what a pattern and a spin were in this context, and didn't have a clue what a Quarter Horse Congress might be. He doubted that these details were important to the story, and so he let the sheriff continue without interrupting.

"Matthew—you have to understand this kid had been riding since he was ten. He'd practiced this pattern so often he could ride it in his sleep. There was no way he should have lost his balance and fallen in a routine spin. The horse continued the spin on his own, and stepped on Matthew on the last part. Crushed his throat and drove two ribs through his lungs. Kid was dead before the paramedics came."

Raven winced. He'd spent a little time around horses while he was in hiding in Australia—enough to have developed a healthy respect for their size and strength.

"The crowd was in shock, of course. At first the assumption was that the kid had been riding too long and too hard in the heat without staying properly hydrated. Teenagers think they're immortal; you can't imagine how hard it is to make sure they remember to eat something healthy and drink enough water when they're busy having fun."

Raven tucked the thought away for future reference, to be brought out in twelve years or so. He himself had been a serious, studious child, but to hear Ana tell it, Cassandra had been a handful.

"I suspect Morgan must have counted on that assumption. He didn't realize that when an apparently healthy young man collapses and the fall leads to a fatality, there's a full autopsy, including not only a full Mundane tox screen but also an inspection for any signs of dark magic. You probably know the spell. It's mild as dark magic goes. The common name is Rasputin's Confusion."

So named for the historically inaccurate belief that it had been used by the mad monk Rasputin to weaken the last of the Russian czars, to make him malleable and controllable. In fact, if Rasputin had used it on the Czar, he would have been too incapacitated to act as a figurehead for Rasputin's nefarious but ultimately futile schemes.

"Morgan had never been in trouble before, but he had the most motive of anyone, and so they called in one of his teachers to see if he recognized the magical signature." The sheriff shook his head. "Morgan claimed he didn't realize that it would make Matthew fall, let alone get trampled. He claimed that he thought it would just put Matthew off his game."

Raven snorted. "That's crazy. Anyone who thinks that knows nothing about that spell."

"He thought he could control the effects."

"Not even a practitioner far more experienced could hope to have so much precision with that sort of spell."

The sheriff shook his head. "Kids get cocky. And really, they *don't* teach a lot about dark magic these days at school. Supposed to keep the kids from being tempted to experiment, but ignorance isn't always bliss."

"Not something I'd expect from a pillar of law enforcement." Though Raven didn't exactly disagree with the position.

"You weren't there when this pillar of law enforcement watched a twelve-year-old girl die in his arms from an overdose. Puff the Magic Dragon, they call it. Cannabis laced with magically-enhanced crystal meth. Kids figure they drink and smoke cannabis and nothing bad happens, so they can believe their friends who tell them this stuff is safe, too. Maybe truly accurate drug information in health classes would have prevented her death, and all the others, maybe it wouldn't. But trying to keep kids ignorant sure isn't keeping them safe."

They had strayed far from the topic, but Raven couldn't help his curiosity. "I wouldn't have thought drugs would be much of a problem in your jurisdiction. Devil's Crossing is hardly the inner city."

The sheriff gave a dry, bitter laugh. "You have no idea. Illegal drug use is the dark underbelly of rural America. These farm towns are drying up and blowing away. There's no jobs, no money, and, for the kids who can't get out, no hope. I'm not championing Lansing's golf resort because I'm some evil fuck who wants to destroy the beautiful, rural harmony for a few extra bucks from back-East billionaires with too much time on their hands. Devil's Crossing needs jobs, needs hope. Even if it takes, pardon the pun, a deal with the devil to get there."

"So what happens to the golf resort with Lansing dead?" Raven asked.

"Hard to say. Technically, it was the corporation, not the individual, building the resort, but Lansing was the majority owner. With him gone, it falls to the lawyers and the probate courts. It may get tied up for a while, it may not."

"So if Lansing's death isn't stopping the thing, that somewhat weakens the motive for Morgan, or any other opponent," Raven said.

"Maybe they didn't realize it wouldn't go through anyway. Maybe they just wanted revenge and it just didn't matter."

"Vastly different MO from what Morgan was convicted of before," Raven hazarded. "I saw the photos of the victim from the cave. It would take a powerful dark mage, and a hardened one, to leave a human being in that condition. The incident at the championship might not have been intended to be fatal. And it takes a very different sort of person to commit what is essentially cold-blooded political assassination as opposed to an adolescent impulse to level an unfair playing field."

"You almost make it sound like you think that what Morgan did to Matthew was justifiable."

"Justifiable, no." Raven said. "Understandable, somewhat. He needed that scholarship. His rival didn't. And from everything you said, it sounds like Matthew's parents' money, more than Matthew's skill or hard work, would have become the deciding factor."

"I can understand the point of view," the sheriff said. "But let me put this question to you. Just answer it in your own head. I won't put you on the spot by asking for your answer, now or ever. Take a good long time and think about it. You have a son. He's just a baby now, but that will change all too soon, I promise you. You're a good dad, which means you are going to use all the resources at your disposal to give your son every advantage you can. And you're a Ravenscroft, which means your resources are considerable. Now picture your boy as a teenager, nearly a young man. He's had all the advantages, yes, but he's also worked hard on his own to develop his talents. Hell, with you and Cassandra Greensdowne as parents, I can't imagine he'll be anything less than impressive."

Provided that I don't utterly fail at fatherhood, Raven didn't say. He'd been assured that all first-time fathers had the same fears, but not all first-time fathers had as much reason to doubt.

"Now imagine that some other kid with fewer advantages decides to level the playing field. Maybe he intended to hurt your son, maybe he didn't, but the result is the same." Craig met his eyes, held his gaze steadily. "The boy you held in your arms as an infant, the boy that contains the best parts of you and his mother, lies broken on the ground, and none of your extensive wealth and power can change that. What would you do?"

I would flay him alive and burn his writhing body to ash. The dark magic within him, long-suppressed but never truly gone, surged at the picture painted by the sheriff's words.

Raven said nothing, and not even William could have sensed magic not yet released, and yet Craig's smile said *yes, now you see.*

"I understand your point," Raven said. "But there's a reason why judges and juries are not allowed to rule on cases in which they have personal involvement."

"Agreed," the sheriff said. "And if Morgan had come out of his stint in the juvie program and lived out his life as a productive and law-abiding citizen, I would have been more than happy to let bygones be bygones."

"It sounds like you're presupposing his guilt and then using that presupposition as evidence."

"Maybe so," the sheriff said equably. "But it's not the only evidence we have. I presume you've seen the file."

"I have. It's all circumstantial."

"Still valid." The sheriff shrugged. "But I'll let you talk to Morgan and make your own mind."

FOUR

Raven had more familiarity with interrogation rooms than he had ever wanted, and the one in Devil's Crossing was pretty standard. Institutional gray walls, sealed concrete floor, no windows. One wall was composed almost entirely of a mirror that anyone older than five had to know was one-way glass. A CCTV monitor stared down unobtrusively from one corner, a blinking red light warning that it was recording. Since Raven was not defense counsel, he had no claim to confidentiality with the boy.

Morgan was dressed in an institutional denim shirt and jeans. He looked up as Raven entered, his dark eyes assessing, cool but not hostile. Raven paused to take his own stock of the boy—no, young man, for Morgan's build and bearing said that he had left childhood behind. The file said he was nineteen, legally an adult, though lacking the experience and maturity of a full adult. Morgan had the broad shoulders of someone raised with hard farm labor. Time spent out-of-doors may account for some of the deep tan, but Raven suspected that either Mexican or native blood had some influence as well. His file had only said he was adopted.

"Hello, Morgan," Raven said. "I take it your counsel advised you who I am and why I'm here?"

"You are Corwyn Ravenscroft, infamous dark mage now working for GII. One of the counselors at the ranch has a friend in GII and pulled some strings to get you here," Morgan recited in the sort of monotone usually reserved for algebraic equations.

"Close. I am not employed by Guardian International Investigations, though I do consult with them from time to time. I am here as a friend-of-a-friend, not in any official capacity. And please, call me Raven."

"Raven, then," Morgan said. "I suppose I should thank you for coming out to the outer reaches of Nowheresville, but honestly, I'm not sure what good you think you can do."

Morgan stared past Raven as if the topic held no interest to him. Raven suppressed the urge to grab him by the collar and shake him. Had he been this annoying when he was this age?

He reminded himself that Morgan was at the stage of life where hormones soared and being seen as weak was a fate worse than death. The more frightened a young man was, the tougher he acted. Morgan had to know how serious his situation was, how badly things could go for him.

"What I can do for you depends entirely on what I can find out," Raven said. "What can you tell me about the day Magnum Lansing died?"

"Hey, I don't know anything about it."

"I never said you did," Raven said evenly. "But you were seen in the area. Pretty remote place to be taking a walk."

"A lot of people like to hike out by the butte. It's quiet there. Peaceful." Morgan's eyes swept from Raven's old-fashioned cravat and tailored jacket down to his well-shined Italian shoes. The look clearly said *not that you would know.*

Raven ignored the silent derision and focused on Morgan's word choice. He had no formal training in the art of interrogation—did this even count as interrogation, if he was here unofficially and supposedly on the boy's side? But he'd heard enough Guardians talking shop over microbrews (theirs) and pinot (his). He knew that, outside the classic sociopath, most people tried to avoid telling an out-and-out lie, even when they were being mostly untruthful.

"So a lot of people like to hike out by the butte. What about you? I don't remember hiking being listed among your interests. I'd have thought you got enough exercise, between riding and farm work."

Morgan shrugged and looked to one side, clearly uncomfortable with being caught in a near-falsehood. *Ah, probably not a sociopath, then. Good to know.*

"Footprints in the cave match your boots, right down to the fault in the tread on the left." Raven pressed.

"I was in the cave a few days before Lansing died. Technically, it's still public land. I burned a little sage to honor the spirits of the petroglyphs."

"I thought you practiced Art, not Craft."

"And I'm sure you know mages who go to Mass on Sunday. I wanted to honor the traditions of my ancestors."

So, Native American, then. That would explain his protectiveness toward the petroglyphs. Though he had no indigenous blood, Raven understood the impulse. He respected antiquity, especially things of magic, whether it came from his culture or another. But he also respected the laws against murder.

"Your truck was seen near the Devil's Boneyard about the time they think Lansing was killed."

"I was looking for other caves," Morgan burst out. "Other hidden petroglyphs. Potshards. Whatever. More proof that Devil's Boneyard and the area around it should be preserved as a culturally significant site."

The boy spoke with the truthfulness of passion; Raven was inclined to believe him. Still, it didn't hurt to probe.

"Did you come across anyone else?"

Morgan's eyes narrowed. "You mean, did I come across Magnum Lansing and murder him?"

Raven took a deep breath and reminded himself that practice in dealing with teen-age snark would probably make him a better father to an adolescent Ransley, gods help them both. "I meant exactly what I asked."

"There was a man and a woman walking a dog about a quarter-mile in. They were heading out as I was going in. Doubt that they'd made it as far as the butte, though. The dog was one of those fluffy little lap dogs. Never saw the point to them. If you're going to get a dog the size of a cat, you may as well get a cat."

Raven didn't have much of an opinion on dog breeds, having never owned a dog. Of course, he'd never been much of a cat person until he'd come out second-best in a battle of wills with a scruffy stray kitten. Nuisance now slept on their bed, shed white hairs on his black wool coat, and subsisted mostly on lobster and grilled salmon.

If the young man had wanted to defuse suspicion, he could have left out the size of the dog and any other details that might exculpate the strangers. "Did you see anything else? Notice anything at all unusual?"

"No—wait—yes. There was a, gods, I don't know how to describe it. A whump, something I felt more than heard. Like the start of an earthquake, only it was in the air, too. I might have thought it was thunder, only the sky was clear. It happened so quickly, I thought I might have imagined it. I'm not entirely certain that I *didn't* imagine it."

"You didn't mention this before," Raven said, voice carefully neutral.

"No one asked before. I guess they were too busy thinking I was a suspect that they didn't bother to consider me as a witness."

"You could have brought it up on your own."

Morgan hunched his shoulders, drawing into himself, not meeting Raven's eyes, suddenly looking much younger. The change in body language forcibly reminded Raven that Morgan was just a year or so out of General Academy.

"Like I said, I thought maybe I imagined it. Mentioning some indescribable, unknown phenomenon that might or might not have happened isn't likely to make anyone any more impressed with my truthfulness."

Which may or may not be a valid point, but Raven thought it had more to do with a young man's fear of appearing foolish. Raven would like to believe he'd never been this idiotic, but he'd been around Morgan's age when, largely out of spite, he'd sworn loyalty to the most powerful dark mage of their time.

"Well, I came here explicitly to give you the benefit of the doubt, so tell me more."

"There isn't any more to tell. Like I said, it came and went. Could have been all in my head."

Something had happened, of that Raven was almost certain, but to press harder was to risk having the boy dig in and convince himself that he had imagined the whole thing.

"So you were looking for petroglyphs and potshards. Did you find any?"

"Nah. Not so much as an arrowhead."

"How close did you get to Devil's Boneyard?"

Morgan paused to think. "Hard to say a distance. Everything out here is so wide open, and the butte's so big. You think you're closer to it than you really are."

"If you had to guess?" Raven prompted.

"Maybe a half-mile? Maybe less?" Morgan didn't seem to be deliberately prevaricating.

"What time did you leave?" Raven asked.

Morgan drummed his fingers as he thought. "The days are still pretty short, and I didn't want to get stuck out there after dark, so I started back as soon as the light started getting that orangey-gold that means it's almost sunset."

Clearly the boy spent more time out-of-doors than Raven ever had. "And that would have been?"

"Five-thirty, maybe, when I turned around. Wait—I remember looking at the dashboard clock and thinking I wouldn't have time to stop at the library on the way back."

"Why didn't you just teleport?"

Morgan's look told him he had just been dismissed as an idiot. "I had the farm truck. Picked up a load of hay on the way out. Parked it in the barn to unload the next morning. You can check the invoices at the feed store, and I think one of the boarders saw me unloading the truck the next morning, if you don't want to take my parents' word."

"Did you hear anything else unusual while you were in the park?" Raven asked.

"No." Morgan's answer was quick, off-the-cuff. He'd probably answered that question so many times that he answered now without thinking.

Gods. He wanted Cassandra here. He'd even settle for Rafe. Raven knew an obscene amount about dark magic and nothing at all about conducting an interrogation. "All right. How about anything that seemed normal at the time, but in retrospect could have been something else?" He refused to examine the sentence too closely, in case it made even less sense on inspection.

Morgan's brow furrowed, as though he were pondering the question. Maybe he wasn't doing too badly after all.

"There was—I heard something like a rabbit scream, off in the distance. And then what sounded like coyotes yapping, so I figure they'd made a kill." He shuddered. "They have a right to eat, same as anything else, and they help keep the balance since people killed off all the wolves, but the sound gets to me, and I grew up out here. Sounds like some weird spirit creature cackling."

"You're sure it was a rabbit you heard scream?" Raven hadn't even known rabbits *could* scream, but he wasn't about to admit his ignorance.

Morgan opened his mouth for an automatic reply, but remained silent, paling. "I assumed that's what it was. I mean, I've heard it before. It's the sort of thing that freaks out city slickers, because it does sound like someone's killing a baby. You don't think—?" The boy looked sick at the thought he may have heard Lansing's death, so sick that Raven glanced around for the location of the nearest wastebasket.

Whatever Morgan's intention may or may not have been toward his classmate, Raven doubted him capable of the cold-blooded focus of will necessary for the type of spell that would cause a death as gruesome as Lansing's had been.

"It couldn't have been," Morgan whispered. And then, in a stronger voice, "It *couldn't* have been. The scream was too high-pitched. It might have been mistaken for a woman, or a child—they always say a rabbit's death shriek sounds like a screaming baby. Lansing was a grown man."

Raven left the boy to his comforting self-delusion. No need to tell him that the screams of a man dying in agony bore little resemblance to the pitch of the same man speaking, or even shouting in anger. Raven wished he could rid himself of that knowledge and the memories that it brought.

FIVE

After interviewing Morgan, Raven wanted to look at the scene. Craig introduced him to the deputy-Guardian who would act as a teleport anchor to the base of Devil's Boneyard Butte. The deputy looked like he was fresh out of General Academy, although surely they didn't hire them *that* young and inexperienced. Brad? Chad?—Raven had already forgotten the name—made a valiant attempt to hide his unease at the assignment, and succeeded at least in making it unclear whether the nervousness sprang from Raven's past as a dark mage or his current celebrity as one of the best-known consultants of Guardian International Investigations.

Whichever it was, the young man gamely allowed Raven to anchor to him. Raven followed the connection through the ether until he faded back into being at a flat spot about a quarter-mile down the trail from where the recently-discovered cave opening gaped like the dark mouth of hell. Cassandra's voice spoke from his memory—*Raven, behave.* He gamely resisted the temptation to deliberately loom over the deputy just to watch the reaction. It had been a couple years, at least, since he terrorized junior members of law enforcement just because he could. Hadn't even wanted to, for the most part. He was just ill at ease because he was out of his element; he refused to take it out on what was probably a perfectly nice young man.

"The boss said that I should wait here for you," Chad—yes, it was definitely Chad, he remembered now—said. "Any closer is rated for master mages only—they're being that cautious, even though the signature must be largely faded now. And, of course, they're keeping the civilians out."

Raven didn't bother to point out that *he* was a civilian. Although, he supposed, only in the most technical sense. The GII director had snuck up on him, damn her. Cassandra had probably seen it all happening and hadn't warned him. Shaking his head, he took off his black suit jacket, folded it, and gave it to Chad for safe-keeping. He'd heard that it could be hot out on the high desert, but hadn't paid the warnings as much attention as he might have. He rolled up his sleeves and started up the trail to the cave.

It didn't take long before a niggling sense of *wrongness* settled over him. Raven had more experience with dark magic than almost anyone now living, and yet this felt different from anything he'd ever known. The closest thing he could compare it to was the aftermath of a dark magic ritual, but this was less concentrated and yet more pervasive. Josiah, his Mundane bookseller friend and chess partner, had once tried to explain the concepts of antimatter and dark matter. At the time it had seem nonsensical, but this, what he sensed, it felt like anti-life. Not death, no. Death was a natural part of life. What he sensed was a hint of something antithetical to life, as though it and life could not exist in the same space.

He strengthened his shield and continued to the mouth of the cave, the wrongness weighing more heavily the closer he got to the cave. And yet he knew somehow that what he sensed was still the echo of the thing, not the thing itself.

With magic, what you didn't know could very definitely hurt you. Could kill you. He moved slowly, carefully, reaching out with his magic to look for traps, to look for an ambush. The high desert was still, so still that he could hear his own pulse like thunder in his ears. The gravel on the path crunched beneath his feet. Was it always this quiet? He'd thought the Craft lands up on Chehalem Mountain near-silent, but there had been the rustle of small animals in the underbrush, the chittering of birds and the occasional buzz of insects, the high-pitched call of a hawk announcing its territory.

He startled at the blur of movement as something yellow-brown and rodent-sized darted from behind a rock of the same color. It was across the path and down a hole almost before he registered its form in his mind. Prairie dog? Did they have those in Oregon? It seemed too small to be a groundhog, or at least it was smaller than that improbably-named creature they dragged out every year in Pennsylvania in a superstitious bid to predict how late Spring would be in arriving. Nothing dangerous, at least. It had probably been frozen, camouflaged by its surroundings, until his approach broke its nerve and it bolted for a more secure sanctuary.

Perhaps the other creatures in this dry, spare place were just wary as well, not emboldened as forest-dwellers might be by the more abundant cover provided by the woodlands. It was a more comforting hypothesis than the possibility that most of the wildlife had been driven off by the oppressive feel of darkness that grew with every step.

Could this be a residue of whatever magic that killed the developer? It would have had to have been a powerful working, indeed, for its aftermath to be spread so wide and linger so long. A more powerful working than he could imagine coming from a young man barely out of boyhood.

There were places in the world known for their dark power. Usually it was a remnant of large and horrific events that had repeated over and over again. Sometimes the energy was so strong that even Mundanes sensed it, and named the place haunted or cursed.

This place *was* called Devil's Boneyard, for reasons no one ever satisfactorily explained, though there were conflicting folk tales about fossils being found or notorious bandits being run to ground. The research Raven had done prior to the trip turned up neither significant fossil finds nor any record of desperados meeting violent death in the locale. Several sources claimed that Devil's Boneyard was an almost literal translation of the indigenous name for the place. For all he knew, the place carried a bad reputation back to Neolithic times. Hard to believe of a place that had become a popular destination for weekend rock-climbers.

No. Even the most magic-blind of Mundanes could surely sense the dark power that rolled off this place like fog off of dry ice in a production of *Macbeth*. Whatever was going on here must be a relatively new development.

He reached the mouth of the cave, which was barely high enough for him to enter without stooping and narrow enough that if he reached out to either side his fingertips would brush the black volcanic rock on each side. The place reeked of a dark power wholly unfamiliar to him, and he realized that he was afraid.

Fear, personal fear for himself, was not something he was used to. He knew the wariness-mixed-with-adrenaline of magical combat, yes. And the last years had taught him the helpless, desperate fear that his wife and his child were in danger and he might not be enough to save them. He had faced death and, though he did not want to die, the prospect had not brought this gut-sick, heart-pounding terror that threatened to rob his will. Not even William had triggered this level of fear in him, and Raven had been afraid of his late master in a way that he had feared no one since his father had been killed when he was a child.

The early years of his childhood and then, later, his time serving William, had molded him (some might say warped him) in such a way that he did not have the instinctual fear-response that most people sensitive to magic felt in the presence of dark power. But this was something different, something alien.

If Morgan had been responsible for this, it went far beyond any training the young man had, beyond anything he could have found in any book he would have access to. That would make Morgan the most powerful wild talent ever to live. And though the wild magic that erupted sometimes at adolescence was a thing so different from trained magic that people once blamed it on ghosts and demons instead of realizing its true source, still Raven could not imagine that the boy could be that powerful without him sensing *something*.

He had come to investigate the cave. He would not let his mind take him wandering down paths meant to distract himself from that goal. He had trained his will to the practice of his Art; it was stronger than his subconscious, no matter how wily the latter might be.

He took a few deep breaths, grounding himself, and moved forward, deeper into the cave. When he had left much of the daylight behind, he pulled from his coat pocket the crystal sphere he'd charmed to act as a portable light globe. Was it his imagination, or was the radiance of the globe dimmer than usual?

His hand slipped to his waistcoat, where the Ravensblood once would have been. The artefact had saved his life more than once, but it was no more. Its creation had cost the life of his apprentice, and he would not pay that price ever again.

The cave didn't smell like he had expected. But then the caves of his imagination were damp things full of dripping stalactites. This cave was dry, with a flat, dusty smell almost, but not quite like that of a library. It reminded him of old, powdery wood and cold granite, with a hint of something almost—garlicky? Oh, of course. Naturally occurring arsenide compounds.

A little further in, he saw the first of the petroglyphs. It was vaguely anthropomorphic, with stick-figure arms and legs. Its oval body had two rows of downward slashes that could have been meant to represent ribs, wounds, or body paint. The head was a triangle, the mouth gaping open to reveal large, sharp teeth. The eyes were spirals set in circles. In each hand it held—a stick? No, a spear, to go by the inverted *v* shape at the top of each one. The power emanating from it took his breath away. Fear shivered down his spine, and he took a step back.

It took a few breaths to center himself and realize that this was not the source of the dark power that filled the cave. Whatever this was, it was strong, dangerous in its own way, but not inherently evil. The little bit he'd found in the files said that the archeologists called in by law to assess the site had said that the petroglyphs were old, older than Stonehenge or Newgrange, old enough to have passed from the knowledge of the tribes that lived here when the Mariner first landed. And yet the power had not faded.

The tribes spoke of the petroglyphs as though they were living things with wills of their own. Raven had thought it just a metaphor, a way of translating what these images meant to those not raised in their culture. Now he knew that these things were real in a way he could not articulate, born of power outside of his understanding.

A memory came to him, another cave with strange beings painted on the walls.

"What did you do to me?" Raven had asked Bran Tarrant in that faraway cave in Australia.

"Sent you on a shaman's journey. I knew you'd either come back a new person, and healed, or die on the journey. You were dying anyway, so it seemed worth the risk."

Raven shook his head at the enormity the gamble Tarrant had taken, the audacity of what had been forced upon him. "So this is what you do to people someone brings you to heal? Make a shaman of them?

Tarrant only laughed at his outrage. "Never before. And probably never again. For one, most people don't have what it takes to survive the journey. For another, I only did it because I saw that this is what you needed, the reason you came to Australia."

"I came to Australia because a group of people who insisted they knew more than me thought it was the best way to avoid arrest."

"Of course, that was the reason. And it wasn't. Things happen for more than one reason, you know."

This was why, for all his respect for Mother Crone, he tended not to spend much time with Craft people. Too much exposure gave him a headache.

"You don't have to worry about being a shaman, you know," Tarrant said. "You aren't. Well, you are, but not really. Being a shaman is about being true to your deepest self, and you, my friend, are a mage straight to the core. You just had a deeper need than most mages to come to terms with all of who and what you are, and this seemed like the way to do it. Maybe not the best way, but the only way I could come up with."

Raven had trained in Art where learning was vital and trusting to pure, uncontrolled instinct could lead one to a horrible death. But this petroglyph was something older and more powerful than his Art. Raven touched the pendant he always wore around his neck, a silver raven with a red stone in its beak, a gift from Bran Tarrant.

He closed his eyes and trusted in a power he had only tapped once and scarcely believed he had, trusting in Tarrant's words where he did not trust his own training. He, who had only knelt before to William his master, knelt now before this strange and eerie image. *I know my ancestors stole this land from the people who you protected. I know I am likely trespassing on sacred ground where I have no right to be. But if you are, indeed, sentient, you surely must feel the darkness gathering. I seek only leave to investigate that darkness, to stem the tide before there is more death.*

Both the gesture and the words came out of some deep well within him that he'd had no awareness of until this moment. He sensed a—softening? Easing? A wordless permission to continue.

He had no Craft training. Possibly he was imagining everything. But he wouldn't dare think that too loudly while he was within this cave.

He went deeper into the cave, passing more and more petroglyphs, some overlapping others. Some were recognizable— stylized bighorn sheep with curling horns, birds, saber-tooth cats long extinct. Others were abstract—lines and circles in patterns that he could not make meaning of. There were more human-like figures, but none held the power that the sharp-toothed, spiral-eyed one did. All, however, struck in him a sense of awe. *These are older than every book in my library, older, probably, that the Ravenscroft name.* He could understand why someone would kill to preserve the petroglyphs.

Understand, but not condone. Especially as they were too cowardly to acknowledge the deed, leaving an innocent young man to take the fall.

You can't be certain he's innocent.

He shook his head. *Focus.* There would be time for that later. He needed to keep his mind on the here-and-now. Too much magic present that he didn't quite understand to let his mind wander. Besides, if he didn't pay attention, he risked missing clues, and he didn't have a Guardian at his side to compensate for his weaknesses.

He had thought that the desert outside had been quiet, but the cave's silence reached a new order of magnitude. It was as though the silence itself was a sound, a pressure against his eardrums, like the weight of the air before a thunderstorm. He found himself straining for the *drip-drip* of water, the scuttle of a small creature hiding among the rocks, anything but the oppressive nothingness.

The tunnel took a gentle curve to the right, and the darkness seemed to dim. Raven stopped, reaching ahead cautiously with his magic to sense another power, a new signature, anything to explain the light that should not be there. Nothing. He took a careful step forward, and then another.

And then looked up and laughed at himself. His steps had brought him close enough to the cave roof that had been cracked by heavy equipment to see the sun that streamed through. That sun was the bane of archeologists who had not yet determined if these petroglyphs were as hardy as She Who Watches, who presided over the Columbia Gorge from her high cliff wall for ages uncounted, heedless of the wind and rain. Intellectually, Raven understood all the problems of exposing to the open air artifacts that had been for centuries preserved in a sealed environment, but at the moment that ray of sunlight brought a wholly illogical sense of wholesomeness into the dark, grim cave environment.

The cave opened up into a wider underground chamber. In the center of the cave floor was the chalk outline where a body had lain before it was removed. Raven could practically hear the archeologists scream at the disturbance of the sensitive site. He winced. The dark stain of blood that had dried on the cave floor had done at least as much damage as the chalk. Petroglyphs covered two of the walls, now in regular patterns that surely had had some meaning to their creators. The third wall, a large, flat surface directly opposite the cave and at least as tall as a single-story house, held what could only be the stylized petroglyph of a raven, chiseled deep into the wall, black on black like a shadow against the night sky. It stood with wings outspread, its claws designed to create the illusion of clutching the boulder on the cave floor and its beak open in a silent scream to the cave roof.

The wall exuded a darkness that flowed forth like contagion from a wound. Betrayal washed over him. After all the times he had insisted that the raven was not a symbol of evil. . . But no. He sensed the signature of the raven itself—strong, yes, dangerous, yes, but only in the same sense that the spiral-eyed figure near the mouth of the cave was dangerous. It felt a little bit like a ward. A ward that had been weakened, about to break.

Halfway down the wall, a deep fault appeared, scarring the widest part of the raven. Damage, no doubt, from the same earth-movers that had caused the crack in the cave ceiling. Raven spared a thought for the geologists that had declared the cave physically stable enough to enter, and wondered from which college they had received their degrees. Could the crack be what weakened whatever protective spirit the raven represented? Perhaps the petroglyph had been placed here to hold back the darkness he felt all around him?

But that made no sense. The petroglyphs in this cave dated back to the dawn of history, maybe to the days when humans hunted mammoths and occasionally fell prey to saber-tooth cats and dire wolves. No matter what folk tales and superstitions hung about various places in the world, dark magic was a human creation. He could not believe that the workings of any dark mage could be so powerful after so many years.

Explain the petroglyphs, then. They were not dark, but they were ancient, and still powerful. He'd been worried about being out of his depth when it came to investigative procedure, but he hadn't expected to be in over his head when it came to magic.

None of this made *sense*, though. None of it fit with his understanding of how magic worked. The petroglyphs he had tucked into a corner of his mind labeled Craft-works-different-than-Art, but the darkness he felt, it was something more, something dangerous, something unlike any Craft working he'd ever known.

He backed out of the cave, stumbling occasionally as he went, but not wanting to turn his back on the darkness. When he reached the spiral-eyed guardian petroglyph, he paused to face it respectfully. *Who made you? Who called you into being? Are you here to protect us from the darkness in that cave, and if so, will you serve even though the ones you were to protect are long gone?*

Stepping out of the cave and into the sunlight felt like returning to the land of the living after a sojourn to the underworld of the dead. Odd, how the desert that had seemed so still and lifeless before he stepped into the cave seemed, by contrast, a soothing symphony of sound. The wind rustled softly through the tall grass. A crow called in the distance and was answered by a neighbor. Far down the trail, the bored young deputy-Guardian tossed stones at a hollow, sun-bleached log; a dull thud scored each hit while a sharp crack of stone-on-stone betrayed each miss. Raven started down the trail, squinting in the bright light.

When Raven got closer, the deputy stood to greet him. "Learn anything?"

For one, adolescent outburst or no, I don't think there's any chance that boy you have in the station could have generated that much power. But he

47

was working independently this time, and on a course contrary to the one the local Guardians had taken. Should he show his hand so soon? For that matter, how could anyone believe that Morgan had managed that level of magic on his own? It seemed counter-intuitive that any Guardian would chance letting whoever was behind that much dark magic go free solely in the interests of a quick close to a case, even one as high-profile as this one. Contrary to his own expectations, he had not found Craig Schmidt to be the sort of ignorant rural sheriff who would railroad a young man against logic solely because of his past. But even a Mundane could not miss the sense of dark power rolling out of that cave. How could they not realize that it couldn't possibly have been Morgan? None of this made any *sense*.

"I haven't come to any conclusions yet," he hedged. "But I'd advise Schmidt to continue to keep the cave closed off to the public until we figure out what's going on."

SIX

Rafe's friend Scott wouldn't be available to consult with him until the evening, so Raven returned to the bed and breakfast. It had been a long day so far, and he decided to try for a nap so that he'd be alert and clear-minded when he went to talk to Scott. Raven seldom slept well in a strange place, especially when Cassandra was not with him. He had planned to take a nap before going out again, but sleep eluded him. Memories of the dark, dangerous power he had sensed in the cave would not leave him. Odd that the residual magic remained so strong while the magical signature had, as predicted, faded to uselessness. Soul stealers had that effect, but Raven knew soul stealers, and this felt different. Similar in a way he could not articulate, but different nonetheless.

He stared at the wall, or rather at the landscape painting that hung on the wall. Again, he found himself wishing Cassandra was here, and not only for the company. Though he loved her like plants loved the rain, they were never the sort of couple that needed to live in each other's pockets to survive. But Cassandra was a trained investigator; he was merely a consultant with more knowledge of dark magic than anyone came by honestly. He'd thought he'd come out here, meet the boy, look over the crime scene, give his assessment and, if necessary, make himself available as an expert witness at the trial. But now he had a feeling that there was way, way more going on than met the eye, and they needed a real GII agent down here as soon as possible.

The host had provided a message crystal for guest use. Raven disliked using a crystal not personally warded and keyed to him, but the alternative was that gods-awful Mundane phone which Sherlock had finally foisted upon him. He was sure Cassandra had slipped it into his bag somewhere even though he himself had deliberately 'forgotten' it.

Since he was using an unfamiliar crystal, it took longer than usual to convince Cassandra's work crystal that he was an approved contact. Cassandra wasn't available, and he ended up leaving a message. He tapped his fingers on the polished wood of the small dining table, thinking. He was on his own, at least for the time being. Where would Cassandra go from here?

Of course. If Cassandra only had one suspect and had serious misgivings about that suspect's guilt, she would start looking around for who else had reason to want the victim dead. Lansing had been CEO of a high-powered company. Not only did he have a substantial fortune of his own, but he controlled even more millions. Billions, probably. When the numbers got that high, the precise figure ceased to matter, at least to Raven. Enough money, anyway, to provide a strong motive. But for whom?

He activated the crystal again. "Chuckie?" He cringed a little at using such a childish name, but Chuckie insisted that *Charles* was his father. "It's Raven."

Chuckie answered immediately. "Raven, buddy, how ya doing? I'm just finishing up that research that your sweetie asked for."

Chuckie had been Cassandra's partner before Rafe. Most mages had little use for Mundane technology, although things like cell phones and televisions were slowly making inroads, much to Raven's disappointment. Chuckie was an exception; the self-styled techno-mage specialized in magical/computer interfaces and was GII's go-to for any research best done on a computer.

"Ah, yes. I'm not working with Cassandra on that one. I have a little side project I was hoping you could help me with." He explained about Lansing's death, skirting the fact that he was looking into it as a side-project for Rafe, not for GII.

"So basically you want to know who might want Lansing dead?" Chuckie said. "You want the whole list, or just the top hundred or so?"

"I'd heard he was an unscrupulous profit-monger," Raven said. "But you're making him sound like he was as bad as William."

"Nah. William at least had class."

True enough.

"Listen, perhaps the man's only saving grace was that he was a Mundane. Limited the amount of damage he could do."

"I'm beginning to wonder if I should put *you* on the suspect list."

"Hey, I'm only someone willing to dance on his grave. You need to move up the list to the people who were willing to put him there. Better yet, the people who wanted to see him die *horribly*. That should narrow the list down to a thousand or so."

"Starting with?"

"Off the top of my head? His first wife. His second wife. His th— No, make that the family of his third wife. She committed suicide, and he's widely believed to have driven her to it. The shareholders of his first two companies, many of whom lost small fortunes, some of whom were left destitute when the companies filed bankruptcy, while he skipped away with his off-shore holdings that no one could *quite* prove were acquired illegally."

"Wait. Why would people buy shares in a third company if his first two companies went bankrupt?" Raven didn't pay too much attention to the stock market—he left his lawyer and his accountant to hash out the details of his own portfolio—but he knew enough.

"People are greedy and gullible. Sociopaths are charming and convincing. You do the math."

"His current company is—"

"Smoke and mirrors. Same as the first two. The shareholders don't know yet, of course. My guess would be most of the board does, but they're probably hoping to grab their suitcases of money and jump clear when the tower falls."

"What about the environmentalists?"

"Personally, I'd put them pretty low down on the list. Not that they're likely to be mourning his passing, but statistically they're more likely to picket his luxury hotels or haul his ass into court. Even the direct-action types are more likely to pour sugar into the gas tanks of the bulldozers than they are to resort to inflicting bodily harm, let alone murder most foul. But I'll talk to Suzy. Her thing's the oceans more than the desert, but she might know someone who knows someone who heard something."

"Wouldn't that be asking her to betray her own?" Raven asked.

"Not even close," Chuckie said. "You should hear her rant about anyone who discredits the cause by resorting to violence."

Chuckie sounded perilously close to a rant himself; Raven headed him off with a description of Morgan, finishing with "By your analysis he's unlikely to be the murderer?"

Chuckie made a non-committal sound that Raven had learned meant that he wasn't willing to disagree with Raven, but wasn't fully committed to his point of view.

"No?" Raven prompted.

"Kids are unpredictable." Chuckie said.

"He's nearly twenty."

Chuckie snorted. "Maybe you were all grown up and responsible at twenty, whatever responsible means for a dark mage. Hell, you were probably a responsible grown-up when you were *five*. But most of us were still pretty stupid at that age. I mean, I was nineteen when I hacked the Mundane's central security system. On a dare."

Raven had heard allusions to the incident, which had caused days of nationwide panic and years of strained relationships between the Mundane, Art, and Craft communities. He'd never heard the full story, though. Someday, he'd have to drag it out of Chuckie. Should be easy enough; Chuckie was fond of microbrews and couldn't hold his drink nearly as well as he thought he could.

"So you're saying. . .what, exactly?" Raven asked.

"Only that it's still an open field."

Raven gusted a sigh of frustration.

"Yeah, sorry, my friend. Welcome to the life of a Guardian."

"I'm not a Guardian," Raven protested.

Chuckie laughed. "You keep telling yourself that. I'll poke around in LansingCorp's finances and see if I can find anyone with a particularly strong motive, see if I can track the whereabouts of those with more personal motives. But first I have to get dinner on before Suzy gets home. She's been out counting sea otters all day, so she's going to be tired and hungry."

Counting sea otters. Raven couldn't quite tell if Chuckie was joking or not, and he wasn't going to open himself up by asking. "I shall talk to you later, then."

His host had left a bowl of fruit on the table. Raven helped himself to an apple on his way out the door to stroll among the orange California poppies and yellow St John's Wort that seemed to thrive even in this arid landscape. He fed the core of the apple to a small, shaggy-maned black pony that had come to poke its head between the fence rails to beg for a treat.

He replayed his conversation with Sheriff Schmidt—with Craig, since apparently even law enforcement was casual out here. The thing was, the man's report on what caused young people to turn to dark magic was. . .interesting, but a little narrow in focus. Raven had never faced not having the funds to do, well, *anything*, and so he hadn't spent much time thinking about how limiting it could be, how frustrating it could be for a talented young person who would otherwise be facing a bright future.

The Ravenscroft Foundation contributed to a few scholarship funds. Alexander Chen, who had been his lawyer since before his age of majority, handled the details. When Raven got back from this trip, he would make certain that at least some of those had a strong needs-based component.

The pony nudged his arm, and so he obligingly scratched under its mane and along the crest of its neck. The pony stretched out its rather coarse head, upper lip twitching in pleasure. Raven was not and would never be a horseman, but while in Australia he'd come to not mind the company of at least the smaller, tamer representatives of the equine species.

His mind kept coming back to one thing. The dark magic residue in the cave was so very strong. Craig Schmidt was neither stupid nor corrupt. How could he possibly believe that something that took that much power had been done by a boy not yet twenty?

SEVEN

After showering, Raven dressed simply in a white cotton button-down, tailored to fit but not bespoke, and a pair of black jeans that was one of the few denim items Cassandra had persuaded him to buy. He'd been warned that the style in a place like Devil's Crossing tended to be more low-key and that he might raise hackles if he showed up at a bar in a bespoke suit and tie. Generally, he favored darker colors, but hoped the white shirt, at odds with his usual image, might be disarming.

Raven was surprised that Scott chose The Devil's Pitchfork as a meeting place. He was even more surprised to find that Craig was tending bar after having presumably worked a full day at the station. Scott had not yet arrived, and so Raven took a seat at the bar that gave him the best vantage of the door and waited. A jukebox stood in one corner, either a carefully restored vintage model or a detailed replica. It blared a type of music one of the younger GII agents had told him was called *country rock*. Raven had no desire to make any closer acquaintance with it, then or now, but it seemed he had little choice in the matter. He doubted very much that the jukebox offered anything by Mozart or Liszt.

The polished wood bar was clean, at least, and the patrons, though loud, did not seem overly rowdy. In fact, he suspected that much of the volume resulted from an attempt to be heard over the music.

"What's your poison?"

Raven turned to face Craig, who tossed a coaster in front of him in anticipation of a drink order.

"You don't look like much of a beer drinker," Craig said. "And our wine selection is a choice of house red or house white. I doubt either would meet your standards."

55

Raven was certain that they hadn't discussed wine at any point in their short acquaintance.

His confusion must have showed on his face, because Craig chuckled. "When you've tended bar as long as I have, you learn to read your customers. I do have an imported absinthe you might find to your taste."

Raven had imbibed far more absinthe than was good for him during his time serving William. He'd only indulged in the stuff a time or two since then. He hadn't intentionally avoided the wormwood liqueur, but perhaps his subconscious had associated it with memories best forgotten.

"Absinthe would be fine. I'm surprised you carry it." He suddenly found he missed the strong licorice flavor, the bitter of wormwood balanced by the sweetness of the dissolved sugar. He'd buried William almost two years ago now; time to lay the memories to rest as well.

"There used to be a small goth crowd in town, and they drank it. Most of them found their ticket out of town, one way or the other. Moved to Portland or Seattle."

Raven looked around the bar. Most tables were occupied by men and women in faded and worn jeans—the fade and the wear honestly come by, not like the ridiculously expensive and artistically torn denim that went in and out of fashion every few years. Baseball caps and t-shirts advertised feed stores and rodeos, and the occasional cowboy hat looked like it actually may have seen a cow.

"You get goths in here?"

Craig grinned. "When you're the only game in town, you'd be surprised who turns up."

The man prepared the absinthe in the traditional way, measuring the deep green liqueur into a tall glass, balancing a slotted spoon across the mouth of the glass and placing sugar cubes over the slots. He dribbled water slowly over the sugar, allowing it to carry the dissolved crystals into the glass until the resulting mixture was an unearthly shade of pale, clouded green. The challenge in his smile as he placed the glass on the coaster in front of Raven seemed to say *See? Not so much a hick as you thought.*

Raven reached for his wallet, but Craig waved for him to put it away. "On the house. Worth it to someday tell the grandkids that I served absinthe to the famous Corwyn Ravenscroft."

"Famous? Or infamous?"

"Oh, I'd say the best legends are a bit of both." A Trickster gleam lit his eyes, and Raven realized then that law enforcement was lucky Craig was on its side.

"A legend? Gods, I hope not," Raven said sincerely.

Craig clucked his tongue. "Bit late for that, I'd say."

"Sister's kids keeping out of trouble?" Raven asked to change the topic. *See, Cassandra, I can do small talk. When I want to.*

Craig sighed. "At least since this morning. So far as I know."

Raven chuckled. "Ever thought of settling down yourself."

Craig's smiled was wistful. "Someday, maybe. Haven't had much luck with women. Or men, for that matter."

Before Raven could respond, Craig cut him off. "I'm guessing the person you came to meet just walked in the door."

The newcomer did bear a resemblance to the description Rafe had given of his new *friend.* His curly mop of hair was so blond that it shone nearly white in the strong light near the entrance of the bar. He wore a faded concert t-shirt, at least three strands of stone beads, and a hemp necklace with a peace sign. He saw Raven at the bar and strode up to him, holding out a hand to shake.

"Corwyn Ravenscroft?"

"I go by Raven."

"Scott. Thanks for coming."

Scott had a strong handshake; Raven could easily imagine him climbing rock walls with ease. He didn't however, use that strength to try to crush Raven's hand in a macho dominance game, so that earned him a point, at least.

"Let's get a booth where we can talk privately." Scott shot a significant glance toward the sheriff.

Why come into the man's establishment if you are so worried about him eavesdropping? Perhaps he was trying to make some sort of obscure point. Perhaps he meant to annoy the sheriff with his presence—though, if so, he was a bit wide of the mark, to go by the sheriff's bland, unruffled gaze. Perhaps, as Craig himself had said, it was simply that Devil's Pitchfork was the only game in town.

Raven carried his glass of absinthe, following Scott to a corner table. A waitress in dark jeans, a fitted white t-shirt, and a nametag that read Cyndy promptly arrived. Scott ordered some brand of beer Raven had never heard of, presumably some sort of microbrew. Scott made small talk about the problems he was having fixing the old beater of a truck they had on the program's farm. Raven knew nothing about automobiles and cared less, but the younger man was an engaging storyteller and managed to entertain him until the waitress came back with a chilled glass and a bottle with mountains and trees on the label.

"So you talked to Morgan?" Scott said.

"I did."

"And?" Scott prompted. "Surely you can see that he's no killer."

"I don't think I can make a judgement on his character on such short acquaintance. But one thing that I do think—he might be talented for his age. He certainly has a lot of potential. But I cannot believe that he's powerful enough to be behind what I felt up on that butte." Even now, with the babble of the people all around and the most prosaic of music blaring from the jukebox, the memory of that darkness made him shiver. "I can't imagine how the sheriff could think he is."

He had to talk to Craig about the cave, but the bar was not the place.

"He's a cop. He doesn't care so long as he can call the case closed."

Raven had his share of problems with law enforcement, sometimes even when he was working *with* law enforcement. But Craig didn't seem like the type; he actually cared about justice.

Even if he didn't, he had better start caring about whatever was going on up in that cave. Because anyone that dark and that powerful was dangerous, and Raven didn't think the problems would stop with the death, however gruesome, of one greedy land developer.

"If there's not the evidence to convict, surely they will have to let him go," he said aloud.

Scott fiddled with his beer glass, already almost half-empty "Unless they simply manufacture whatever they can't find."

"And I thought *I* was cynical about law enforcement." Raven shook his head. "Sheriff Schmidt may be a bit short-sighted, but I don't think he's actually corrupt."

Scott's mouth twitched like he wanted to argue but didn't want to piss off the consultant who was currently working on his pet cause. "Time will tell. Time that a young man who's trying to turn his life around will spend behind bars, getting even more cynical about his chances of success in life."

Raven's brow furrowed. "Haven't they set bail?"

Scott snorted. "Far higher than Morgan's parents could pay, even with a bail bondsman. The farm is already mortgaged to the hilt to pay the legal fees from the last time. The prosecutor argued against setting bail at all due to the serious nature of the crime. The judge said that he had to take into account Morgan's exemplary conduct, outside of the juvenile conviction, which no longer bore legal relevance now that Morgan was an adult. I understand that the same prosecutor had wanted to try Morgan as an adult for the first manslaughter charge, and was not too shy to share his feelings on the judge's refusal to do so. I think that the grudge match between them is the only reason the judge set bail at all."

Well. One of the few advantages of being a Ravenscroft; if it was the sort of problem that could be resolved merely by throwing money at it, it soon ceased to be a problem.

"I'll speak to my attorney in the morning and he'll have bail arranged by the afternoon. Meanwhile, our best hope is to find out what *did* happen in that cave. It seems like the evidence seems mostly circumstantial. It might help if we had another solid suspect. I have a friend from GII looking into the financials. You're active in the Stop the Resort movement. Is there anyone you know of who has a particularly short fuse, or a history of dark magic?"

Scott's eyes narrowed. "The idea here isn't to save Morgan by ratting out someone else."

"I thought the idea was to get to the bottom of what really happened, thereby clearing Morgan's name." *If in fact he is innocent,*

Raven didn't add, knowing that it would only set Scott off and make the conversation even less productive.

He himself had very few doubts left as to the young man's innocence. Not because he had that much faith in his ability to judge character, but because he had faith in his ability to judge power. Whatever the hell had happened in that cave, he doubted very much that Morgan was strong enough to be behind it.

"Law enforcement's just looking for any excuse to come down on activists."

Raven raised an eyebrow. "You are aware that Rafe is with GII, yes?"

Scott shrugged. "He was also with Cam. I figure he had to be one of the few open-minded guys on the force."

Raven took a sip of his absinthe. Yes, Rafe had come a long way from the days when he believed that there was no such thing as a *reformed* dark mage. Raven and Cassandra had had something to do with that. Cam had done more. Yet Rafe still gave the cold shoulder to Tony Borzoff, refusing to accept that Tony was trying to turn his life around after his long-ago conviction.

He finished off the absinthe and tried to decide if he wanted another. Rafe could do so much better. He fought the urge to drop a few well-chosen facts about Rafe that would cause Scott to break off all contact. Rafe was a grown man who could make his own decisions.

Cyndy stopped by to ask if they needed anything else.

Raven looked over to Scott. "Did you want to eat while we're here?" Raven, for his part, figured he might as well—the only other option in town, so far as he saw, was the corner convenience store/bait shop/deli, which Raven considered dubious at best.

Scott hesitated.

"My treat, of course." Raven said.

Scott brightened. "Yes, then, thank you."

"Two dinner menus, then," Raven told Cyndy. "And another absinthe. Another ale?"

Scott nodded eagerly.

"And another ale."

The waitress returned quickly with the menus and the drinks. "I'll be back in a moment to take your orders."

Raven made his own choice, then used the opportunity to watch Scott. The blonde man didn't spare more than a glance at the front of the menu where the burgers and sandwiches were listed, but went directly to the full dinners at the back.

Cyndy returned as promised, and Scott ordered the Surf'n'Turf and added a side of mozzarella sticks. The Surf'n'Turf, Raven noted, was the most expensive item on the menu.

The money didn't matter to him personally, but Raven still made note of how easily the man let him pick up the tab on such short acquaintance. Rafe, like Raven, had been raised with an old-world sense of what it meant to be a gentleman, even if Rafe's sensibilities were less elegant. It would be too easy for Rafe, heart still mending, to be taken advantage of by an unprincipled suitor.

EIGHT

"Your friend was right," Alexander Chen's voice said through the message crystal the next morning. "Bail's been set high, but it's been set, which is a miracle given what this kid's been accused of. There's enough money in the Cam's Kids fund, no problem there."

The Cam's Kid's fund was something he'd set up after about the fourth or fifth time Rafe's late boyfriend had come to him asking him to bail one of his projects out of jail, or pay for emergency housing when it wasn't safe for one of Cam's clients to go back to the home they were living in, or to throw money at a hospital that balked at providing necessary medical care for an uninsured minor. After he'd done the latter a few times too many, Raven made it a practice to make a donation to the campaign of a random politician in favor of national health care every time Cam or someone from the foundation woke him up in the middle of the night to guarantee that a bill would be paid.

"I just want to make sure you're certain that this is what you want to do," the lawyer continued.

In truth, Raven was far from certain. He had not forgotten the sheriff's hypothetical, nor his failure with Adam. And yet. . .*innocent until proven guilty.* He believed in the precept, the more so because it had seldom been applied to him in his youth. Morgan was right; coming from a family without money was often treated like as big a crime as coming from a family of dark mages. It wasn't fair, in either instance. The *world* wasn't fair, but where he could Raven would change that.

This wasn't like before, like Adam. He wasn't taking the young man on himself, he was sending him back to his parents who knew him and could deal with him. The court had an approved method of releasing someone until his guilt or innocence could

63

be appropriately judged. Raven was just correcting for economic injustice.

"Do it," he told the lawyer.

He wished he felt as certain as he sounded. The younger Raven had been so much more self-assured. Of course, the younger Raven had sworn himself to William. No matter what his test scores said, the younger Raven had been a bit of an idiot.

Jasmine had dropped by with breakfast in a basket, and the scent of baked goods wafted from beneath the blue gingham towel that covered it. The kitchen contained a respectable selection of teas, including both plain Earl Grey and an Earl Grey with lavender. Raven decided to sample the latter. The fragrance of black tea, bergamot and lavender provided the perfect counterpoint to the smells of warm apple and cinnamon rising from the basket. Raven allowed himself to push away his doubts about Morgan and his concern over the dark magic he felt on the butte, focusing instead on the simple and splendid repast.

Thus fortified, he teleported to the sidewalk in front of the closed tavern and crossed the street to the library housed in a white Victorian structure that reminded Raven just a bit of a wedding cake. He strode up the steps, stopping on the porch to read the engraved metal plaque on the door.

Chadwick Memorial Library

Our town's library resides in what was once the home of Doctor Michael Chadwick, Devil's Crossing's very first medical doctor. The wealthiest man in town, most of his money came from timber and mining interests inherited from his father, not from his medical practice. They say he never turned away a patient and never charged more than someone could afford to pay. Legend has it that, as well as money, he accepted as payment: a Smith and Wesson revolver; a turkey fresh-plucked and dressed; a jug of homemade hard cider, and a bull terrier pup he named Terror.

Doctor Chadwick and his wife Julia were never blessed with children. Doctor Chadwick predeceased his wife by less than a year. Julia's will bequeathed their entire estate to the town of Devil's Crossing. She stipulated that, in memory of her husband who loved learning and loved his neighbors, part of the funds be put in trust to build and support a library.

Raven put his hand to the doorframe. Warmth spread in his chest, warmth toward the doctor and, by extension, the town.

The library smelled of books and old-fashioned linseed floor polish, and Raven felt at home in a way he hadn't since coming to this infernal town. It was blissfully, blessedly quiet—none of this library-as-community-center nonsense where library staff said nothing to parents who let their children run screaming through the aisles. Not that he had a problem with community centers. He'd even contributed generously to campaigns to build them in disadvantaged neighborhoods. (At Cam's behest, but still.) He didn't even have a problem with children in libraries *per se*. The neighborhood library had been his favorite refuge from the time he was old enough to walk there on his own, at a considerably earlier age than most children today. But to him the library had been a special place, a sacred sanctuary of quiet and books, a haven from loud, bullying peers. The world was filled with places for people to be loud and boisterous. He felt sorry for introvert children today, growing up without a quiet place to just *be*, as well as adults stuck in thin-walled apartments or shared living situations who had no place they could go to hear themselves think.

The library carried back issues of the *Crossing Guard*, the local paper. Raven scoured these for any information on the cave in the Devil's Boneyard and the controversy over the golf course. Raven discovered that, despite the newly-found petroglyphs' age, the sealed cave environment had preserved the pigments so well the archeologists who studied them believed that the colors looked much the same as they would have the day they were applied. It seemed inconceivable that they could be endangered for something as tawdry and unnecessary as a golf resort. Had people no respect for antiquity? Had they no *soul?*

Being trained in Art rather than in the Craft tradition, Raven knew only a little about petroglyphs in general. The local tribes believed that the ones in the cave had been created by a people so ancient that they had little or no direct connection to the tribes that dwelt there when the white men first came. Some papers made reference to the Old Ones or the First Ones, but Raven couldn't be sure if these were terms that came from the tribes, or if it was a bunch of romantic clap-trap with origins only as old as the imaginations of the white reporters.

Raven found an article about the Devil's Boneyard petroglyphs in one of those glossy news magazines and studied the pictures. The photographer had won a lottery to be allowed to go into the cave and do flash photography—it was feared that too many flashes could destroy the pigments. His eyes kept going back to the warrior figure near the cave entrance, and to the huge raven at the cave's end. *The warrior protects the raven and the raven protects the world.*

Raven shook his head sharply. Where had those words come from? He felt as though he was in one of those dreams where he just *knew* things he had no way of knowing, the dreams that made so much sense until he woke.

His thoughts strayed to that long-ago cave in Australia, to the images on the walls there, stylistically different but with the same feel of ancient, unfathomable power. The cave brought thoughts of Bran Tarrant, the odd mage-shaman whose lineage was as mixed as his magic. Of Tarrant's words, which Raven had tucked away in his memory with other unsettling things.

Raven couldn't discount Tarrant's assessment. It had a ring of truth. It spoke to his soul in a way he couldn't quite put into words. Yet Tarrant himself had said that being a shaman is about being true to one's deepest self, and that Raven was a mage straight to the core. Had, in essence, given him leave not to do anything with the knowledge, and that had seemed like the wisest and most comfortable approach. Except now he wondered if Tarrant had known all along that Fate would call to whatever strange, latent abilities he might have.

Raven wasn't a strong believer in destiny, but sometimes the universe fell into patterns that made him wonder.

Perhaps he should reach out to Mother Crone. Although her background was Old World Wiccan, she at least understood Craft, which put her closer to the needed learning. More importantly, she had contacts among the shamanic subset of Craft and could make an introduction. Many of the Native American Craft practitioners were understandably suspicious of Europeans inquiring into their traditions, and with his family history, well. He couldn't blame them if they warded their crystal against his signature after his first attempted contact.

Best to glean what he could from the articles first; at least he would not annoy any contacts Mother Crone could secure him with questions easily answered elsewhere.

He read the article carefully, including the sidebars. With the librarian's help, he located the source material quoted in the journal *Antiquity.* It seemed that the local existent tribes all claimed to have no knowledge of the significance of the petroglyphs, who made them and why they were in the cave that seemed, even before the slide that sealed it off completely, to be little-trafficked.

He looked through the local papers for the accounts of Lansing's death, and for articles on the proposed golf resort and about the activists committed to stopping it. He even paged through a small, locally-published book titled *Legends and Folklore of Devil's Crossing.* For a small town, it seemed to have more than its share of hagiography, most of it surrounding the Butte. The book claimed that the tribes had warned the first settlers away from the butte, stating that the place was cursed. The story was that the tribal name for the place, which the settlers translated as *Devil's Boneyard,* came from an epic confrontation between a long-ago medicine man and the devil himself. The devil lost, and the tribe buried him and piled rocks over his grave to keep him down, and that pile eventually became the butte.

The tale had more holes in it than a family-size pack of swiss cheese, of course. Geologists knew the butte was a large section of hard rock, probably the core of an ancient volcano. Erosion carved away the surrounding softer rock and dirt layers to leave the impressively large, block-like structure to stand alone. So far as Raven knew, the devil never figured into the original spiritual beliefs of the local tribes. And, if one took into account the stories of people who *did* believe in the devil, Satan was alive and well, leading innocents astray and losing bets to fiddlers at any number of crossroads.

The book contained tales of eerie chanting at night that ended abruptly when someone went to investigate; a quiet, reliable family man who came home and murdered his wife and children after a night camping on the butte, and then went mute, never saying a word until the day he was hanged for the crime. There was the *de rigueur* ghost of the maiden who leaped to her death from the top of the butte rather than betray her true love by marrying the man her father chose. The road to the butte even had the classic disappearing hitchhiker, tales of which supposedly went back to the horse and buggy days. Raven mentally flagged that one for Josiah. His chess partner was interested in origins of folk tales. If the book had the provenance of that particular ghost story correct, the Devil's Crossing hitchhiker may in fact be the earliest instance of that particular tale.

Regardless of the unlikelihood of the individual tales, Raven did not dismiss the collection out of hand. Josiah tended to ramble about folklore over the chess board, and from him Raven learned that the most outlandish folktales often had a grain of truth. The bloody tyrant Vlad the Impaler became Vladimir Dracula of vampire legends. Unfortunate individuals with extreme hirsutism were killed as werewolves by their superstitious neighbors. Places that in early times were said to be cursed in modern times were found to have unnaturally high levels of arsenic in the soil. Some so-called haunted castles in Europe had been so contaminated by centuries of dark magic that they would likely never be fully cleared of the emanations.

The library closed up for the day much earlier than he was used to, but he supposed even with an endowment a small-town library had to be careful with its budget. He felt like he'd gained very little new knowledge for the time he'd spent. He sighed deeply. Perhaps Cassandra and Rafe would wrap up the case they were working on soon and one or both would come out here for a weekend. Scholarly research, ward-breaking, magical improvisation, those he could do, but he was by no means a trained detective. He was beginning to feel utterly useless here.

He left the library and crossed the street to the tavern for a late lunch—or was it an early dinner? Maybe by the time he ate and returned to his temporary home Cassandra would be off duty and he could pick her brain, if not convince her to teleport to him and rescue him from his own incompetence. With that hopeful thought, he crossed the street to the tavern.

Craig wasn't behind the bar. This early in the day Raven would have been surprised if he were. He was, however, on the customer's side of the bar, accepting from the waitress a large to-go bag with grease stains starting to show near the bottom. His hair was ruffled, his face tired and uncharacteristically grim. He smelled like a fireplace.

Raven stepped forward to greet the man, but as soon as Craig turned and saw him, his eyes narrowed.

"You have a lot of nerve coming in here!"

NINE

Raven stepped back in surprise at the cold rage in the man's voice. He'd guessed that Craig wouldn't be happy about him making Morgan's bail, but he had no idea that the man would take it this personally. "What I did was within the law, both the letter and the spirit." Out of the respect the sheriff had previously won from him, he kept his voice conversational, his posture unthreatening. This was not the time for Bad Old Raven to resurface, no matter what instinct demanded.

He did, however, strengthen his shield to combat-readiness. There was no sense being a fool. By the way the sheriff's eyes darkened, he had sensed the change. Everything Raven knew about the man said that Craig wasn't stupid enough to have a go at him if Raven didn't make the first move. He hoped he was right. Not that the sheriff's magic would pose any challenge to him in a real fight, and not that he would likely end up in any trouble that couldn't be managed by the combined forces of his GII contacts and Alexander Chen, attorney at law, but he didn't want to break the longest streak being out of tabloid headlines in his adult life. Not to mention that he had an aversion to being imprisoned behind magic-dampening fields, and third time was definitely not a charm. Besides, he rather liked Craig.

"Legal." The sheriff spat out the word as if it were a curse. "Oh, yes, it was all legal. Why don't you explain that all to Morgan Jansen's parents? Though you'd have to dust off your necromancy."

"What?" Raven hadn't cared much for necromancy even when he was a practicing dark mage, but he let the verbal slap pass in his shock at the deeper implication. "What has happened?"

"The local hay man was making a delivery over at the Jansen's farm. He found Sam and Lucy Jansen in the front yard of their

71

house, exsanguinated. Their house burned to the ground. The whole place reeked of dark magic. Morgan is nowhere to be found. There's an APB out. I warned my officers to consider him extremely dangerous."

"What? None of that makes sense." Raven realized he sounded like the civilian he was, and naïve, which he was not. "But why?" Sam and Lucy had always stood by Morgan. They were the only family he had ever known.

"Who knows?" The sheriff growled. "Maybe they asked him to take out the trash before he could use the truck. We all know Morgan doesn't like to be thwarted."

Thoughts whirled through Raven's mind, too fast for him to make sense of them. "I'm sorry." It was the one thing of which he was certain. "If I had known—I had no way of knowing."

"Of course not," the sheriff said. "And, of course, you couldn't listen to me. Or the prosecutor's office. I'm guessing you knew they argued against bail at all."

Raven nodded. No point in making things worse by playing dumb.

"Just because I've known the boy for longer than a day, just because I'm a law enforcement professional, well, that's no reason to listen to me. Not when you're the great Corwyn Ravenscroft."

Raven flinched. "I'm sorry," he said again. "If there's anything I can do to help—"

"I'd say you've done enough."

All eyes in the bar turned to him. It had been a while since he had felt such weight of public condemnation. He hadn't realized that one could fall out of practice with bearing such things.

Under the circumstances, he didn't linger to ask if the bar sold bottles to go. He schooled his face to an emotionless mask, squared his shoulders, and strode from the bar with a confidence he did not feel. Daring the deli-and-bait store, he found they offered a surprisingly acceptable wine aisle. He selected a bottle of Willamette Valley merlot and another of pinot noir, then picked up some packaged Tillamook cheddar and a box of crackers. Wine selection or no, he wasn't about to dare the questionable-looking chicken nor the Jo-Joes, which were apparently fried somethings.

72

He returned to his temporary refuge. The message crystal was flashing the clear light that signaled a non-urgent message. He tapped the base of the crystal and felt instantly better for hearing Cassandra's voice.

"Raven, love. Sorry I missed you. I just wanted to let you know that it doesn't look like either I or Rafe are going to get loose from here to come out any time soon. Things are crazy. We've been working with the locals. . .there's a weird surge in magic-related crime in Portland. No one can figure out what's going on."

Raven poured himself a glass of wine, and stared at the food. He had no real appetite, though he knew wine *with* dinner was healthier than wine *as* dinner.

Raven stared morosely at the ceiling of the cottage, letting his eyes follow the grain of the wood on the exposed timbers, trying to let his mind numb itself.

No help coming from GII. He wondered if he should just go home. He had been worse than no help here. The sheriff was right. He didn't know the community, didn't know the dynamics.

Maybe he wasn't a dark mage anymore. That didn't mean he was a good man.

He had tried to be, these last few years. He had tried. He longed for home. Not just the comforts of Ravenscroft Manor, though shutting himself up in his study with his books and his brandy certainly had its appeal. He missed his city. He knew it streets, its politics, its people. Even when he was notorious, at least he knew where he stood.

Despite the immodest amount of wine he consumed, he had trouble falling asleep. He rose several times to pace the floor, trying to no avail to wear himself out. He even considered going outside to walk, but he'd heard that there were venomous snakes in the area and had no idea if they were active at night. It hadn't been the queasy feeling in his stomach that kept him lying awake, staring at the ceiling long after the clock on the wall had chimed midnight, however. He kept on playing over the events of the last day. His interview with Morgan. The discussions about Morgan he'd had with both the sheriff and with Scott before he made his decision to make the boy's bail. The harsh and very likely warranted accusations from the sheriff last night.

Raven woke the next morning with his stomach reminding him that it preferred a better food to wine ratio. He got up, poured himself some water, made himself drink it despite his stomach's opinion on the decision. He flipped open the napkin that covered the basket on the center of the table and decided he didn't have the will to eat right now, no matter how tempting the coffeecake within would have been otherwise. He made a cup of Earl Grey, and tapped on the message crystal, reaching out to the crystal on his mantel at home. It was early enough that Cassandra might not have left yet for work.

"Raven?"

Cassandra's voice always felt like grace, a benediction. As though he could not have possibly have screwed up all that terribly, not have been such a terrible person, and still have her in his life. Love welled up within him. Would he ever fail to be reduced to a sappy teenager by the mere sound of her voice? He hoped not.

"Things are a mess here, Cassandra," he admitted. "And I fear that I may have just made them even worse. Something big is going on though, bigger than one boy could account for, even with a lot of talent and some major sociopathic tendencies."

He filled her in on the events of the last day and half.

"I know you're to say it's just like Adam. I guess I haven't learned my lesson."

"Oh no, love, you can't blame yourself. Not this time. You did everything you should have done. You have the opinion of his parents and a social worker familiar with him. You considered things carefully, discussed them with the lawyer. Yes, it turns out that the sheriff was right and the social worker was wrong, but you couldn't have known that."

"I really think the situation warrants an official GII investigation," Raven said.

Cassandra groaned. "I wouldn't want to be the one to have to explain that to Sherlock. She's already ripping her hair out."

It took a lot to rattle Cassandra's supervisor; she was normally as cool-headed as the fictional character from whom her nickname derived. "What's going on?"

"It seems like every nutcase and wanna-be dark mage in the Portland area decided to go off at once. We have some sort of a doomsday cult situation out in Molalla. Up until Monday they weren't even on our radar—just an ordinary-looking organic produce co-op. I think I even have a flyer for them around here somewhere. I was thinking about signing us up for a fresh produce subscription delivery. Now there's been shots fired and they're talking about the end of times. They've barricaded themselves in and set booby-traps, Mundane and magical both. We reached out to the Seattle office for reinforcements, but they have a situation of their own, a fundamentalist group that's gone from annoying to dangerous with no prior warning. And those are just the highlights. The Eugene office just messaged *us* for help and we had to turn them down."

Raven sighed and ran a hand through his hair. He couldn't expect Sherlock to send someone out to investigate something he could not even define while there was an active situation going on.

"Look at it this way," Cassandra said. "You always wanted to be a Guardian. Now's your chance."

"When I was in General Academy. What, are you going to give me one of those gold-badge stickers they hand out at classroom visits?"

"I'm sure I could track one down. Look, I hate to do this, but I have to dash. I was supposed to be meeting Rafe, like, five minutes ago."

"Right, then." Raven said. "Stay safe."

"Always do." The crystal went dark, signaling that Cassandra had deactivated at her end.

It was so, so tempting to pack up and teleport home. He was a civilian, not even here as a consultant. No duty held him here. So far, he couldn't even claim he had done anyone any good. Except that *something* involving dark magic was going on. While any legal obligation from his pardon ended when he brought down his former master, Raven felt a duty to use his rare and ill-gotten knowledge of dark magic for good whenever he could.

Even if that knowledge, though extensive, fell short of the current demands.

Raven showered, dressed, and returned to the library. Fortunately, there were no other patrons and, if the librarian had heard of last night's disruption at the Devil's Pitchfork, she was too professional to glare. Raven poked around the town's historical records for a while. Other than the local myths and legends, none of which seemed terribly out of the ordinary, he could find nothing. No credible history of curses. No recent or even distant record of notable dark mages. He gave up and teleported back to the B&B long before the library's closing time.

Jasmine had left a packet of local information for guests, sitting on the desk by the landline telephone. There was a pizza place in the next town that would deliver as far as Devil's Crossing for an extra surcharge. While he wasn't a fan of pizza, it was the only option other than the convenience store and Devil's Pitchfork, and so he called in an order.

The pizza arrived an hour and a half later, small for the price but surprisingly edible. His growling stomach reminded him of the number of meals that he had skimped on or skipped altogether, and he found himself finishing the whole thing. In the resultant food coma, he eyed the bed. Though it was only late afternoon, he thought maybe he could catch up on some of the sleep he had missed.

A flash of red drew his eyes; the message crystal, signaling *urgent*. Had he caused some other disaster?

No sense trying to avoid the news. He heaved a heavy sigh and went to the crystal, hesitating only before a moment before tapping the base to activate it.

"This is Raven."

TEN

"This is Craig. Sheriff Schmidt. There's a situation. I need you to come out right away."

"I'll consider it if you tell me where, what, why, and whether I should have my attorney present."

"What? No, it's nothing like that. Look, I owe you an apology, and you'll get one, in full and in detail. But there's no time now. I have a hostage situation. No time to explain on the crystal. I could really use a combat magic heavy hitter with reliable accuracy."

Trap! Raven pushed the thought away, blamed it on his early history. He didn't think the sheriff would use such tactics, especially when Raven had done nothing illegal and had the might of GII behind him. Besides, the sheriff sounded frantic. If he was playacting, then he could replace the best actors at the Shakespeare festival in Ashland. Raven did not think he was acting. He was certain enough to stake his life and his freedom. Or at least certain enough not to risk the life of an innocent.

A better person than he, someone like Ana or Cassandra, wouldn't have hesitated for even one moment.

Raven thought for two before he answered. "Where are you?"

"It would take too long to explain. You're an out-of-towner. On these back roads, it'd take an hour, hour and a half by car if you didn't want to risk tipping over the edge and into the ravine."

Raven wasn't bloody likely to get in a car anyway if there were another option.

"Just use me as a teleport anchor," the sheriff urged. "Please. Come quick."

Raven closed his eyes, reached out through the ether until he found the sheriff's solid presence. The sheriff felt like an ancient stone warmed by centuries of sun, belonging to this land, this desert, this community. Raven followed the pull and found himself at the end of a rutted dirt road, facing into a clearing.

As soon as he had faded in fully a hand grabbed his arm yanking him behind the rusted wreck of a car. "Get down."

Before he had fully oriented to his situation a bullet whizzed overhead passing through the space he had been occupying to take out a piece from the trunk of the juniper behind him.

Gods. That's all they needed. Mundane firearms tended to behave erratically around magic for reasons that no one had ever fully explained.

"Is he a Mundane?" Raven asked in a whisper.

"Craft," the sheriff said in the same hushed tone. "Lots of Craft here have 'em, even some of Art practitioners. For hunting and such. Putting an animal out of its misery when it's suffering and the vet is three hours away by truck. 'Course most folks in this town grew up around guns and magic and they have more sense than to combine the two."

Raven dared inch up the side of the car, just a little, just enough to catch a glimpse of the shooter through the dust-filmed windows of the wrecked car. He saw a tall, broadly built, red-haired man with the red-red skin that comes with sunburn, not genetics. He had one arm over Morgan's shoulder and across his neck, not quite a chokehold, but not far from it. In his other hand he held a nasty-looking revolver pointed at Morgan's head.

Raven ducked back down again, hiding behind the door of the car before he could draw the attention of the gun man. "What the hell is going on?"

"That's Harvey Heilman. Harvey the hay man."

"The one who reported finding Morgan's parents?"

"Yes. We're still not sure if he had any involvement in that mess. The magic seems too strong for what we know of Harvey's abilities. As I said, he's a Craft practitioner, not Art, and not terribly powerful at any rate. But what we know for sure is Morgan found out what happened at his parents' farm and drove like a bat out of hell to Harvey's hay barn. Harvey had just finished deliveries for the day. Our one surviving witness says Morgan had heard that

Harvey reported it and just wanted to know what happened. What Harvey had seen, knew. I guess word had reached Morgan that he was wanted and he knew better than to come to the police. Or maybe not better. If he had come to us at least he wouldn't he wouldn't have a gun to his head right now.

"The only surviving witness said that Harvey went nuts. It was like he didn't even hear what Morgan was saying, what Morgan was asking. He started shouting crazy things, accusing Morgan of being after him, of accusing the police force of being after him, of half the people in the Valley being after him. There was something about demons and a rain of blood. There'd already been gunshots by the time Morgan got there, and one of the neighbors had already called the police.

"As soon as Harvey heard the sirens, he grabbed Morgan and the gun and hauled them into the truck. One of my deputies pursued and that's how we ended up here. The deputy followed him this far. We think Harvey's truck axle broke on the rocks up ahead and he decided to make his stand." The sheriff shook his head. "I don't understand it. I just don't understand it. I've known Harvey for going on twenty years now. Bought hay from him every year back when I kept a pony for the sister's kids. Everyone knows Harvey. Everyone likes Harvey."

"You said the last survivor. So people were killed up at Heilman's place?"

"Yeah. Good thing that one of our deputies got out of the car and looked around to see if there was anyone who needed help instead of joining in the chase with the truck. Harvey's wife and his four kids were all shot. Only the eldest one survived by playing dead. She was in shock, and I'm not sure how much sense there is in the tale she told. I almost hope she doesn't completely understand what happened. There was blood and brains everywhere from what the deputy said."

Gods. Raven's thoughts went unbidden to his own little Ransley Zachary. He couldn't imagine what would drive someone to kill his children like that, to kill his wife like that. Even Raven's father had had enough natural instinct not to kill his own offspring.

"It's still feasible that Morgan could have killed his own parents and that was a separate incident," the sheriff said. "But in light of this afternoon's events I'd have to say that looking less likely."

It was not the time for *I told you so.* "How do you want to do this?"

"I'll be honest, I'm not really sure. But I figure with all your experience with the GII you've seen a lot more of this than we ever see in a lifetime out here. I think I've only heard of one hostage situation my whole life in Devil's Crossing and that was a man who got drunk and beat up his wife, and panicked when the cops came. My dad was sheriff then, and he said it was the toughest situation he'd ever faced in his life. That man was drunk, yes, but he wasn't acting like he was lost in a totally different reality. Anyway, I was hoping with your experience. . . At the very least I'm guessing you've had much more practice at targeting spells."

As a matter of fact, he was one of the best in the field, beating out even seasoned GII agents on the target range. But still, *no one* could be certain enough of their aim for this scenario.

"They're coming," Harvey screamed. "The shadows. You think I don't know, but I can feel them coming closer."

"What shadows?" Raven whispered to the sheriff. "Do you know what he's talking about?"

The sheriff shook his head. "As far as we can tell he's delusional."

"You've been working for them for years," Harvey continued. "You think I don't know what you're up to? You and the Jansens, the men in black coats, you're all in league."

In league? Raven was fairly certain that *in league* was not a phrase in Harvey's daily vernacular. It sounded like a phrase he might have picked up from a book, or a horror film.

"You see why we believe that we're not going to be able to talk our way out of this one. And it would take too long to get a sharpshooter from the state police or the Feds. We can usually get support from Bend, but they're dealing with an unusual spike in serious crime for some reason. Harvey could snap and kill the kid at any moment. Targeted combat magic may be our only hope of a positive outcome," the sheriff said.

"No one is good enough to guarantee the results in this situation," Raven said. "We would be risking the kid's life. Even if I was able to aim the spell lightning to avoid hitting Morgan while trying to take out Harvey—and mind you that's with less than six inches margin of error. I don't know many people who are that confident, even in GII, and most of my early training was not intended to avoid casualties. Even if I could make the strike, there's the risk that Harvey could still get off a shot, intentionally or as a reflex. His finger could pull on the trigger as he fell."

"But it could be a bigger risk to Morgan if we do nothing." The sheriff looked over his shoulder. "In about another five minutes the sun is going to start slipping down the horizon, and the glare will be full in Harvey's eyes. That will be our best chance to strike. Otherwise, I'm afraid Harvey will get more and more desperate as fatigue sets in, and shoot the kid no matter what we do."

There was another option. If Raven were anyone but himself, this choice, this test, would not be before him. If he had been anyone else, he wouldn't be standing here with the power of the dark magic still flowing in his memory and his veins, and the desperate need to atone forever burning in his soul. For his work in bringing down his former master, Raven had been granted a full pardon by the Joint Council of the Three Communities, provisional on his forsaking dark magic. He had only broken that vow once, in the heat of the pitched battle when William had resurfaced to threaten all that Raven loved.

Many of the laws regarding what was and was not dark magic were somewhat arbitrary. Combat spells such as magefire and spell lightning, even Hammerhand, were not considered dark *per se*. Like Mundane weapons, their use was legal or illegal based on circumstances. Raven didn't disagree with the classification of some dark magic; death magic had left a stain on his soul that might never wash away. The law said that any magic that subsumed one person's will to another was automatically dark. In some ways, Raven understood where the lawmakers were coming from. To completely lose one's will, to have one's mind and one's power taken over by another, that was one of the worst nightmares

Raven could imagine, and his years with William had given his imagination plenty of fodder. Not to mention that the addictive nature of dark magic meant that a strict ban made sense. Once a mage found justification to take over someone's will once, it became that much easier to find a reason to do it again, or to perform some other act of dark magic. Raven, having spent much of his adult life as a dark mage, still policed himself for signs of recidivism although several years had passed since his return to the light.

It was far easier, far safer, to reject dark magic altogether. But in circumstances like these, where the alternative would risk the life of at least one civilian as well as a number of law enforcement officers, the choice seemed less clear.

"So, given your assessment of Harvey's magical abilities," Raven said, "I should be able to overpower his will, even from this distance. Take control of his thoughts, make him drop the gun."

"You can do that? From this distance? Without prior contact?" The sheriff sounded suddenly wary and Raven couldn't blame him. It was a frightening thing to think that your thoughts and decisions might not be your own.

Usually it took familiarity with and some cooperation from the victim, even if that cooperation came from either coercion or subterfuge. Or else the mage casting the spell had to rely on a charmed object somehow slipped into the victim's possession to boost the magic.

"I couldn't manage it with anyone with any real power. And not for any length of time. Mind control like in a Mundane's silly vampire movie doesn't exist. Harvey appears panicked, exhausted. I might be able to grab him for just a few minutes, long enough maybe for Morgan to get clear and your men to move in."

The sheriff said nothing for a moment, but his voice when he spoke held no hesitation. "Do it."

"It's dark magic," Raven reminded him.

"I don't care." The sheriff took a deep breath. "Look, half the men here are Mundane. The others have been around the block long enough to know that good policing is — situational."

Raven hesitated. He agreed that it was the right thing to do. What would Cassandra or Ana tell him to do? Or Sherlock, the director of GII and Cassandra's boss, who pulled him out of his isolation and proved to him he had a place as a consultant? They had put their own reputation, their own careers on the line, to stand up for him. Was he risking all that if he used dark magic again, here in front of strangers and near-strangers?

"I'm senior officer here," the sheriff said. "I'll take responsibility."

For a lot of reasons, it was not that easy. For one, obeying orders did not give absolute protection when one knew that the orders were illegal. For another, Raven was a consultant with GII and not here in it in an official capacity. Arguably, he either outranked Craig Schmidt, or was not in the chain of command at all.

Alexander Chen had gotten people off with a lot less to work with. But that really wasn't even the point. He hadn't been able to save Adam. He could save Morgan, maybe. He was damned if he would let him die over what was illegal but not, in this instance, actually wrong.

He was trusting the sheriff to keep his word. It would be easy enough for Craig to deny that he had told Raven to go ahead with the dark magic. It wasn't even twenty-four hours since this man all but threw him out of his bar. A few years ago he might not have accepted the risk. But trust came easier to him these days. He believed that Craig was a decent man, an honest man.

He closed his eyes, focused his own will, then reached out to Heilman's. He found no resistance, not even the natural barrier of a Mundane. Instead, the man's consciousness grabbed onto Raven's will like a drowning man clutching a lifeline. Fear clutched Raven's throat. The man's mind was a maelstrom of terror, confusion, and a strange dark hunger that seemed alien to the rest of his thoughts and emotions. And that maelstrom was drawing Raven in.

ELEVEN

He pulled back, panicked, only managing to stop from fully disengaging when he realized that he was freed from the danger. *What the hell was that?* Did Heilman have multiple personalities? Is that what Raven sensed? Or was something equally strange going on, beyond even Raven's experience?

No matter. Time enough to analyze that later.

He reached out, twined his will with the panicking, confused part that he identified as the primary personality, let it cling to him. *I know you're scared. I have a plan. Yield to me.*

Right now, he needed to get Morgan safe. He held Heilman's will gently, but firmly. It was as though he were picking up a wild animal, and didn't want to scare it but didn't want to risk it is escaping. Just as gently, he molded that will with his own. *Let Morgan go. You're safest if you let the boy go. Let the him go, and all will be well. You'll be safe from the guns, safe from the shadows. Just let him go.*

It wasn't working. The anger, the rage, the darkness in Heilman's mind fought him, clamoring for violence, for blood. Shrieking that the only way to be safe was to kill the threat.

No. You're safest if you give up the boy. You're safest if you give up Morgan. The shadows will leave you alone if only you give up Morgan. You can be at peace. It wasn't working. Gods damn it, it wasn't working. And then suddenly Harvey shoved Morgan away, sending him stumbling toward the officers on legs shaking with shock. Morgan tripped, fell to hands and knees, scurried to cover behind the wrecked car without taking time to get to his feet.

It had worked. Oh, powers of light and dark, it had worked. Now all he had to do was convince Heilman to put down the gun. Raven took a deep breath, and then another. Focused his will, shaped what he wanted in Heilman's own thoughts. He saw the gun hand lower, just by an inch or so, then lower again a few more inches. He almost had it. Almost there.

The maelstrom madness in Heilman's head spun even faster in fury, too fast for Raven to parse out individual thoughts. Heilman's will jerked away from Raven's hold. Raven's thoughts were still too close to Heilman's; the man's darker emotions almost overcame Raven's own, almost *became* Raven's own. Raven sensed the fear, the despair, the horror. Their gun hand, no Heilman's gun hand moved faster than thought. Raven reached out with his own thoughts, but before he could exert his will the barrel found its place under Heilman's chin, and a finger moved on the trigger.

A bang like the amplified slamming of the door echoed against the rocks as Heilman's body dropped to the ground and was still. The silence that followed was deafening. No one moved, no one even spoke. It was as if the world itself held its breath.

Raven's feet took him forward, the gritty soil crunching beneath his hard-soled shoes until he stopped just short of the body. The spirit he had so briefly tangled with, had struggled with, had tried to help, was gone. Gone as surely and completely as if William's most spectacular and most destructive spells had hit the man and torn him apart. Except this body was intact, nearly unchanged except for a singed hole under his chin. Scarlet blood poured from his open mouth. From his ears a yellow fluid leaked. Brain matter? Spinal fluid? The yellow fluid had streaks of pink. More blood, mixed into other fluids.

The gun was still in Heilman's hand. Mostly metal, a little wood, some black powder and the bullet. No power as Raven understood power, and yet it had achieved one of the oldest, most common and yet in its own way the most profoundly dark magic the world had known since its beginning. This Mundane object had taken a living thing, a living man, and transformed him into nothing more than meat and bone.

The sheriff and his deputies were surrounding the body now. They kept a careful distance as though an invisible line around the corpse must not be crossed for fear of destruction of evidence, or out of respect for the life that had once been and now was no more. Raven heard them talking quietly. The voices seemed so very far away, as though he were hearing them from a television screen in another room. Something about the type of ammunition that was used, a type commonly sold to farmers who loaded their pistols for snakes and other small vermin.

Raven was no stranger to death. He'd seen more people die in more horrible ways than most human beings could see and stay sane. He never managed to become immune to its effects; he supposed that was what had divided him from William. Yet this death, relatively quick and clean, shocked him in a way he had not been prepared for. Maybe because it *was* quick and clean, just a brief second, a brief twitch of a man's finger, and the border between life and death, that inexplicable border that no scientist and no mage had fully explained, that border had been crossed. The border had been crossed, the gates closed, and for this man there would be no return. Oh, one could get into the metaphysics, the possibility of planes beyond this one, beliefs about reincarnation. But the fact remained that this man, Harvey Heilman, Harvey the hay man, this man would never exist as he had been on this plane. It seemed wrong that something so quick, so simple, so utterly without magic, should be so utterly irreversible.

Raven had seen death often enough that it should not make him queasy. But he had never been tangled in a dying man's thoughts before. It was like touching his own mortality. He willed down his gorge, straightened his spine, and reminded himself that he was still alive.

Nothing he could do for the dead. His responsibility was to the living, and he was more certain than ever that they were facing something much bigger than a dead real estate mogul and a mentally unstable hay farmer.

"Are you all right?" The sheriff asked.

"Fine. I didn't — what happened, I didn't want him to do that."

"I didn't think that you did," the sheriff said with more faith than most people gave to Raven on such short acquaintance.

"We need to talk." Raven's voice sounded strange in his own ears. Flat, slightly unreal. "Once this is all cleaned up, we need to talk."

"We'll need a statement from you. Do you want to stick around while we wait for the techs to come and take charge of the scene? I should really be here until the van comes to take the body to the morgue. It could be a while, so if you want you can come in tomorrow. . ."

It was a courtesy for the sheriff to give him a choice. He probably only extended the offer because of how he had treated Raven the previous evening. Raven considered just teleporting back to the B&B and have a good night's sleep, or try to. Easier to lick his wounds in private, and come to the police station in the morning with his masks and his mental equilibrium intact. But he had sensed something familiar in the darkness within Heilman's mind. In the heat of the moment, he had not recognized it. Now in hindsight he knew what he felt. It was akin to what he had sensed in the cave at the Devil's Boneyard. If he was right, they'd already spent far too long to realize a danger that was only growing worse.

"I'll stay."

Raven trailed the sheriff as he approached Morgan. The boy was sitting on the ground, hugging his knees to his chest and rocking back and forth. Someone had gotten out one of those silvery blankets that emergency personnel carry and wrapped it around his shoulders. His whole body shook and he was breathing hard but too fast.

"How are you, son?" the sheriff asked. "At some point we need to talk about what happened."

Morgan just shook his head. "I— I— Just give me a minute."

It was very clear to Raven that it would take more than a minute for the boy to get himself together. He had seen enough crime scenes to see the effects of severe emotional shock.

Apparently, so had the sheriff. "All right, son. All right. I'd like to take a statement as soon as possible, but I don't think you're going to be in any shape for a while. Are you hurt at all?"

Morgan glanced at up at him once, and then returned his gaze to the ground. "I wasn't hit or shot or anything like that."

"All right," Craig said. "I think you should be looked over anyway. I'll have an ambulance here to take you to the hospital.

One of my reserve deputies will meet you there. She'll take your statement after the doctors clear you."

The sheriff walked a little distance, indicating that Raven should follow him. "The deputy I'm sending is good with trauma situations. She's trained to act as a family liaison for the families of victims. She'll take good care of him."

"Should I arrange to have a lawyer present for the boy?" Raven asked.

"It's up to you and him, of course," the sheriff said. "But I don't think that's really going to be necessary."

"You no longer think he had anything to do with his parents' deaths." He phrased it as a statement, but he still wanted the sheriff's confirmation.

"My money's on Harvey at this point," Craig said. "If Morgan were one of my nephews, I'd want to keep the interview as low-key as possible. Do it at the hospital, rather than having to bring him in to the station, like we would if we did a formal interview with the lawyer."

"So where does he go after that?"

"That's a good question." The sheriff frowned. "As far as I know, there is no other family."

"Damn." Raven thought for a moment. "There's a hotel in town, isn't there?"

"Yeah, the Hotel Grand. A little run down, but they're clean and safe. I don't know that Morgan has any money though. I'm assuming he will inherit everything from his parents, but that'll take a while. I'm not sure he's on any of the farm accounts."

"You can help me make arrangements with the hotel. I'll pay the bill for a few nights. Give him a chance to figure things out."

The sheriff sighed in relief. "Thank you. We're not really set up for this sort of thing here. Too small, not enough resources. I may not be Morgan's number one fan, but I still don't want to make him sleep in the barn a few yards from where his parents were killed."

TWELVE

In the end Raven gave two statements that night. The first he gave at the scene, the official one in which he was little more than a witness to the tragedy that had happened. The second he gave later, in Craig's office at the bar, after hours.

The sheriff poured a scotch for himself and made up a glass of absinthe for Raven. Raven took his drink without comment. He had never been on official duty here; it was none of his business whether the sheriff considered himself on duty or officially clocked out. They both needed the drink.

Raven didn't start talking until they were both well enough into their drinks to have the alcohol buzz take the sharpest edge off of what they had seen. And then he told the sheriff what he had sensed. "Either the man had multiple personalities—rare, I know, but it's possible—or there was something else there. In his head."

The sheriff shook his head. "Heilman was never known to have any instabilities before this moment. 'Course sometimes it's all boiling under the surface and then it just erupts without warning."

"Right." Raven leveled him a steady gaze. "And in real life, how often does that actually happen?"

The sheriff smiled grimly and shook his head. "Not often. Not often at all."

"So, it must be somehow related to what happened in the cave."

The sheriff shook his head again. "I don't see how it could be. I mean yes there's two unusual occurrences, well, three if you count the Jansens' deaths and Heilman's suicide as two separate incidents. But you know as well as I that correlation does not mean causation. That's just sloppy police work."

"I would agree with you if correlation were all we had. But the darkness, whatever it was, it felt like a separate personality. It makes no sense, but that doesn't make it any less true. And that darkness felt the same as what was in the cave."

"So you did sense a magical signature after all?"

Raven took another long sip of the absinthe. Though it had been well-blended with sugar, it was the bitterness of the wormwood that he tasted. "Not a magical signature. At least not like anything that I have encountered before. It was—the whole thing makes no sense in terms of anything I've ever known about magic. And I flatter myself that I do know quite a bit."

"No flattery if it's true. You have quite the reputation, and not all of it bad. GII doesn't hire consultants on a whim."

Raven rested the empty absinthe glass against his chin. "It all comes back to that damn cave. We need to take another look at it. First thing in the morning, preferably. I have a feeling that time is running out, and we don't even know what we're fighting against."

It took him a second to remember that he was not here officially, this was not GII, and the sheriff had no reason to take direction from him.

"That's what we'll do, then," the sheriff said before Raven could finish the thought. "Do you think you and I will be enough, or do you want to call in more support?"

"Let's just keep it to the two of us for now," Raven said. "No offense, but if we run into something there that I can't handle alone, I don't think there is another mage within two hundred miles who can be a damn bit of help. There's a huge unusual surge in magical related crime in Portland, so we're not getting any help from GII anytime soon. I already asked. So I'm all you've got, if you wish to let a civilian walk all over your case."

"I'm a big enough man to admit when I'm in out of my depth," the sheriff said "I can handle the regular sheriff thing just fine, but this is something beyond that. My county doesn't have a budget for consultants. It barely has enough budget to pay for me, my car, and my deputies. But if you would consider working for nothing more than gratitude, I would be happy to consider this your case in all but name."

"It's never been about money for me." Raven gave an ironic chuckle. "Easy enough for me to say that, I know, with all of the

Ravenscroft ancestral funds behind me. But if the side of the light comes to benefit from the blood money of my ancestors, then at least that may lessen some of the stain on my family's name."

"You're a good man," the sheriff said as he took Raven's empty glass and mixed him a fresh drink.

The words forced an amused half-chuckle from him as he accepted the drink. "Those are words I don't hear too often." He knew Cassandra thought him a good man, as did her aunt Ana who had bargained for his pardon. Rafe probably believed the same, though the man would rather die than admit it. He, himself, didn't think himself a good man so much as he was a man with a past trying to do good to atone. A fine distinction, yes, but an important one.

"No, really, you are." The sheriff passed him his new drink. "I'm not sure I would be as willing to take on possibly dangerous work at no pay after someone insulted me as I did you."

"What? You mean earlier, at the bar? You were positively polite compared to others that have torn into me at various times, and those others include my wife, my current nanny, and one of my closest friends."

He could call Rafe a friend while he was out here; it would never get back to the smug nuisance.

"Besides," he added, "at the time you thought you had every right. For that matter, at the time I thought you had every right to, as well. I mean, this is your town and your people. It made sense that you had a clearer read on the situation."

"You would think so. Instead, I nearly got an innocent boy killed. Innocent of his parents' deaths, anyway. Although if you're right about everything being connected —"

Raven leaned back in his chair. "You had no way of knowing that Heilman was going to lose his mind, let alone that he would take Morgan hostage."

"I'm talking about the APB. If I hadn't made Morgan so afraid of the authorities, he would've come to us, instead of trying to find the details of his parents' deaths from Heilman."

"Still, unless you have a talent for clairvoyance that you've not told me about, you had no way of knowing how things were going to turn out."

They finished their drinks in silence then.

"Are you all right to teleport back to your lodging?" the sheriff asked.

"Oh, I've drunk far more absinthe than this and teleported."

It had been a while, and he had been serving under William. William alone was a reason to drink to excess. Never mind that he encouraged the practice. Those days were long behind him in more senses than one. Still, some of that frightening alcohol tolerance remained.

He took his leave of the sheriff, after inquiring and being assured that the man could safely make his way home himself. Then he teleported to his temporary home, where he capped off the night with a glass of wine before seeking his bed.

The morning came all too soon, bringing with it—he wouldn't call it a hangover, exactly, but he definitely wished he had indulged a little less the night before. He settled his sour stomach with some of the hostess' excellent baking and cleared his head with several cups of Earl Grey before using the message crystal to talk to Mother Crone. She was one of the representatives of the Craft Community on the Joint Council, but he was more interested in her position as leader of the wiccan community and her knowledge of Craft. He explained to her what was going on at Devil's Crossing.

"I wonder if that has something to do with the amorphous sense of danger that a lot of covens have been reporting lately," she said. "I've never heard about anything like it, personally."

"Look, the archeologists and the tribes all agree that these petroglyphs were—created, brought into being, however you want to say it—by a culture even older than that of the Native Americans who live here now. But I also know that the tribes have sacred lore that they do not share with outsiders. I absolutely respect their right to withhold their knowledge, but if there is anything they know that can help me turn back this shadow, I'm begging here."

"I understand," Mother Crone said. "I will talk to my contacts among the elders. I do not think they would withhold information when doing so could endanger lives."

THIRTEEN

Raven teleported out to the agreed-upon site a little way away from the cave. Even before he fully regained corporeal being, he could feel the immense, dark power roiling out of the cave. Not only had it not faded with time, it had gotten far, far worse.

The sheriff was there. "It wasn't like this. It was barely a brush of dark magic when I investigated the scene. I thought it was just residue. No wonder you insisted that Morgan could not be responsible for this."

Raven shook his head. "This is far worse than when I investigated the scene. At least twice as bad, I'd say."

"Then what you felt the first time you looked at the cave was still stronger than what I had sensed investigating the scene. That's why there wasn't a meeting of minds when we first discussed it. It's like we were talking about two different things entirely."

"So whatever it is, it's getting worse steadily. At an exponential rate, if I had to guess."

Whatever it was, it was darker and more deadly than any human mage Raven had encountered. More powerful even than any mage of legend that he had read of, even if the strength of those legendary mages had not been exaggerated over time.

"Do we go forward?" the sheriff asked.

Raven could hear the fear in the man's voice, and didn't blame him. He himself had not been this afraid when he faced down William, even though at the time he wasn't certain he would survive that encounter. At least William had been a known quantity. He didn't know what the hell this was, but he now doubted that it could be human, nor the direct product of any human mage's power. He thought about soul stealers. Though called forth by a mage, they were not created by mages and could not be controlled by them. He knew well the feeling of soul stealers, and this was not that. Nor did this behave the way soul stealers behaved. And yet that was the closest analogy he could come up with to what they now faced.

Soul stealers came, so far as anyone who studied the matter could tell, from some dimension adjacent to their own. Early magic tomes called them demons from hell, but Raven believed neither in demons nor in hell. What they faced now almost made him reconsider that belief.

Oh, it would be convenient to be able to believe in demons, and hell, and in a god or gods that would protect them. Raven believed gods to be metaphors for the spiritual powers of nature in the universe, as channeled and directed by Craft practitioners. To his knowledge any indication of their direct involvement in human affairs was nothing more than a fairytale.

"I go forward," Raven said. "If anyone has shields strong enough to protect against that darkness, it is I. Your strength lies in your knowledge, your training, and your badge. Not to denigrate any of those, but I don't think they're going to be much help here. Your shields are not strong enough for whatever is pouring out of that cave. Hell, I don't know if *my* shields are strong enough for whatever is pouring out of that cave. But one of us has to get a closer look into what's going on and I am the most obvious candidate for that task."

"It goes against every bit of that training for me to hang back and let a civilian go forward," the sheriff said.

"We both know that this is not any sort of situation that your training was meant to meet. And we both know that I am no ordinary civilian. If nothing else, if I don't come back, that's where your training, your badge, and your connections will come into play. If I don't come back, you'll need to go through official channels. Maybe evacuate the town, definitely cordon off a larger area. Make an official request to bring GII in and not just as a favor to their wayward consultant."

The sheriff nodded, clearly relieved and just as clearly guilty about that relief.

Raven willed his shields to full strength and started walking towards the cave. The closer he got, the more certain he was that the darkness he felt related somehow to what he had sensed in the mind of the poor, doomed, hay farmer. The closer he went to the cave, the more he could feel it, pressing against his shields. Like some ravening animal it stalked him, sniffing at the edge of his defenses for some weakness. And still he kept on. He had survived full battle with William. Twice. He would survive this or die trying. No one else stood a chance. Cassandra, maybe, in the fullness of her powers, but he still had almost nine years on her in terms of experience. Not to mention, if it came to a choice between sacrificing her and sacrificing himself, well, he knew what the right choice would be. Not only because Ravenscrofts were gentlemen as well as dark mages, but also, because if anyone deserved life, it was his beloved. And if anyone had crimes that could only be washed away with blood, it was he. That she would never agree with this assessment only proved how accurate it was.

Step-by-step, up the trail. He was breathing hard before he made it halfway to the cave. He was not that out of shape, but the struggle went beyond the physical. And still he pressed on. At the rim of the cave, now, and his heart pounded in his chest as though it would bruise his ribs. And still, he continued into the cave. Made it as far as the spear-holding petroglyph warrior. Was that a trick of the light, or was it actually glowing? Power pulsated out of it, white in the darkness, pushing back at him.

He bowed to it. "Do you remember me? You and I, I think, are on the same side. I need to pass, to get into the cave, to learn what is going on here." He turned, took another step into the cave, and hit a wall. Literally. He saw nothing between him and the darker recesses of the cave, but something stopped his progress as though a stone wall stood in his way. Just like, what did they call them? Force fields, in those mundane science fiction shows that Chuckie and Cass sometimes made him watch when Chuckie came from the coast for a visit.

He turned back to the warrior. "You must let me pass. Those you are charged to protect are gone, for the most part. But I think, over all, you ally more with human life than whatever is beyond to this barrier. You must let me pass."

It wasn't like hearing words in his head, no, nothing like that. It was more like knowing someone's thoughts as though they were his own. Someone, or something, whichever category the warrior fell into. *I have no enmity for you. And for that reason alone I would not let you go further. But the barrier is all that holds the darkness at bay. Letting anything cross the barrier would only weaken it. You are not strong enough to hold back the shadow that threatens here. Only one human has ever done so, one woman and the borrowed strength of her tribe, back in the long ago. Even then she paid with her life.*

"Perhaps you mistake me," Raven said. "I am myself not without power."

Oh, I know who you are. The Raven who tricked his own master to bring light back to a darkening world. You are powerful, yes. Nearly as powerful as she was, but you do not have the will and strength of the tribe behind you. Nor would you know what to do with it, for your tradition is a solitary one.

It was, perhaps, a simplification of the difference between Art and Craft, that he was not here to split hairs with a disembodied spirit. Was the warrior trying to tell him he should bring in Mother Crone? Much as he respected her, this did not seem to be her sort of thing.

The craft of this time is different. They have ceded battle magic to the Art, yours is a world with its soul split in two.

There was a case to be made for the value of specialization, but he was not going to get into that here and now.

Besides, the shadow returns now stronger than ever for the ages it waited in silence. Stronger for all of the other worlds it has devoured since last it was turned back from this one. I will hold the line as long as I can, for when I fail, it will devour this world as well. And all the bright life this world holds will fall into the darkness.

This felt like a nightmare, a nightmare or some bad movie that Cassandra's Guardian friends would watch, throwing popcorn at the screen in his parlor while he was trying to read in the study. And yet. . .

It felt real. It *was* real, as real as William had been. He knew it in his bones. He could feel, too, the darkness behind the invisible wall. It leaked through in spots, leaked through and flowed forth like some horrible invisible mist. Felt, but not seen. When this wall failed, and it would inevitably fail, what came through would be too powerful for him to stop.

He backed out of the cave, then turned and fled, going as fast as he dared in his city shoes down the uneven rock-strewn path. A retreat, not a surrender. He would research, he would consult, he would find a way.

Not familiar with firearms, it almost took him too long to recognize the sheriff's shooter stance, feet shoulder-width apart, arms outstretched, both hands supporting the gun aimed directly at him.

FOURTEEN

Raven skidded to a stop and struck with spell lightning. Only at the last second did sense override instinct so that he aimed just at the Sheriff's feet, a distraction rather than a killing blow. Fast as Raven was, he would not have been fast enough, except for the way that firearms often went a little bit wrong around magic. The bullet that had been aimed at his chest went wide, and he felt a sharp slice like the sting of a knife blade grazed his arm. *What the hell?*

Rage and betrayal only lasted long enough for him to look into the other man's eyes, which were wide and wild. Something was very, very wrong.

The sheriff stepped back, shaking his head, and dropped the gun. It clattered on the stone path. And then the sheriff himself fell to his knees, shaking, his chest heaving like a bellows as he gasped. Raven approached him slowly, step by careful step, never taking his eyes off the man, nor off the gun that lay on the rocks between them.

"Get up," Raven said, voice calm and commanding. It was a voice he heard dozens of Guardians use at at least half a dozen crime scenes. He held his magic to hand, ready to defend himself, to kill if need be. "Get up. Move away from the gun."

The sheriff's face was white beneath the tan. He did not stand, but scuttled backwards like a child doing a crab walk. When the man was far enough back for safety, Raven stepped forward slowly. He picked up the gun and clicked on the safety, glad that the Mundane liaison had insisted on that much training before allowing Raven anywhere near a joint operation a few months back. Raven looked down the black metal thing in his hands, having no more idea what to do with it than a rookie Mundane cop would know what to do with an ancient tome on necromancy. An ancient tome written in Greek. At last he threw it to the side, as far away down the hill as he could. Possibly not the most responsible way to dispose of a firearm, he supposed, but that was not his chief concern at the moment. Probably at some point the deputy lowest in the Devil's Crossing hierarchy would be sent to look for it. If the gun had been damaged, well, most people who took aim at a Ravenscroft did not come off so easy. If the sheriff kicked up a fuss, Raven could buy him a new gun.

"I don't know what happened," the sheriff gasped, shaking his head as though he didn't believe his own words. "I mean I do, but I don't. It was like in a nightmare. I was watching myself act but it wasn't me. Something using my knowledge of weapons, the muscle memory I developed on the firing range. It was overwhelming my mind, saying that you were a danger that needed to be destroyed. I knew that the *something* was wrong. But I just couldn't, I couldn't —"

Raven held his hands out placating only. "I know, I know. Deep breaths, calm down." This was not a part of policing he had any training in, nor, to be honest, any particular skill. Gods, what he wouldn't do to have Cassandra here, or even Rafe at this point. "How about now. Are you all right now?"

"Yes, I think so. Yes. But how can you trust that, how can I trust that?"

"Because you are stronger than Heilman, far stronger. In both magic and in will. And because we are going to be moving away from the sphere of influence. Can you get up on your own, do you think?"

He hoped like hell the man could, because he didn't feel confident enough to get within striking distance until they were a bit further away and the sheriff had proven himself a little more stable.

The sheriff got slowly to his feet, still a little unsteady.

"Can you walk?"

The sheriff nodded.

Raven had his doubts, but they'd see. "Lead the way then."

Neither of them was in any shape to teleport just yet, and he was not going to be turning his back to the man for a long time. He didn't think the sheriff had actually intended harm to him, and he was fairly certain the dark influence had gone. Still, he was rather attached to his life and he was not going to give it up carelessly.

They hiked about a mile in silence, Raven's arm hurting with every jolting step. It was something one didn't think about until now. How connected the body is, how every movement from every part of the body could hurt a seemingly unrelated limb. He looked down at his arm. There was a dark, wet patch surrounding the torn fabric of the black Brooks Brothers shirt. At some point they would have to do something about that.

The trail widened, and the sheriff slowed so that Raven could walk beside him. He did so, still keeping a cautious space. The sense of oppressive darkness had faded to nearly nothing, to where it might be nothing more than imagination.

"How bad did I hit you?" The sheriff's voice was raspy, and a little too soft, as though he were the one who had been hit.

Raven suppose that, in a sense, he had been, just not with the bullet. "Not bad. A graze."

"Let me see." The sheriff stopped, and Raven halted beside him, hesitating only a moment before letting the man close enough that he could part the torn fabric to see the wound beneath.

The sheriff breathed in sharply, the air whistling between his teeth. "You'll need to get that seen to. There's a Mercy Medical over in the next town. Healers and Mundane physicians both. Supposedly it's to give you a choice, but practically speaking, for urgent care you take who you can get and are glad for it. Hard to staff out here. Most people who have put that much time into a healer's or doctor's degree want a little more out of life than a movie theater showing third run movies and an hour-long drive to a grocery store that mostly carries staples."

"We both know I can't go to a hospital," Raven said.

The sheriff scoffed. "Why? You got a warrant out I don't know about? Thought all that got cleared up years ago."

"You know damned well there's no warrant, just like you know why we can't go to the hospital. Even I know they're required to report gunshot wounds, and I'm only a consultant."

"Never took part in a cover-up in my life, I don't intend to start now. I did what I did, and I can own up to it."

"Noble," Raven growled. "Noble, but stupid. We both know it was not your fault you shot me. If that weren't the case, you'd be a smoking corpse a mile back and I'd be facing a lot of paperwork with GII."

"I don't lie on my reports."

Raven started walking back down the trail. The sheriff stood his ground a moment, and then trotted his few steps to catch up.

"We're not lying," Raven said. "Just omitting unnecessary facts."

"Maybe when you were a dark mage, you got in the habit of playing fast and loose with the truth, but—"

Raven stopped walking and rounded on him. "If I hadn't learned to play fast and loose with the truth, William would've made a book cover of my hide and gone on to take over the whole of Three Communities," he snarled. "You think I care what a country sheriff does with his career? We're looking at something big here. Something that could be a threat to the whole state, perhaps the whole country. Maybe even the world. GII isn't sending anyone, and I don't have time to break in another sparkly-clean sheriff too blinded by his own radiance to see beyond the end of his nose. You're more tolerant than what I expected to find, more intelligent, too. I don't expect to get that lucky a second time. So just swallow your self-righteous pride so we can get the situation managed before more people die."

For a moment, he expected the man to continue arguing with him. Maybe insist on grinding his career into the ground with the heel of his honor, to hell with what would best serve his community.

The sheriff made a choked sound that might have been a laugh. "You always this complementary with local law enforcement?"

Raven chuckled. "Not always. Some of them I wouldn't bother saving from themselves, and good riddance. But you are right that I do need this taken care of." He nodded toward his arm. "How good are you with healing magic?"

"Mmm, not so much. I mean I took the basic first-aid course as part of my training. I know some healing magic, but surely not up to your standards."

Raven smiled grimly. "I doubt that, seeing as I have no standards at all. Healing was never my strongest skill even before. . ."

Before he knelt to William and became a dark mage.

"You're kidding right?" He paused. "Oh."

"Yes. Oh."

Everyone in the magical community knew that if one did enough dark magic, they would lose the ability to do healing magic. Raven had done a lot of dark magic in his life, and could attest that one did not lose *all* healing magic. The raw power for healing was greatly diminished, not gone entirely. But the ability to handle that healing energy in any meaningful way, that was another story. When you factored in that it was always harder to doctor one's own wounds and the fact that he hadn't used healing magic in decades for any purpose other than banishing soul stealers, his healing abilities were as good as non-existent.

"Doesn't it come back? Eventually, I mean," the sheriff asked.

Raven shrugged one shoulder. "Probably not. No dark mage has gone long enough without using dark magic to test the theory."

"But it's been years for you. Surely —" the sheriff said, and then stopped talking abruptly.

No doubt he was remembering yesterday's incident. Probably wondering if there had been more. He wouldn't be wrong to wonder. Raven stiffened his shoulders, waiting for the accusations, or questions at the least. He heard the sheriff beside him draw breath to speak, and then blow it out again a long, smooth, exhale.

"Well," the sheriff said with forced aplomb. "We'll just have to see what I can do for you then. But if there is any sign of infection, any at all, you're going to the hospital and no arguments."

Raven gave a noncommittal smile. "We'll see."

FIFTEEN

After a brief discussion, they agreed that they'd recovered enough from the shock of the events to be safe to teleport. At least he hoped that they were. Truth was, they were too far out to hike back to civilization, and on a weekday, they were unlikely to encounter anyone who could give them a ride. After some discussion, Raven teleported back to the bed-and-breakfast, and let the sheriff use him as a teleport anchor in order to follow. Raven set Craig up on the couch with a tall glass of water, and a smaller glass of wine, figuring that the man could use both. Honestly, of the two of them, the sheriff looked more like the one who had been shot.

As an afterthought, he set out the cheese and crackers. It wouldn't do for either of them to drink on an empty stomach. He picked up the receiver of the old-fashioned landline phone and pressed the number that said *your host*. When Jasmine picked up, he explained the situation and soon she was at the door with a first-aid kit. She offered to stay and assist but Raven waved the offer away, explaining it was just a little scratch that he'd gotten in an unfortunate incident that occurred on a hike. She looked him up and down but said nothing.

"Yes, I know I'm not dressed for it," Raven forced a rueful and somewhat sheepish tone into his voice. "I've already been told so. Apparently, city shoes aren't good for hiking. It, ah, may have contributed to the accident."

She left him then to his *faux* manly embarrassment and went back to her painting. He didn't know if she would recognize the bullet graze for what it was, but he wasn't taking any chances.

The sheriff snorted. "You may have left off dark magic, you may be married to a GII agent and work for them, but no one can say that woman of yours made an *honest* man of you."

Raven turned to him and shrugged. "Well, we *were* on a hike, there *was* an unfortunate incident, and I *have* been told in the past that hiking in city clothes is not a good idea. I merely said it *may have* contributed to the accident. It also might not have."

The sheriff got up, took the first-aid kit from Raven, and pushed him toward a stool. "All I can say is, I guess we're lucky you're on our side now."

Raven laughed. "All my magical skill and training and what you appreciate is my ability to lie with a straight face." He shook his head in mock disappointment. "I see how it is."

Craig reached out and ripped the sleeve from Raven's shirt. At Raven's offended look, he shrugged. "The shirt was ruined anyway. I can't imagine that either you or your little lady spend much time sewing and mending."

Little lady? Now the man was just being deliberately provocative. He was fortunate Cassandra wasn't here. Of course, he didn't think Craig would use the phrase in her hearing, even as the joke he intended it to be. The man had to have *some* sense of self-preservation to survive in law enforcement.

The sheriff opened the first-aid kit and rummaged through its contents. He selected a small package, ripped it open and—

"Ouch!" Raven exclaimed. "Try a warning next time." He had a fairly high threshold of pain, but he hadn't been prepared.

"Just a little antiseptic. Wouldn't have thought you'd be such a baby about it. When you're not actually a healer, it's best to use as much mundane stuff as you can before you apply the mojo."

"They taught you that in cop school, did they?"

"Right you are," the sheriff said. "Comes in useful sometimes. Should have tried it yourself."

"Yes. Well. I did apply when I was a fresh young thing right out of General Academy. I believe the results are a matter of record."

The sheriff winced. "Sorry. You're right. Didn't mean to touch on the sore spot."

Raven shook his head. "Water under the bridge at this point. And I will admit my response to rejection was less than exemplary."

"Mistakes were made all around. As you said, water under the bridge." The sheriff crumpled up the antiseptic wipe and tossed it at the wastebasket, making the shot in one. Of course the man had good eye-hand coordination. Probably in school he'd played football in the spring and basketball in the summer. Or was it the other way around? Raven never kept track of those things.

Raven had thought the subject dropped, but the sheriff continued on. "Guardian Academy is not the only path, though, especially for returning adult students. There might be other options."

Raven chuckled. "At this point in my life I think I am too used to being the master to return to the role of the pupil. It's not an experience I would want to inflict on myself or any potential teachers."

"Well, something to think about, anyway," Craig said. "Okay, let me give a try at healing. Since you asked for a warning, and all."

Raven shook his head. *Smart ass.*

For a man who declared himself not very good at healing magic, the sheriff wasn't half bad. First came the tingle, then the warmth, bright and clear as sunshine and just this side of too hot. Raven took a deep breath, relaxed into it, and tried not to wish for Cassandra.

"Well, that's as good as it's going to get," the sheriff said. Raven glanced down at his arm. How much of it was the cleaning, and how much of it was the magic, he couldn't say. But the wound already looked smaller and less angry.

"Have to do without stitches, obviously," the sheriff said. "Personally, not too happy about that, but there's some butterfly bandages in the kit that should hold it closed well enough. If you think you can handle the pain."

"There was a time when no one less powerful than William himself would dare to taunt me," Raven said.

"Yeah, well, there was also a time when your picture hung on the station wall with the words *wanted dead or alive*," the sheriff said as he applied the butterfly bandage. "Things change."

Raven smiled. "Point taken."

Cassandra was a talented healer; good enough that she could have chosen it as a career had the Guardians not called more to her soul. It would be so easy to use this as an excuse to get her to come to him. To see her for even a little while. If he played it just right, she wouldn't even be annoyed. But he and Cassandra had the sort of love that did not require constant proximity to keep the flame alive. She was busy with her job right now, and he had more respect for her work then to call her away for something so purely personal.

The sheriff sat back, scrubbed his face with his hands. "I guess I should be more grateful that you've forgiven me for shooting you."

Raven expected this moment, the point where the adrenaline had worn off completely and the reality of the incident hit. "That wasn't you. We both know it. It was the——" he waved a hand. "The whatever-the-hell is going on."

"I can't believe it took me over so easily," the sheriff said. "And here I've always prided myself on my strength of will. I thought my magic—oh, hell, I've never even aspired to be in your league, but I thought I was at least a reasonably strong practitioner for an old country sheriff. And here I was, just as weak as poor old Harvey."

"You are strong," Raven said. "The thing controlled you for mere moments before you were able to shake it. And we were close to the heart of the phenomenon, where its power was strongest." He picked up the sheriff's empty glass and refilled it without asking.

The sheriff accepted the glass with a shaking hand. "I really shouldn't be drinking on duty."

"You're taking the rest of the day off. Personal trauma, or whatever you want to call it." Raven said decisively. "Drink."

The sheriff knocked the wine back with much less respect than the vintage deserved. Raven filled the glass with the dregs of the merlot, and opened the pinot noir to breathe.

"What the hell was that? Back at Devil's Boneyard?" He met Raven's gaze with haunted eyes. "What the hell is going on in my town?"

"I have no idea, and that's the scariest thing of all." Raven described what he had sensed in the cave. "If there were any practitioners strong enough to create something like that, I would know about them. GII would know about them. I can only guess that someone found some way to bring a darker power across. We can only hope they didn't understand what they were doing."

"Across from where?"

"Damned if I know. We know that there are other planes, other universes. The existence of soul stealers tells us that. This," he waved his hand, "quantum mechanics that the Mundanes keep talking about tells us that. Whoever is behind this, whoever brought it across, they aren't necessarily powerful in and of themselves. They could be just lucky. Or unlucky. At this point we don't know who it was or what happened to them."

"So what now? What the hell now?"

"To be honest, I don't know," Raven said "I've never seen or experienced anything like this before. Never even contemplated anything like this happening."

The message crystal flashed. Raven went to it, tapped it to activate it. "This is Raven."

Maybe it was Chuckie with some answers. Gods, let it be Chuckie with some answers. If they could find out who was behind this, maybe they could find out what they did, how they did it, find some way to undo it. At this point Raven was less concerned about punishing the guilty or getting Morgan off. He just wanted to stop the shadow before it grew.

"Mr. Ravenscroft, this is Chad. Pardon, but you said this crystal was a possible contact while you're in town. Do you know where Sheriff Schmidt is? He hasn't come back. Last we heard he was with you."

At Raven's nod of permission, the sheriff leaned in. "I'm here with Raven. Is there a problem?"

"Sir. Sorry, sir, but there's been incidents. Plural. Murder-suicide by the old Brooks place, that we can handle on our own. Unfortunately, no one is going anywhere on that one. But then there was a hit-and-run out on Arrowhead Road by the old lumber mill. No skid marks. Looks deliberate. And, okay, this is gonna sound weird, but there was a knife fight in drama club at the high school. For real knife fight, not props. They got the kids separated, but they're not sure that they have everyone involved in custody, and they're still trying to sort out what it was about and who started it. None of the incidents seem related only. . ." The deputy trailed off.

Craig looked over at Raven, and Raven could see in his eyes the finish to the deputy's frantic statement. Rare enough to have one of these things happening in Devil's Crossing. Unheard of for two such incidents to happen in a week. For everything to happen on the same day, and only a day after the Jansens and Harvey. . .

"Magic involved?" The sheriff asked the question that had been on Raven's lips.

"Not so far as we can tell, sir." The deputy's voice was frantic. Poor kid had probably never handled anything more exciting than a DUI. "At this point, who can tell?"

"Right. I'll take the high school. At least my sister's kids aren't involved in theater, so I don't have to worry about any conflict of interest, and that sounds like the most volatile situation at the moment. Call out the posse to get Arrowhead Road cordoned off until we can process the scene. They've trained for things like this. And see if you can talk Buck into coming out of retirement temporarily. He's got to be tired of fishing by now."

The message crystal went dark. Craig turned to Raven. "So much for the rest of the day off."

Raven hesitated. "I'd offer support but. . ."

"You're not trained in this, you're not here in an official capacity, and this certainly isn't your area of expertise as a consultant. Got it. You've already been more help than I have any right to ask. Just one thing. Could you check in on Morgan, see how he's doing? See if he needs anything. And should he happen to give you any information that helps—I'm not talking about anything that would help with the prosecution. Right now that's the last thing on my mind. Anything he says you pass on to us would be hearsay anyway. But if you can help if you can find anything that will help us with the bigger picture, unofficially—"

"Absolutely," Raven said. "And then, well, I hate to feel like I'm leaving you in the lurch, but at this point research is possibly the most important thing I can offer. I've already exhausted your town's archives. I have an extensive library at home, and access to the GII' s archive as well. I promise I'll be back in a day or two, and in the meantime if you need me for any reason, you can contact me through GII."

The sheriff smiled despite the grim situation. "Trust me, you're the last person I would accuse of running from a fight. I appreciate all you've done, all you're doing. Get some rest before you go anywhere. Getting shot is a shock to your system, and the hike back in the sun couldn't have helped. Not to mention whatever you faced in the cave." With that, he teleported, presumably to face the chaos ripping apart his town.

SIXTEEN

The shower in the AirBNB had a hand-held spray attachment, and so Raven was able to wash off without getting the bandage wet. It felt remarkably good to be clean of the dirt, sweat, and blood he'd accumulated on the day's adventure. It also relaxed him enough that could acknowledge how tired he was. He'd intended to go directly to visit Morgan and then teleport home, but Craig had been right, damn him. They'd finished the cheese and crackers, so there was nothing to eat, but the cool, white sheets of the bed called to him. Whatever was in the cave, it wasn't a problem he could solve immediately, and he'd be better for a rest. He stretched out on the bed, intending only a short nap, but it was nearly dinner-time by the time he woke and dressed.

Raven teleported to the street outside of the saloon and walked in to get directions from the waitstaff. The sheriff had left instructions to feed him when he showed up, and so the waitress insisted that he sit down to a meal. He hadn't fully realized how long it'd been since he'd eaten, nor how hungry he was, until the hot, housemade bowl of chicken soup found its way in front of him. Before he finished the soup, the waitress was back out with his French Dip sandwich. The sandwich was on thick-cut slices of toast, and the broth for dipping had just the right amount of seasoning. The meal came with something called curly fries on the side. Raven poked them with his fork in suspicion, but the sandwich and soup had left him still hungry enough to nibble at one tight-curled fried spiral. To his surprise, they weren't half bad — thin cut spirals of potato that had been dipped in some spicy breaded concoction before being fried. He finished almost half the side serving before the heaviness of the grease left him feeling too full to continue.

He offered to pay, was told again that his meal was on the house. He thanked the waitress and tucked a generous tip beneath the plate before heading out. The hotel was a block and a half behind the bar, a two-story Victorian affair that had seen better days. The gingerbread had been painted with blue and red accents that, when the paint had been fresh and new, must have contrasted brightly with the white of the building. Clearly, the hotel had once been someone's entrepreneurial dream, lovingly planned and built, but the paint was now long faded. The wood of the front steps creaked just a little under his tread, but the porch itself had been recently swept and well-tended geraniums grew in pots along the railing. The chandelier in the main entryway gleamed with polish, and the worn Persian rug in front of the reception desk might have been genuine. The young woman behind the desk looked straight out of central casting —wholesome, fresh-faced country girl, blonde hair pulled back into a ponytail. Stacked beside her were a number of anatomy textbooks, and when Raven craned to see the screen of the laptop perched on the desk, it showed what appeared to be the map of the human central nervous system.

She jumped when he cleared his throat to announce his presence, but recovered with a bright customer-service smile. He returned her polite greeting and asked for Morgan's room number.

"Ah, I'm not certain. . ." she trailed off. "That is, are you from. . ."

It took him a moment to realize that she was concerned he might be a reporter or someone who had a grudge with her guest. "I'm Corwyn Ravenscroft. You'll see that I'm the one being billed for the room. I just wanted to check on Mr. Jansen's well-being before I left town for a while. Feel free to check with him, to see if he's disposed to receive a visitor."

Her troubled face cleared. "Oh, Mr. Ravenscroft, of course. You can go ahead and knock yourself. He's in room five. Just down the hall, turn the corner and it'll be the first door on your left."

He followed her direction, and found himself standing in front of the door with a numeral five neatly painted in gilt.

He tapped on the door. "Morgan? It's Raven. I'm just stopping in to see how you're doing. Do you have a moment?"

The door opened. "Yes. C–come in."

The boy's eyes were bloodshot and swollen, his hair uncombed. He still wore the same clothes he had on yesterday. Well, of course he did. Everything else he owned had been burned up in the fire that destroyed the only home he'd ever known.

"Have you slept? Eaten?" Raven found himself asking. Found himself thinking that if this were his son, he'd want someone to take care of him.

Morgan sat in one of the chairs at a little table that looked the same vintage as the hotel. He gestured Raven to the other chair across from him. "I slept some. Couple hours, I think. The deputy who took my statement last night brought food by earlier, but I wasn't really hungry. Girl at the desk let me put it in the hotel fridge for later."

"Do you need anything?" Raven asked.

Morgan choked on a laugh edged with hysteria. "Nothing. Everything. I—" he waved his hand. "It's all gone. Everything, my family, my. . .everything." He took a shaky breath. "I borrowed the phone at the desk, and got hold of the Armstrongs who live down the road from the farm. They'll look after the horses, make sure that they're fed and watered until I can. . ." He took a deep steadying breath. "I still have my parents' truck. I mean, I guess I do. It must still be at the Heilman's. Oh, God—" a few more breaths. "I don't know if I can go there. I mean even if they don't have it cordoned off. They probably have it cordoned off. But how can I. . . Man, I just. . . Mrs. Heilman, she used to feed me cookies and lemonade when I was a kid and came up with my Dad to get hay. She was just. . .blood everywhere and the three little boys, too. They say the girl lived. I didn't see her."

"I haven't been up to the scene," Raven said. "They said she played dead that's the only reason she made it. I'll ask someone about the truck. Probably a deputy can drive it over here eventually. But no one expects you to go back to your parents' farm until you're ready."

"It's my responsibility. My parents raised me to be responsible, or they tried to. But I don't even know how this is supposed to work," Morgan said. "I, I don't even so much care for myself, but things have to be straightened out. For the horses. There will be, I guess there will be funeral arrangements, or something, to make when police release. . .And I, I don't even know where I'm supposed to live."

The law said that Morgan was a man at nearly twenty, but the boy he had been was still close to the surface even as he struggled to be a real grown-up with responsibilities he should never have to face at this age.

"Was there any other family?" Raven asked gently. "Anyone who can help with," he hesitated just a moment. "Arrangements?"

"No, no one. Mom and Dad were both only children. Dad's parents died in a car crash when he was in his twenties. Blow out, bridge, they said it was no one's fault. Mom's family came from some weird religious group. They disowned her when she left the church. As far as I know they're still alive down in South America somewhere, but she hasn't spoken to them since before I was born. I don't think they even know I exist. Mom and Dad just had me and, well, we know what a disappointment I turned out to be. I mean here I was with my test scores, and my grades, and everyone thought I was destined to have this bright, bright future. And I threw that all away. No scholarships for me now, and no college would ever want me. The only reason I had anything like work is my parents owned the farm. Nothing but failure as far as the eye can see. Even worse, I killed someone. A classmate, if not a friend." He met Raven's gaze with blood-shot eyes. "Do you have any idea what it's like to have done something you can't take back, something you can never forgive yourself for?"

"Oh, yes."

Morgan looked down for a moment, flushing a little. Raven didn't blame him for forgetting who he spoke to; grief drowned the young man's usually quick mind.

"I wanted to make it up to them somehow," Morgan said after a moment. "Not that my parents ever made me feel like I needed to. They were nothing but supportive through everything with Matthew, the court case, everything. But I just felt like I had let them down. I swore I would spend the rest of my life making it up to them, only I never got the chance."

The boy's voice choked off on that last word. He turned his face away, but not before Raven could see the tears. Raven felt totally out of his depth. This was a sort of thing Cassandra was good at, or Ana.

He tried anyway. "You were their child. They weren't going to stop loving you, stop being proud of you, just because you made a mistake." He knew it was true, because he knew it would be true of him when Ransley got old enough to make mistakes of his own.

"It's just that," the boy swallowed. "It's just that my own mother, my biological mother, signed me away before I was even born. Insisted on a closed adoption. Walked away from the hospital as soon she recovered from the delivery and never looked back. If she even knew who my father was, she wasn't saying. The only thing I know for sure is I'm a mix of English, Spanish, and Native American, and I only know that because my parents bought me one of those 23 and me DNA kits for my eighteenth birthday since I kept on asking questions that they didn't have any answers for. There's no way even to know what tribe. I could be local or who knows." He waved at the air to indicate a universe of possibilities.

"I know it's ridiculous, but I always wondered if there was something wrong with me," Morgan continued. "Something so bad that even my own mother didn't want me. And after I screwed up with the, well, you know, I wondered if somehow she had sensed it about me, in the womb, that I was just no good from the start."

Raven had wondered something similar as a child, when he had grown just old enough and experienced enough to realize that other fathers didn't discipline their children by tormenting them with dark magic. Wondered if there was something in him that caused his father not to love him. Wondered if he was somehow the reason that his father had killed his mother. His uncle had certainly acted as though he were somehow at fault, even if he never explicitly said. Raven spoke from those memories, from that old pain, combined now with the knowledge of a new father.

"If your biological parents failed to cherish you as you deserved, it was their failing, not yours. If you want to believe anything, believe that you are so special that your real parents, the ones that raised you, picked you out of all possible choices to claim you for their own."

119

"I didn't—I wouldn't—I didn't even know that they were dead until I heard it on the radio," Morgan said. "I nearly drove off the road. I had to pull over. And in the next breath the news was saying that the police thought I'd done it. Nothing was making any sense, and I knew if I went to the police they wouldn't tell me anything. I slept in the truck that night, out on the desert. Collapsed might be a better word. My brain just shut down, like reality had become more than it could handle. The next thing I remembered was the sun rising, just like it was any other day. Like my whole world hadn't just ended.

"The morning news didn't have much more in the way of details. The only new information was that Harvey the hay man had been the one to find them. I drove on up to his place. Harvey's known me since I was just a kid. I even worked for him a few times when he needed extra help getting the hay in before rain. I heard the gunshots as I was coming up the driveway. I thought maybe wild dogs. We get those around here. People from the city just take their dogs and dump them out here in the middle of nowhere. The ones that survive pack up and go after the livestock. I drove up and I saw the two bodies in the front yard, and Harvey was reloading the revolver. I should've turned around and taken off. I don't know what I was thinking. I guess I thought maybe whatever happened to my parents had got Harvey's family, or maybe it was wild dogs that got them. By the time I got close enough to see what looked like gunshot wounds, to realize that Harvey was ranting like a madman, it was too late. There were police sirens in the distance, Harvey grabbed me, put the gun to my head, dragged me to his truck, and, well you know the rest."

The boy broke down in sobs, curling up in on himself, pulling his feet up onto the chair to make a tight ball. He seemed strangely small for a tall young man with a lifetime's worth of muscles from fieldwork. Raven froze, not knowing what to do, hoping his silent, non-judging presence was somehow a comfort.

Eventually Morgan uncurled, looked him in the eye. "I didn't kill them."

"I never thought you did," Raven said. "And I'm sure the sheriff no longer believes you did, either, or you'd be in a jail cell instead of this hotel room. Look, I know this is probably the bottom of your list of worries right now, but the hotel room is paid for through the week." That part would be true enough, once he stopped at the desk on his way out. "I'll contact Scott, he'll know what resources are out there. If you need anything else from me, the lawyer will know how to reach me. You don't have to figure this all out at once, and you don't have to face it alone. I promise you that."

Morgan studied him now. "Do you have kids?"

"Just one son. Ransley. He's just a baby. He's back in Portland with my wife, Cassandra."

"He's lucky to have you."

Raven didn't feel good about Morgan being all alone in the hotel room to deal with his grief, but no alternatives came to mind. He'd given up on getting any additional useful information from Morgan. Morgan had never even gotten close to his parents' farm, and by the time he got to Heilman he'd been too wrecked to know the difference between a soul stealer and a sunshade, let alone in a position to parse out information on some phenomena he had never encountered before. And yet this visit felt like anything but a wasted trip.

SEVENTEEN

Raven stopped back at the bed-and-breakfast just long enough to pack his dirty clothes into a carrying bag and let the host know that he might be gone for a day or two, but that he wanted to continue to use the rental for a week and would pay as though he were there. Jasmine was more than happy to extend his stay. The last thing Raven did before leaving was using the crystal to reach out to Scott.

"You have a lot of damned gall messaging me," Scott said without preamble.

It was the second time in almost as many days Raven had been greeted this way, and he didn't particularly like it. "Why? What do you think I did?"

"Your buddy the sheriff had an APB out on Morgan."

"What? That was lifted almost a day ago. And it was a mistake from the beginning." And Raven was not feeling particularly happy with being accused of malfeasance toward the boy he had gone out of his way for as he had Morgan.

"And when Schmidt shot poor old Harvey? Was that just a mistake, too?"

"Harvey shot himself. It was a tragedy but—"

Scott interrupted him. "Yeah, buddy, you just keep telling yourself that."

"I don't need to tell myself anything. I was there."

"And of course you're going to stick up for your cop buddies." Scott snarled.

"You're conveniently forgetting that one of my cop buddies, who is also your cop buddy, is the whole reason that I came to help Morgan in the first place. Look, I don't have time for this. I was hoping that I could get some help for Morgan. He's on his own now. I guess you heard about his parents. I was just hoping there would be some group that might be able to help him out."

There was a long pause. "Yeah. I'll ask around. See what I can do."

Raven thanked him and ended the link, not feeling terribly confident that there would be any help coming for Morgan. Well, the boy should be set for the week at least. Hopefully by then the crisis with the darkness would be over, one way or the other, and Raven would have time to follow up and make sure that he was all right.

Although Cassandra was almost certainly at GII this time of day, he teleported home first, both to drop off his clothes and see Ransley.

"Oh, hey, boss," Tony, baby on his hip, greeted him when he materialized in the parlor. "I was just about to put Ransley down for his nap."

"Give me a moment to take my bags up to my room, and I'll take him for a bit," Raven said. "Don't worry, I'm not going to disrupt his schedule too much. I just want to hold him for a while before I start on the research I need to do."

"No arguments from me. Gives me a chance to start on laundry."

Though Cassandra and Raven had both told Tony that he was not responsible for household chores beyond childcare, he seemed content to pick them up anyway, and Raven wasn't going to complain. With the baby in the house, the twice-weekly visit from the maid service wasn't quite enough to keep order otherwise.

Ransley blinked at him sleepily as he carried the child to the nursery. He sat in the rocking chair with him for a few minutes, staring into green eyes so like Cassandra's. "Were you good for Tony and your mother while I was gone?"

Ransley smiled and gurgled something that might have been "da."

Raven smiled back at his son. "That's right, I'm your dad." Raven had scarcely imagined being a father in his lifetime. Now, he found that he was a dad. It was a strange turn of events, but a welcome one.

He hugged his child closer, thinking of the Jansens. Thinking that they must have held Morgan just like this, almost two decades before. A child theirs by choice rather than by blood, and possibly all the more precious for that. He owed it to them, and to the young man their baby had grown into, to discover what was behind their deaths. He was certain now that Heilman was more the tool than the true killer.

A crime wave in Bend. A crime wave in Portland. A crime wave even in little Devil's Crossing with scarcely enough people in it to make up a wave in the first place. The timing could not be coincidental. Was the darkness roiling out of that cave just a part of what was going on, or the cause of it? Whatever it was, he needed to talk to Cassandra, and to Sherlock. They needed to try to fit all the pieces together if they were going to view the bigger puzzle picture.

Ransley was soon asleep, barely stirring when Raven gently eased him down into his crib. He turned the baby monitor on so that Tony could hear if the baby awoke. It was a bit of Mundane technology that Chuckie had insisted on installing, but Raven and Cassandra both soon came to appreciate the peace of mind it brought. He supposed such a thing could be done with magic, but the Mundanes had thought of it first, and their solution seemed as good as any. Raven had an old-school mage's suspicion of the encroachment of Mundane devices into Art households, but Cassandra had a more modern approach, and he was losing ground fast. He wasn't so sure he even minded so much anymore, as long as no one asked him to get into a car, or, gods forbid, a plane.

Cassandra messaged on the crystal to say that she would be working an extended shift and not to wait up. Practically speaking, this meant she'd be at her desk or in the field until she collapsed from exhaustion and someone scooped her up and dropped her onto one of the cots GII kept for such exigencies.

He let Tony know that he was going to be busy in the home library so that the nanny would know he was back on the first line of childcare. Even though circumstances necessitated employing a nanny, Cassandra and Raven had both agreed that they, not the nanny, were raising their child. When they were home, they took care of Ransley, unless exhaustion or pressing research dictated otherwise.

Raven stayed up long past midnight reading through the Ravenscroft journal for mention of anything like the current phenomenon. His only reward for his diligence was a headache and a sincere desire to develop a time-travel spell so that he could berate some of his ancestors for their poor penmanship. At last he had to admit that continuing to push through despite his sleep deficit would only make him more likely to miss something important.

He turned out the lights and went upstairs to his cold sheets. Nuisance was already curled up on Cassandra's pillow. The cat began purring loudly as soon as Raven settled into his own side of the bed.

"I know, cat. I miss her, too."

Cassandra had not returned to the house by the time Raven woke. He forewent his usual full breakfast and Earl Grey, instead settling for a slice of buttered toast before turning his mind once again to research. GII had an extensive library, and if he availed himself of it he also had an excuse to stop in to greet Cassandra.

Raven materialized just outside the teleportation wards surrounding the GII building. He strode through the big double doors, and nodded acknowledgment to the greeting given by the young man at the front desk. As he crossed the lobby and followed the open staircase to the second floor, he could sense the thrum of nervous energy moving through the building. Here and there he spied signs that this was not just a typical day in Guardian International Investigations. An open door of a conference room showed empty doughnut boxes stacked by trash cans full of the detritus of takeout dinners. Empty boxes from the lunch carts were scattered in the center of the conference table. A pair of worn-looking officers in the uniforms of the Mundane Portland Police Department, mud up to the knees of their dark trousers, stood by the coffee pot waiting for their turn to re-caffeinate. The tension only heightened his own sense of unease, and he took the stairs two at a time before walking with ever lengthening strides to the office that Cassandra and Rafe shared.

Sherlock sitting in the spare chair, was the first person he could see from the doorway. Her normally impeccable tweed skirt bore a stain that might have been spilled tea from earlier in the day, or possibly even the night before. Her jacket was missing, her shirt sleeves rolled up, and her tie loose around her neck. Her normally impeccable updo was escaping its bonds, and her pale English complexion had taken on a gray tinge. Sherlock cradled a mug of tea to her chest as though it contained the elixir of life. She lifted her head when she noticed him in the doorway.

"Raven, thank gods you're here." Her upper-class English accent did nothing to hide the exhaustion in her voice.

Cassandra kept her desk in the corner to the right of the doorway, the better to see the trees and sky from beyond the window. She leaped out of her chair to greet him with an embrace, as though he had been gone for a few months instead of a few days. She was not usually so demonstrative in the workplace, and though he was not over-fond of public displays of affection, he put his arms around her shoulders to support her as she sagged against him in exhaustion and relief.

He drew back a little to look at her. She looked haggard, with dark circles like bruises beneath her eyes. Cassandra held to him a moment longer, then slipped from his arms. He let her go reluctantly, and noticed how she stumbled as she returned to her chair. Had she been eating since he was gone? Sleeping?

Across the room, Rafe held a paper cup from the espresso stand outside, rather than a mug filled from the office coffee pot. Rafe was a dyed-in-the wool drip-coffee drinker. When he moved onto the fancy stuff, it meant he had been awake for at least a full day.

Rafe tipped two fingers up from his coffee cup in a tired greeting. "Hey Raven. If I'd known how badly we were going to get slammed with work here, I would never have sent you off to sunny southern Oregon."

"The situation in Molalla?" he asked.

Sherlock shook her head. "That's been resolved. So to speak. Mass murder-suicide. Even the kids."

Raven winced, saying nothing. Ever since they had Ransley, he found crimes involving children hit him much harder.

"It's like the Portland metro area has lost its collective mind," Sherlock said. "No one can explain it. If senseless violence and dark magic were viruses, then I'd say we were running an epidemic. It would make as much sense as anything."

"Regardless of everything happening here, it might have been a good thing that Rafe sent me down to Devil's Crossing." Raven said. "Whatever's causing the problems there, it's big. I'd say it has to be part of what's going on. Perhaps even the cause of what's going on, only it doesn't make sense. Nothing really makes sense." Raven grimaced. "I'm afraid I come bearing more problems and no solution yet."

"Nu-unh." Rafe wagged a finger at him. "You're a consultant. You're supposed to solve our problems, not bring more."

Raven couldn't remember the last time he'd seen Cassandra's partner punch-drunk with exhaustion. Given what GII faced on a normal week, that was a dire sign indeed.

"I'm sorry," Sherlock said. "I do believe your analysis is correct. The laws of probability don't stretch far enough to cover this many coincidences. Under ordinary circumstances I'd let you take Cassandra and Rafe and anyone else you wanted out to Devil's Crossing. But even if all we're doing here is putting out fires, we still *need* to put out those fires. Portland Guardian Bureau is completely overwhelmed. So are the Mundanes. The most I can do is leave you to it, rather than trying to drag you into the front lines here. Gods know we could use you."

Raven wanted to argue, but he understood her point. "I'll be around for a day or two anyway. I need to talk to Mother Crone, and I need to do some research that's best done here."

Footsteps running down the hall heralded the arrival of an intern who stopped at the open doorway, knocking once on the doorjamb. "Sherlock, ma'am, I'm glad I found you here." He paused to nod to the others in the room. "Ma'am, Sirs."

A new intern, then, one who was not yet familiar with the informality of GII.

The intern took a moment to catch his breath, then continued. "There's been an incident at Wilhelm's mausoleum. Someone tried to use dark magic to break through the wards. The wards held, thank god. The local Guardians want us in on it."

Not surprising. Wilhelm's was the oldest facility for cremains on the West Coast, and remained one of the most prestigious mausoleums in the area. Many powerful mages were laid to rest there, and their ashes would be immensely powerful in any number of dark magic rituals Raven could name. The wards had been created by the famous wards master James Braxton and were monitored and upkept by his heirs. The mausoleum was at least as secure as the GII headquarters and the Joint Council building. It was nearly as secure as the Ravenscroft properties.

"The mausoleum wants to get the Braxtons in as soon as possible to check the wards for damage," the intern continued. "But they figured we'd want to send a forensic mage in first to look for clues as to the perp. After all, it's a slim chance that they might get lucky next time."

"Or have success with a less well warded target," Raven said. "In any case, the people behind this are dangerous and need to be stopped."

Cassandra and Sherlock exchanged glances. "Tell Wilhelm's we'll be there," Cassandra said.

"I'll come along, if that's acceptable," Raven offered. "If nothing else, I may recognize the signature. And I would like to see if there's anything strange about the magic used."

They were able to use the sexton as a teleport anchor, and arrived on the well-kept lawn of the historic building. The sexton was a friendly-looking man, broadly built and ebony-skinned, showing just the beginning of softness of middle age and sedentary living. The day had turned blustery, but the tight braiding kept his collar-length cornrows neatly controlled despite the strong wind.

"Hi, I'm Simon Reeves. Thank you for coming." He shook Cassandra's and Rafe's hands in turn. His eyes grew a little wider when he recognized Raven standing just behind them, but he recovered quickly. "And Mr. Ravenscroft, what an honor. I didn't expect you."

"I'm Cassandra Greensdowne, and this is Rafe Ramirez, my partner," Cassandra said.

"Ms. Greensdowne, yes of course. I should've recognized you from your photos." Simon paused then, wincing slightly as though he wasn't quite sure if he was supposed to acknowledge that he had seen all the newspaper articles on Cassandra and her famous, sometime infamous, husband.

"The report you made with the local Guardians stated that you were woken at about four in the morning by the wards pinging an alert."

"Yes, we're rather old-school here. The wards were keyed to me by my predecessor when I took the position. They're looped into a crystal messaging service as well, as a backup. We're, well, Wilhelm's is a special place. Working here, it's not just a job. It's a commitment, a sacred trust. People put their loved ones in our care. Not to mention the responsibility that comes with preserving an historic site like this. And, of course, there's the danger represented if any of the more illustrious remains fell into the wrong hands."

"You contacted local Guardians right away?" Cassandra asked.

"Yes, and then I came right down to the mausoleum, but whoever was trying to break in was gone. The Guardians arrived soon after."

"Weren't you afraid?" Raven asked. "Coming here before the Guardians arrived. It could have been dangerous. What if the mage trying to break in was still here?"

"Then I would defend the mausoleum as best I could until the Guardians arrived." The man lifted his chin. "I may not look like much, but I can hold my own."

Raven sent out a tendril of his own magic, just enough to test the strength of the man's shields. Simon met Raven's gaze with a challenging smile. Point to him; most people would not have even noticed the intrusion. The man was stronger than Raven had expected, although Raven doubted that he would last long against a dark mage of any serious caliber. *Fool*, was his first thought but then he saw both the humor and the fire in the man's amber gaze. Simon knew his abilities, but he also knew his job. Raven doubted Wilhelm's actually expected or wanted Simon to put his life on the line, but that would not matter to a man like Simon. His commitment was to the mausoleum itself; its history, the art of its stained glass, sculptures and fountains; the preservation of the privacy and peace of those interred within. Raven gave the man a nod of respect.

"May I?" Raven gestured toward the invisible wards. It's what they were there for, to see what they could sense before the signature faded, but it was respectful to ask before reaching out to anyone else's wards.

"Please do," Simon said.

Raven closed his eyes and reached down, brushing against the fabric of the wards. He could feel the ward spring instantly to life, a little extra prickly and wary given the recent attempt to breach it. The wards were over a century old, and yet no less lively for that. They couldn't seriously injure him if he did not attempt to breach them, but they were ready to give him a warning shock if they even suspected he was about to make an attempt. *Ssh, my lovely,* he thought to the wards. *Just wanting to see who else was here.*

The magical signature of the would-be grave-robber was less impressive than the wards. Not a long background in dark magic. A dabbler if anything. No one he knew, probably not even taught by anyone he knew. And there, underlying it all. . .

It was weaker here. He wouldn't have sensed it if he wasn't looking for it, if he didn't know what to look for. But there was, yes, clinging to the magical signature a touch of the same darkness that had overwhelmed Heilman.

EIGHTEEN

Raven returned to GII with Cassandra and Rafe. They needed to discuss his findings with Sherlock, although where to go with the information was not as clear.

"So your sense of the darkness is weaker the further you get from the cave and Devil's Crossing," Sherlock said. "Which would make sense if, as you suspect, whatever happened in the cave is the source of all of this. But if that were the case, one would think that there would be a steady line of destruction between Devil's Crossing and here, and that doesn't seem to be what is happening. Could this darkness be like a virus, infecting one person, who then travels and infects others they come in contact with traveling?"

"Except so far as I know there wasn't anyone traveling from Devil's Crossing to Portland since the incident started and before I came back," Raven said. "Devils Crossing is a small enough town that we could actually confirm that pretty quickly. I'll check in with the sheriff there to see if he knows of any comings and goings. My understanding is that Scott contacted Rafe via message crystal."

"Raven's right." Rafe had made a detour when they first arrived, and held a fresh, steaming cup from the espresso stand. "Scott came to Portland on his way to Devil's Crossing, and he hasn't been back since."

"I definitely think it's an angle worth pursuing," Sherlock said. "Remember, Portland is a hub for environmental activism. It's entirely likely that another of the activists from Devil Crossing traveled to Portland, and perhaps Eugene and Bend as well. Devil's Crossing may *seem* that small, but I'm not convinced its sheriff can know all of its citizens' travel plans. I doubt the activists are going to be particularly forthcoming unless he can persuade them that it's a matter of life or death."

True enough. Raven eyed the cup in Rafe's hands with envy and decided he needed to make a trip down to the espresso stand before settling in to the library. He wasn't thinking clearly.

He realized, too, that Scott could have travelled to Portland on activist business and not visited Rafe or even let him know he was in town. He fought down the temptation to say so in front of Rafe. He had no reason for his suspicions other than his deep dislike of Scott, and didn't know if he wanted to bad-mouth the first person Rafe had shown any romantic interest in since Cam died. On the other hand, wasn't it a friend's duty to warn a man that his potential boyfriend was trouble?

Cassandra was better at these things. He'd share his impressions with her and let her decided the best course. It could wait until they had dealt with the bigger crisis.

But if Scott was somehow involved in bringing this nightmare across? He'd met the man. Could he believe the man capable of ushering such darkness in the world? Not intentionally, no. Could he believe that he would be cocky enough to summon something to tear Lansing apart, believing that he could control it? Unfortunately, he could, though where would he get the knowledge? He promised himself he would at least run the idea past Cassandra or Sherlock at the first opportunity.

Rafe turned to Raven. "It isn't possible for something like this to travel through message crystal, is it?"

"I can't say for certain, since I've never seen or heard of anything like this to begin with," Raven said. "But everything I know about how magic works and how message crystals work says that it's unlikely."

"Not to mention that the virus theory wouldn't account for the nearly simultaneous outbreak in Bend, with Seattle following soon after," Cassandra put in. "If it had started in Portland or Seattle, that might make more sense. But from the way Raven described it, Devil's Crossing is hardly a hub for anything."

"Maybe this thing, whatever it is, is traveling of its own will, for its own purposes," Raven said.

"You talk as though it were sentient," Sherlock said.

"Sentience is hardly a black-and-white quality," Raven said.

"Are wards sentient? They react to any attempt to cross them or dismantle them. They can recognize their ward masters. They can be soothed and quieted into somnolence with a gentle enough touch even while they are being taken apart. Yet I've never had a real conversation with one, nor met one with hopes, dreams, and ambitions. Are soul stealers alive? Experts have been debating that for centuries. Having dealt with them myself more than anyone ever should have, I can only say it depends on how you define *alive* or *sentient*. As with many things, how you phrase the question gives you your answer. And this thing is an even greater mystery than the soul stealers."

Rafe jumped in. "If it's of limited sentience, how is it directing individuals the way you theorize? Making *this* person kill his family and *that* person break into a mausoleum?"

"Keeping in mind that this is all theory and guess-work," Raven said, "I think it's just getting inside people's minds and working with whatever's there. Whatever ambitions or hidden resentments that person has, whatever wild conspiracy theories they saw on the internet."

"What about the person who created it, or drew it across, or however it happened?" Rafe asked. "Could they be directing the spread?"

"At this point I can't discount any possibility," Raven said. "Some things would make more sense if this darkness were something deliberately created or summoned. Set up your base in Devil's Crossing, a remote little town where you're less likely to get caught. Move on to major cities, where you're likely to get the most impact and attention."

"You suspect some kind of terrorism?" Sherlock asked.

"The theory could fit the facts," Rafe said. "Except that there's been no demand, and no claiming of responsibility. What would be the point to an act of terrorism if no one knows that it's an act of terrorism?"

"They could be biding their time, making sure the impact has been fully realized before they make their demands," Cassandra said. "My intuition says we're wandering down the wrong path, though. Although I could be wrong."

"I had Chuckie look into the groups organizing the protests of the golf resort," Raven said. "He would have alerted me by now, surely, if he found anyone with the talent and the tactics that match this sort of thing. Everything I've seen in the news articles I found so far indicates that the protesters have been scrupulous about acting within the law. The worst I found was a citation for trespassing, and that seems to be a result of confusion about where the public land ended and the private land began. Besides, why target Portland or Bend? They have nothing to do with the proposed golf course. So far as I know Lansing doesn't even have any contacts in either city."

"I'll have Chuckie check for any corporate ties we're missing," Sherlock said. "But it does seem unlikely. If someone was trying to make a point, they'd go for something with publicly known ties."

"Some radical back-to-the-land type who has a beef against cities in general?" Rafe suggested. "I know it's reaching."

"Again, I would've expected some sort of statement or manifesto by now," Sherlock said. "And I would've expected the violence and destruction to be more targeted. People more directly involved in development. So far the only victim who really ties in to that angle is Lansing. Still, maybe someone new at the game? Possibly unstable?"

"I'd say definitely unstable," Raven said. "If they're willing to unleash something as powerful and uncontrolled as what I sensed in that cave."

"I'll reach out to Chuckie and make sure he's continuing to look into the political angle," Sherlock said. "I'll let him know that this is now an official GII investigation, not just a side project."

"If it's truly back-to-the-woods types behind it, would Chuckie be able to find anything in the computers?" Raven said.

"You'd be surprised," Sherlock said. "He also might have a feel for who we can talk to in the anti-development group. If someone is using the environmental cause as an excuse to kill people, it's in their interest to nip it in the bud before the whole movement gets discredited."

"Scott has contacts with those movements. He might be able to give us a hand with that," Rafe said.

Good luck with that. Raven bit his tongue on the comment. While he didn't think much of Rafe's new friend, perhaps Rafe could get more cooperation and less vitriol from him.

"Raven, let's keep you on research as we planned," Sherlock said. "If we can't figure out *who* at least let's figure out *what.*"

"There may not be a *who* at all," Raven said. "Except, perhaps, as an inadvertent carrier. Remember what I sensed in the cave. How the petroglyphs seemed to be some sort of protectors. The biggest of them had a crack running straight across. Perhaps the petroglyph was holding back some darkness until it was damaged by the same heavy equipment that opened the cave."

"We're back to hypothesizing some shadow-entity unlike anything known to exist," Sherlock said. "And do petroglyphs even work that way?"

Raven shook his head in frustration, not negation. "I don't know enough about how petroglyphs work. Given the age of these petroglyphs, I'm not sure anyone alive knows enough about them to answer that question.

Sherlock heaved a deep, soul-weary sigh. "You have the best chance of any of us of finding out what we're dealing with. I'd loan you Cassandra to help but we do still need to hold the lines."

"I understand." Raven smiled. "That's why you have a consultant to do this sort of research."

The intern returned, looking more frazzled than before. "Sorry to interrupt, but we just got an urgent request. Kidnapping. British ambassador's daughter. There was blood all over the primary scene."

Raven hesitated. "Do you want me to stay?"

Sherlock shook her head. "At this point I think we need you on research more. I need to know what the bloody hell is happening."

Cassandra looked from Sherlock to Rafe. "Can you give us a minute? I'll meet you outside, beyond the anti-teleportation wards."

As soon as Sherlock and Rafe left, Cassandra closed the door behind them. Then she shoved Raven against the wall, pulling his head down to her, and kissed him very thoroughly. "I missed you so much."

He held her tight to him for a few moments longer, eyes closed, breathing in the scent of her hair. "Gods, I've missed you."

"I need to go," she whispered.

He kissed her once more, chastely this time, an affirmation and a promise. "I know."

Oh, it was hard for him to let her go off into a volatile, potentially dangerous situation alone while he went off to research. *Not alone. Rafe and Sherlock are watching her back.* Besides, Cassandra was strong in combat magic herself, one of the best GII had. This was the price he paid for loving a strong, independent, powerful mage. It was worth every bit of it, and more. Always and forever.

NINETEEN

Raven met with Mother Crone at the overlook in the Craft lands above Newberg. Tall, centuries-old trees stood like a fortress behind them, and laid out before them was a patchwork of pastures, hay fields, and vineyards with clusters of houses and roads in the distance. Though Raven had no fondness for hiking and other outdoorsy pursuits, there was still something about woods, and these woods in particular, that lifted his spirits and soothed his soul., The cool dampness and the deep scent of evergreen and earth was a much-needed balm after the stark, dry emptiness that was Devil's Crossing.

"Raven, it is always good to see you."

A common pleasantry, and yet from Mother Crone it carried the depth and sincerity that wrapped around him like a blanket.

"You as well." He meant his reply as much as she had meant her greeting.

Though he had never studied Craft, Mother Crone had given him access to the Craft lands from the time he was an adolescent. They met through his piano teacher who followed the shamanic tradition. Raven could only guess she'd seen in the younger him a desperate need for the peace and the stillness the Craft lands could provide, and a need for a place that he could be himself, not the son of a notorious dark mage killed by Guardians in the Mage Wars.

She told him after his pardon that she had never revoked that access, not even during the years he'd spent as the right hand of the most powerful and darkest mage of their time. Foolish, he might have said in more cynical moments. The fact remained that Mother Crone's faith in him had stayed more constant than even Cassandra's or Ana's. Certainly she'd had more faith in his capacity for goodness than he had had himself during those years. It was a notion he'd clung to in the difficult times immediately after his pardon when he was trying to reintegrate into a world outside of dark magic. He'd like to think that that faith had borne out in the end, and so who was he or anyone to question her wisdom?

"Walk with me," she said.

Raven fell into step beside her, shortening his strides to match hers. Though Mother Crone was fit for her age, she was some twenty years older than him and significantly shorter in leg.

"I've spoken with the medicine people in the local tribes, and even in some of the tribes further out. I made sure that they understood both the seriousness of the situation and the sincere respect and purity of purpose behind the queries."

He didn't ask her if she told them that she was making the inquiries on behalf of a Ravenscroft. He left that to her conscience and wisdom. He respected the tribes' reluctance to be open with outsiders and accepted any historical suspicion and ill will they might still bear toward his family.

"I'm certain the tribes were being candid with me when they confirmed that they didn't know anything about the petroglyphs in the cave beneath the butte. They also state that, although there's tales of an earlier tribe in some of their oral traditions, the tales really don't give too many details beyond the fact of their existence and that they coexisted peacefully with the tribes that came later. Most of the tales state that they eventually married into them to the extent that the former, smaller tribes no longer exist as a separate entity. Many of the current tribes do consider them to be among their ancestors.

"As you mentioned the crack in the raven on the wall and your concern that the damage had something to do with the darkness coming, I did ask them about that specifically. They did say that, with the petroglyphs they are familiar with, a crack in the stone should not lessen or alter the power of the petroglyph. But they stressed that the petroglyphs at Devil's Boneyard were made by a people unknown to them and may behave differently."

The wind rustled the trees; a far-off burbling spoke of a distant stream. From high above he heard the piercing call of a hawk.

"Thank you for asking," he said. "At least we know that we have not ignored any possible line of inquiry."

It would've been within the tribes' right to decide that they would keep their knowledge to themselves and say so. But they would not have lied directly, and especially not to Mother Crone, and not about something that might endanger lives, no matter what the historic justification.

"What will you do?" Mother Crone asked.

"What else can I do? Research, and hope for a miracle."

They walked a while longer in silence. Raven had once asked Mother Crone whether the Craft community had banded together to preserve and protect the Craft lands because there was an underlying sacredness to the land, or whether the gentle thrum of power that he sensed all around was the result of generations of Craft practitioners using the area for their rituals and their meditations. She'd smiled and said it was a little of both. Though Raven had no particular spiritual leanings and had never practiced any form of Craft, still he realized in this moment that the Craft lands were sacred to him, too. The idea that the darkness, if not stopped, could spread even to here tore his soul. Maybe if he could somehow hold back this darkness, protect the Craft lands as well as the people of the Three Communities, it would go some distance to redeeming the great debt left in his family name by his ancestors.

The trail looped back to the overlook. There Raven took his leave of Mother Crone and returned to the GII headquarters, where he ensconced himself in the library and started to look through indexes of the historic records to see if he could find anything like the current sweep of darkness. Though the soundproofing of the library shut out the buzz of nervous activity that ran through the building, Raven still had difficulty keeping focused. He kept on finding excuses to leave the library—to get a drink of water, to stretch his legs, to pour a mug of undrinkable coffee that would sit at his elbow until it grew so cold that he got up, emptied it into the sink of the break room, and started the process over again.

Each trip to the common areas brought new intelligence and the associated speculation. The kidnappers had carjacked a white van from an elderly couple at a truck stop. Was one of the kidnappers

Mundane? There were mages who learned to drive, but it wasn't common, especially outside of rural areas where vehicles were needed to transport livestock and feed. The involvement of a Mundane would increase the risk of firearms coming into play.

Someday soon, he would have to look into creating some form of magical protection against bullets. Just because it hadn't been done yet didn't mean it couldn't be done. But what form would that protection take? Spell? Amulet? He'd have to find some way to predict and make allowances for the tendency for firearms to behave erratically in the presence of magic. Which meant first discovering *why* firearms behaved erratically around magic. And then he'd have to solve the problem of how to safely test whatever he came up with.

Focus. Countering firearms was a problem for another day. He took himself back to the library and the records. When next he surfaced, there had been conflicting sightings of the van in disparate locations at approximately the same time. None of the witnesses had gotten clear pictures or a plate number. The team had split up knowing that at least some of them were on a wild goose chase, and thinning their resources to dangerous level. Ordinarily they would've pulled GII agents off of other cases, or even called in local Guardians or Mundane police, but right now all available agents were working on crucial and time-sensitive cases of their own. Both the local Guardians and the Mundane police had already loaned them all the personnel they possibly could; they had their own fires to put out.

By early evening, word had come back that Cassandra and Rafe had narrowed the chase down to the right vehicle, but that vehicle had been found abandoned on a logging road outside of Estacada. K-9 officers had been brought in, but it was rough terrain and the kidnappers had a good head start. Rafe and Cassandra had set up a small base of operations near the abandoned van. It promised to be a long night.

Raven gave up on searching historical records and teleported home to see if he could find anything in the vast archive of dark magic that he'd inherited from his family. Late into the evening gnawing hunger drove him out of the library and toward the kitchen. On his way, he noticed the message crystal blinking to signal a call.

Although the light was clear, not red, he rushed to over to tap it. "Raven here."

"Raven, it's Sherlock. Cass just checked in, and she asked me to call with an update. She wasn't able to reach you by cell. Figured you hadn't charged it."

Probably true. He hadn't touched the thing since Sherlock and Cassandra forced it on him and wasn't entirely sure where it was.

"Anyway, one of the dog teams tracked the kidnappers to an empty trailer on logging lands. Unfortunately, it's a recent clear-cut, and so there's no cover for agents and officers to get anywhere close, so now it's a waiting game. Cass wanted you to know that the spokesperson for the kidnappers is going on about encroaching shadows and conspiracy."

"The same as Heilman and that group in Molalla," Raven said.

"This bunch is blaming the British government for some reason that only makes sense to them, but otherwise, yes, virtually identical paranoid ranting. And there's no connection that anyone can establish between the groups, or between either group and Devil's Crossing."

"More evidence supporting the theory that the thing in the cave is somehow influencing events in a way we don't understand."

Sherlock sighed. "Exactly. Have you made any progress with the research?"

"Only if you count the elimination of numerous dead ends."

"Thank you for all your work," Sherlock said.

"It's going to be a long night for all of us, I'm afraid."

"Try to get some sleep," Sherlock said. "You're no use to yourself or anyone else without rest."

"And you'll be taking your own advice yourself, I'm sure."

Sherlock snorted, told him he was a cheeky bastard, and ended the conversation.

Nuisance turned up with an insistent meow as soon as he stepped into the kitchen. He fed her a can of gourmet natural cat food (duck and lentils with gravy, hit with a warming spell to make it more palatable). Then he made himself a cold sandwich and a pot of Earl Grey. He carried these provisions into the library to settle down for yet another research marathon.

He leafed through the Ravenscroft journal for anything that he had missed that might help. He flipped through and discarded dozens of books in his personal library, many of them ancient, some of them technically illegal. There was nothing here that could help him. He had perhaps the most extensive private library of magical knowledge dating back to the arrival of Europeans on this continent. Some older tomes went back even further into the dawn of European magic. Nothing. Could the darkness be something unique to this continent? Something that tied into the petroglyphs, something that predated the arrival of Europeans? In his experience, magic was magic the world over. It might have different names, different theories, but it worked essentially the same. He ran his hands through his hair, thinking of myths and legends, of tales older than written language. Raven had not limited his scholarly education to the world of magic. He knew about Joseph Campbell, knew of his theory of monomyth. His idea that all of human history had a shared collective unconsciousness. Bran Tarrant had said something very similar in a cave in Australia, but Raven had been to dazed by his dream journey-hallucination-whatever experience and his narrow escape from death to fully absorb everything the strange man had been trying to tell him.

Nuisance drifted through the open library wall and rubbed against his legs. When that didn't work to grab his attention, she jumped up on the table to walk back and forth across the book he was trying to read. He scooped her up and held her for a few moments, scratching her chin, and set her back down on the floor. With an indignant meow, she leaped back onto the table and nipped at his hands. Sighing, he picked her up, deposited her in the hall and closed the library door before returning to his reading.

His mind was taking him on paths that seemed a lot more like Craft than Art — only Craft didn't work anything like the deadly shadow he'd sensed. Craft was a gentler, subtler magic, strong in its own way but not so easily weaponized. Craft worked with the forces and flows of nature, and whatever the hell was in that cave it did not feel natural. And yet the petroglyphs. . .And yet the petroglyphs.

All his training and understanding of how magic worked said the petroglyphs were part of Craft, not Art. Anthropologists had long theorized that in the earliest time of human history there was no separation between Art and Craft, there was only magic. Perhaps the anthropologists were right, and perhaps these petroglyphs were created in that long-ago time.

The spear-carrying warrior petroglyph was there to protect against the darkness. The raven image however. . . He didn't want to believe that that could be the source of the strange darkness. He knew from his General Academy literature classes that the raven in literary works was considered a bird of bad omen, a symbol of evil and of death. Lines from Poe's poem had been tauntingly quoted to him in study hall often enough to destroy any respect he might have otherwise had for the man's artistry. And yet he remembered Mother Crone talking to him at a low point in his life, telling him that in some traditions the Raven was the savior of the people, a bringer of light.

His mind kept going back to the crack running across the raven petroglyph in the cave. Part of him still wondered if the raven had been there to hold back the shadow and the crack had undone that protection. But that made no sense. Cracks in cave walls did not lead to other planes, they led to more rock, or at most another cave. And Mother Crone's contacts seemed to think the crack was irrelevant.

If only there was more information about the petroglyphs themselves, who made them, what their belief systems were, what the petroglyphs were meant to do. Mother Crone had been certain that the information reported in the archaeological journals was true. The tribes were not keeping any information to themselves to protect their own mysteries. The oral traditions regarding a people that had come before were all vague stories, the equivalent of fairytales and myths, the original facts lost in the retelling over time. As much a part of the monomyth as the Tuatha da Danaan of the Celts or the multitude of tales of the peoples destroyed by the great flood. The archaeological record agreed that there had been tribes that predated the ones now known. The details of their beliefs, their spiritual practices and magical traditions, had been as lost to the mists of time as any knowledge of the builders of Stonehenge or Newgrange. If understanding the petroglyphs was the key to understanding the shadow, the answers were not to be found in any book, no matter how old.

So what now? Raven wasn't about to join the Wannabe tribe. He had far too much respect for Native Americans to go off on some fake vision quest like spiritual tourists with too much money and too much time on their hands. His own ancestry was mostly British Isles with a little French. When he took the British ancestry further back, he found mostly Saxon and Welsh with a little Scots thrown in. Some family history mentioned Pictish blood even further back along the Scottish line. People with their own spiritual traditions, but those traditions had been mostly trampled into the dust of history when the Romans came.

His hand wandered to the raven that he wore on a chain around his neck, the raven given to him by Bran Tarrant after he'd made it through the vision quest/fever dream/drug hallucination. Made it through the experience in the Australian cave that had led Bran Tarrant to proclaim him a mage with a shaman's soul. He wondered now if a little more attention to the spiritual side of magic would have helped him now. Or maybe he was grasping at straws. Far too late to change, in any case.

TWENTY

Raven had been awake for nearly twenty-four hours now. He'd stopped thinking clearly some time ago, and yet he was way too wound up to sleep. Cassandra checked in at one point via crystal to let him know that she was safe, there'd been no recent developments, and she was likely not going to make it home until sometime in the morning, if then. Tony had put Ransley down hours ago, and was probably asleep by now himself. Raven went to the liquor cabinet, found a dusty bottle of absinthe in the back. He poured a measured amount into a tall glass, balanced sugar cubes on a slotted spoon and dribbled water directly from the tap. He had no patience at the moment for the extended ceremony of the raven-topped absinthe fountain currently holding pride of place in the china cabinet. He carried the drink into the parlor, or the living room as Cassandra would have it. A large flat screen TV hung on the wall above the fireplace where once his father's portrait had stared down on him. Though not a fan of Mundane entertainment devices, Raven enjoyed immensely the thought of what his father would have to say about his portrait being replaced by one. He saluted the dark screen with his glass and took a long swallow. The house was utterly quiet. Nuisance had given up on him hours ago and stalked off in a tiff to find some soft place to sleep, probably the dead center of the bed he shared with Cassandra. The steady ticking of the grandfather clock in the corner grated, even though it was a sound he usually found soothing.

He sipped again at his absinthe. The remote that worked the television set taunted him from the antique Victorian side table. Beside it was a gift from Chuckie, a small, artisan-made notebook he had found at a craft fair on the coast. On the wooden cover the artist had etched a raven's head surrounded by a circle of knotwork. Raven opened the notebook and flipped through pages of instruction written out by Chuckie; explanations of Uber and DoorDash and a lot of other Mundane conveniences that he thought Raven should try. He found the section on how to use the remote to turn on the TV followed by directions on how to find a particular program on something called Netflix.

Cave of Forgotten Dreams. He had watched the documentary once before with Cassandra and Ana, one of the few occasions he found it worthwhile to focus his full attention on the screen. It explored the archaeological theories about the recently discovered Chauvet cave in France. The place was a wonder of cave paintings and strange carvings and generations of handprints on a wall in red ocher. Archaeologists believed that the paintings were no mere decoration, and that the cave had been used for religious ceremonies for hundreds of years, but what the cave and its images meant to the people in that prehistoric time was left to speculation.

Monomyth. Collective unconscious. Early humans around the world with their caves, and their paintings, and the magic that might not have been all that different from the magic of today. Eventually he slipped in and out of a doze, moving from documentary to dream and back again, lost in images and mysteries and the haunting background music that spoke to some deep part of him that his rational modern mind had forgotten. The documentary ended and he came to full wakefulness just long enough to accept Netflix' suggestion for a documentary on the passage tomb at Newgrange. He eased into half-sleep looking at mysterious spirals carved deep into the rock and an opening above the mouth of the tomb that, on the dawn that followed the longest night, allowed the light of the rising sun all the way into the depths of the main chamber.

Eventually he fell into a deeper sleep and a longer dream. He was walking through a spiral underground labyrinth, following its turnings with a sureness he did not question. As the passages joined, he gained companions. A gray-haired Pict that barely came to Raven's shoulders, dark skin painted with spirals of blue woad. A broad-shouldered Viking, tunic painted with runes Raven did not know. An auburn-haired woman in a simple tunic dyed the red of berries, embroidery at the neck and sleeves with a twining pattern of stylized birds and animals. Without greeting, without discussion, he and his companions continued on to the center. They all knew where they were going and why they were here. In the dream, he knew as well.

They reached the center of the spiral. His companions lit torches, one in each of the four directions at the edge of the circle in the heart of the labyrinth. In the center of the space there was a stone cauldron, suspended over a fire pit by a tripod of stone. Dreaming Raven could only spare a moment to wonder about the weight of the cauldron and how the structure supported it all.

"You know what the four torches represent," the auburn-haired woman said.

The woman had not phrased it as a question, but Raven answered anyway. "North, South East, and West. Earth, air, fire, and water." General Academy requirements included craft-for-mages course for students raised in Art so that they would not be completely ignorant about other parts of the Three Communities.

"And the cauldron in the center?"

He was more used to it being represented as the fifth point in a pentagram, but he could make an inference. "The center of all. Above and below. Within and without."

"Light the fire," the woman said.

He hesitated just a moment, then took the torch that burned in the east quadrant. *Air. Intellect. The mind.* The quarter in which he was strongest. He touched the torch to the logs beneath the cauldron, and the fire blazed. The ease with which the fire started did not surprise him. This was a dream, and the rules were different.

The cauldron bubbled, giving off a soft green glow that reminded Raven of springtime and sun-warmed grass.

The woman spoke again. "The center of all is the cauldron of life. The place where Spirit came from unbeing into being. That first magic, that moment of transformation that no one can explain. The breath of the goddess. The dream of Vishnu. The word of the god. Life came into our world, our universe. No one knows exactly how, exactly why. Life came into other universes, other planes, as well. And in other planes, no true life came, but those planes spawned different things.

"There is more to the tale," she said. "Mysteries beyond mysteries. And you, a scholar, understand that knowledge must be earned."

She turned to a recessed shelf carved into the wall, a shelf that until now had been hidden in shadow. She took from the shelf an earthenware chalice decorated with intricate spiral designs, and from a hook beneath the shelf she took a ladle. He watched as she filled the chalice from the steaming cauldron.

"The stakes are higher than you know. The thing that comes from the cave will devour all life if it is not stopped. All of the people, the two-legged people and the animal people as well. And even the grains and grasses."

She passed her hand over the vessel and the liquid cooled and turned dark.

"Never forget that death is just another aspect of life, and life itself is a perilous thing. As a mage and a Ravenscroft you make an unlikely champion, but you are what fate has brought us. The stakes are higher than you know. Will you chance the peril to gain the knowledge you need for the challenge ahead?"

He did not demean the moment by telling himself that the choice didn't matter, that it was *just a dream.* Maybe it was a dream, maybe something else, but he knew one thing with a soul's-deep knowing. If he died here, he would not wake up ever again. He knew with that same certainty that if he not chance drinking from the cup, the world he knew would be devoured by darkness.

Beads of sweat formed on his forehead despite the coolness of the cave. He took the chalice with a shaking hand. It had an odd, earthy flavor, like sage and green tea, but with an underlying bitterness. By the time he drained the dregs, he was swaying on his feet. The auburn-haired woman took the vessel from his limp grasp. He started to fall backward, and two of his companions caught him by the shoulders and eased him to the ground.

It was dark all around, and silent. He could not feel his body. He had no words to explain how he knew he was in another labyrinth, but this time he was alone and could not see the walls. Panic surged through him. That time in Australia he at least had had a dream-body to move through his dream-quest. None of his training and nothing he had learned in his years of study had prepared him for something like this. How could he possibly complete this test if he was nothing in the middle of nothingness?

No. Not quite nothing. He still had his intelligence and his will.

It would make no sense to set their only champion a challenge that could not be surmounted.

He had his will. Certain precepts were the same in all magic; the importance of will was one of those precepts. In a dream-world made of magic, should he not be able to will into existence a body, or at least a near-enough equivalent to work with.

He found a center of calmness, and from there took a few unhurried minutes to remember in deep detail what it felt to have a body. The steady da-dum, da-dum of the heart, so regular that it generally went unnoticed by the conscious mind. The slower rhythm of the breath as the lungs alternately drew in and released air. The temperature difference between the cool air that he inhaled and the warm air that he exhaled, so subtle that he would not feel the change unless he focused. Remembered how gravity gently pulled on the solidity of flesh, how skin passed to his subconscious mind dozens of messages that would combine before passing a judgement on to the conscious mind. *It's hot. It's cold. This bed is soft. This ground is hard.* He blended and shaped those memories and charged them with his will until he no longer had to focus to hold it into being.

He had a body with which to act.

He tried and failed to will sight into being by the same method. After the third attempt, he realized what was wrong. He could will a body into being because a body was a physical thing. Sight was a sense. Furthermore, it needed light to function. For all he knew, he *had* sight and there was simply no light by which to see. Or nothing there to see.

He had, without thinking, conjured clothes along with his body, perhaps because his memory had added the feel of cloth against his skin. He focused now on the memory of a cool, smooth, rounded weight of a light globe in his hand. But though he brought the full weight of his considerable will onto the thought, no light globe came. Maybe he just needed to rest first—willing one's body into being had taken a great deal of concentration. And so he gave himself time to recover. . .fifteen or twenty minutes, maybe. He had only his own subjective sense of time to judge by, and he'd read somewhere that complete darkness confused internal clocks more than almost anything else outside of actual drugs. When he judged himself ready, he focused again on the memory of holding a light globe. No, *his* light globe. The small, portable one he had spelled himself. Surely the specificity of the recollection would help.

It didn't.

Though no one had mentioned a time limit to complete this unknown task, Raven felt in his bones that he needed to hurry. Needed to finish this task and return to his real-world body before his tie to it weakened. Needed to return and stop the darkness from the Devil's Boneyard cave before it devoured the world.

So he would continue without light. He could do this. Carefully he got to his hands and knees. He slid one hand over until he found a wall. *Hmm.* Either this place had not been an absolute void to begin with, or his willing a body into being had also brought into being a floor and walls. His initial instinct that this was another labyrinth had at least some support. At minimum, one needed walls in order to have a labyrinth. He used his hand on the wall as support as he got to his feet. Either the complete darkness disoriented him or the potion he had drunk had left him a bit light-headed still.

He started to walk, one hand on the wall for support. Its surface, rough and uneven, felt as though it had been hewn from solid rock. He felt with his foot on each step, making sure the floor was solid before trusting his weight to it. In the Guardian adventures he'd read as a boy someone was always falling through the rotted timbers of a mineshaft or stumbling into a sinkhole. He wasn't sure either danger applied to his current situation. He was no more a spelunker than he was a Craft practitioner. There were many, many things at which he counted himself competent, and yet this last week the universe seemed determined to throw in his face all the countless things for which he had neither skill nor knowledge.

He made slow progress, fighting the urge to move with more speed and less caution. He took each left turn he came across, remembering the hero-Guardian in some story using that trick to successfully navigate the villain's maze. Whether the strategy actually worked or whether it was some hack-writer's invention, he dared not hazard a guess. He refused to think too hard about the other holes in the logic of that story, starting with why the villain dropped the hero in the maze in the first place when it would have made far more sense to incinerate the man with magefire.

His limbs grew heavy with exhaustion, and the darkness seemed to press down on him with the weight of mountains. He had no idea how much time had passed. *Too much, surely.* He became more and more certain with each step that he was utterly and irrevocably lost. A time or two he stopped, hesitated. Turned back the way he had come for a few steps, only to reverse himself and continue in his original direction. If he were the protagonist of the sort of Guardian adventure tales he'd read as a child, he would know the right path by the way his footsteps echoed, or the way the air smelled, or from some slight breeze that only the hero noticed.

Damn. He wondered if he'd be just as well off sitting on the floor and waiting for whatever end came to those who failed a vision quest, or whatever the hell this was.

Only he couldn't. Giving up was another of those things he'd never developed a talent for.

He continued on, wondering with every step if he might be going further in the wrong direction. Maybe he should turn around and try to find another route that might take him—wait! Was that faint light ahead, in the distance? He picked up his pace, going as fast as he dared toward the odd blue-white miasma, ignoring the part of his mind that urged caution of the unknown source. Closer now, he could make out human figures in the light. Closer still, and some of the figures seemed almost familiar.

And then he stopped with a gasp and took an involuntary step back.

In front of him were men and women he had killed at his late master's behest, upright as in life, but showing horrible burns from magefire and spell lightning. A few were little more than gory, bipedal masses, as though they had been hastily reassembled from disemboweled and dismembered corpses. Some eyes held sadness and betrayal. Some held mindless rage.

"No," he whispered, shaking his head. "No, no, no."

He had never forgotten who he had been. What he had done. But to the best of his ability, he had put that past behind him and tried to move on. Except now the past was literally in front of him, barring the way.

The dead shuffled forward, closing the distance, forming a semi-circle. He could no longer keep his eyes on all of them at once.

"No." He raised his voice. "You can't be here. This can't be real."

A dark, rich laugh came from somewhere in the middle of the ranks of the dead. "Real? My dear Raven, my dark star, my betrayer, you of all people know that nothing is real here, not even you. Which means everything is real."

He knew that voice, knew its gently chiding tone and the deadly danger that lurked beneath it. *William.* The front lines of the dead parted to reveal the blond mage, as handsome in death as in life, blood still staining his left side. He was flanked by the students Raven had led to their deaths in a Guardian trap.

Raven fell back another step and licked his dry lips. "You can't be here. I drove the blade into your heart, and I held you while you died. I saw your body interred in my own family's cemetery as there was no one else to claim it."

"And yet here I am." William spread his arms. "Here we all are."

Raven took a deep breath and drew himself up, standing firm now against William's sauntering approach. "No. You are things pulled from my own memories, playing upon my guilt. But I do not feel guilty for your death, William. I do feel sorry for the life you led, though it was none of my doing. And those who I killed in your name, their blood stains my soul, yes, but it stains yours as well."

"And for the students who trusted you, the students you led like lambs to the slaughter?"

Raven flinched. "They were hardly lambs. They would have murdered countless innocents had I not tipped off the Guardians to the coming attack."

"Ah yes, you were already wagging your tail for your new masters, even then. Was it so easy to betray a trust?"

Raven swallowed hard. "Nothing about that night was easy. But I did the best I could to prevent as many deaths as possible. I will not let guilt over past actions stop me from what I must do."

"What about this man?" William reached behind him to pull forward a pale, dark-haired young man without any visible wounds. "Can you forgive what you did to your own loyal apprentice?"

Daniel. Raven's breath left him as if he had been punched in the solar plexus. He stood motionless as the young man approached.

"Remember him?" William said. "Remember how you demanded that he give up his own power, his very life, to charge the Ravensblood?"

Remember? He could never forget, no matter how hard he tried to keep this particular sin to the back of his mind. Not only had he betrayed Daniel; that in and of itself had been unforgivable. But Cassandra had been his apprentice before Daniel. Had she not had the strength and fire to leave, it would have been her death that charged the Ravensblood.

Raven wrapped his arms around himself, suddenly cold. "You commanded me to do it."

"I commanded you to do it," William repeated, mocking. "A convincing argument, except that you failed to turn the Ravensblood over to me as I asked. Instead, you lied to me about your success and kept the Ravensblood for yourself, to use against me."

Daniel spoke to him then for the first time. "I would have followed you, you know. I would have gone over to the light with you, had you only asked."

Whether this was truly Daniel's ghost or just a product of his own memory and guilt, Raven could not say. But he knew in his heart that the specter spoke truth. "I hadn't planned to leave before that. Your death, and my part in it, was the final tipping point. I knew then that I could not go on."

"Convenient, that," Daniel said with a bitterness he had never shown in life. "Considering that it left you with the Ravensblood."

Raven lowered his head, taking several deep breaths before he found the strength to meet Daniel's gaze. "I have many, many regrets from that time in my life, but your death weighs the most heavily on my soul." He stepped forward, offering his hands to the specter of his apprentice. "I know that there can be no forgiving the depth of my betrayal, but I *am* sorry. I am so very sorry."

Daniel reached out his hands to clasp Raven's. For a moment he felt the warmth and solidity of flesh against his own. And then the touch was gone, and the ranks of the dead before him were gone as well. He stood alone once more in darkness, his own heartbeat thundering in the silence. He continued on.

That first the encounter, unsettling as it was, encouraged him. At least he had proof that he was not trapped in endless emptiness. And if he had met a challenge, surely that must mean that he was on the right path? But as the dark paths seemed to lead only to more dark paths, he began to doubt. Perhaps his encounter with the dead was meant as a reminder of his past crimes, before he faced the sentence of eternal nothingness.

No. He refused to believe that. If nothing else, the universe was not wasteful. He was more use in the real world actively trying to do good than he was down here wandering in endless darkness. He remembered the warmth of Daniel's hands in his. It felt like a final farewell, yes, but it also felt like forgiveness.

And then, up ahead, he saw a dim red light that grew brighter as he approached. It took him longer to recognize the figures that stood out against the muddy crimson glow, but then he had never known them in life. He had only seen them in oil portraits that had hung on the walls of Ravenscroft mansion. With the exception of a few Victorian portraits of outstanding artistic merit, most of those portraits now gathered dust in the attic. Cassandra had replaced them with local artists' renditions of the mountains, forests, and waterfalls of the Pacific Northwest, a change which made the house feel more like a home and less like a mausoleum.

He squared his shoulders and lifted his chin defiantly. "You aren't here. You aren't real. Your time is long past."

"We are as real as you are. Our blood runs through your veins." The man who spoke had steel-gray hair and Raven's hawk-like nose. Age had not withered the strength of his carriage nor the proud tilt of his chin.

Raven put a portrait to the face and a name to the portrait. Gwiliam Ravenscroft, Raven's great-grandfather.

"Your power, your mind, your strength of will, all of that came from us," Gwiliam continued. "Do you really think you could use those gifts against your forefathers, you disobedient child?"

Raven shivered, breath catching in his throat, feeling like a child indeed. A child awaiting punishment by the dark magic of his father and helpless to escape his wrath. His legs felt weak, as though at any moment he would drop to his knees to beg for mercy that would not come.

No. He should have recognized the sense-of-dread spell sooner. He'd never known it to be this powerful; it was augmented, perhaps, by the place, by the conjoined effort of some of the most powerful mages who ever lived, by the blood ties—who knew what the rules were here? But he would not be defeated by mere fear. If they were able to hurt him, they would have done so by now. His ancestors had never hesitated to use dark magic in the entire history of the Ravenscroft family.

He took a steady breath and forced himself to match Gwiliam's proud stance. "I acknowledge the gifts I have inherited from the Ravenscroft line. They make up a large part of who I am. But just as the oak is not the acorn, I am not my ancestors. I am what I have made of myself from those qualities. If you do not care for what I am, then I am sorry. But you can no more control the future of our line than I can control its past. I hope, wherever you are and in whatever state you exist, you can someday make peace with that as I have made peace with your memory."

He hadn't known what he was going to say until he said it, but he felt this new truth down to his bones. He closed his eyes and stepped forward. The flash of magefire flared bright even against his closed lids.

He held his breath, waiting for the pain. It didn't come. He released his breath slowly and opened his eyes. He was not burned.

There had been no magefire, and his ancestors were gone. Had they ever been there? He leaned back against the solidity of the stone, weak with relief. Was any of this real?

"What is reality?" he asked aloud, just to hear the sound of his own voice.

His legs ached from walking. No matter what their definition or degree of realness, each encounter had taken much of his strength. And yet he had no choice but to go on.

Gradually he realized that the quality of the darkness had changed, or else his eyes had finally started to adjust to the dark. There were shadows now, shapes, as if this nowhere place were growing more real somehow. From one of the dark alcoves stepped a shape, a man dressed head to toe in buckskins. He wore a loose-fitted tunic, beaded elaborately, like a ceremonial shirt he might have seen in a museum. No glow surrounded him as it had his predecessors. Raven knew, without words to explain why, that this man was real, or at least as real as Raven himself was in this place. Did he hear breath echoing off the walls? Or maybe it was the subtle rattle of the beads. If he had paid more attention to these things on his General Academy field trips, he might have even recognized the tribe by the style of beadwork. This was no cheap re-creation; it felt authentic. Raven would bet his whole library that those beads were antler or bone and polished stones. The stranger was a young man. Morgan's age, maybe a little older. His skin was a deep reddish tan, his long hair in two simple braids that hung down each shoulder. His eyes blazed with anger.

Raven felt the thrum of the stranger's magic. Craft, not Art, and yet more powerful than any Craft practitioner he had ever met, and more dangerous. Raven took a step back, hands up in the universal sign of peace.

"Are you my next challenge?" the stranger asked. "Or am I yours?"

TWENTY-ONE

The man was not speaking English, was not speaking any language that Raven ever recalled hearing, and yet, as in a dream, he understood everything the man said. He added sudden comprehension of unknown languages to the uncomfortable mysteries of the place, and disregarded the paradox. His every instinct told him that the man before him required all of his attention.

"I mean you no harm," Raven said.

"That would be a first," the stranger responded. "Your kind always means harm and the more words of peace you say the darker your intent."

It occurred to him then; from the man's warrior stance, the archaic dress, and the unknown language, this stranger had not come from the same century that Raven had. From the little Raven knew of Craft and ceremonial time stated that in the trance-world and the vision-world, time didn't flow in the same way that it did in the waking world of everyday. What Raven counted as unfortunate history was to this man fresh wounds. Unforgiven and unforgivable.

It was a young shaman-to-be, almost certainly, here to face tests and challenges as the final step to prove his training and take up the mantle of his calling, even as Raven was to face tests and challenges to prove himself a worthy champion.

Raven bowed his head. "I can't deny what my people have done to yours. My people, and my family in particular. Where I come from. . when I come from, these things happened a long, long time ago."

Not strictly true, but Raven wasn't about to go into the more subtle issues of discrimination, economic injustice, and treaty rights infringement. At least one of the foundations he gave to supported legal defense funds for indigenous peoples. He silently promised that if he got through this encounter alive he would increase the donation.

"I'm not here to debate guilt." Raven continued. "You have every right to hate my kind. But there is a danger out there in my world, in my time, a danger that will wipe my people and your people off the planet. That will destroy life itself. I've come seeking a way to end that danger. If you kill me here, there will be many, many innocent deaths."

"Why should I trust you?"

Raven could come up with nothing, nothing that would not sound like the lies his ancestors told to this man's people over and over again. But what could he do? If his magic was as strong as it was in the waking world, he would have no trouble defeating this man. But could he be so sure that it worked that way? More importantly, if he killed this man here, the man would not wake from his vision quest in his own time. Raven felt certain that the stranger was destined to be a powerful shaman. What would it do to the flow of history if Raven ended his life here? What right did he have to deal that sort of blow to a people his family had already wronged?

Ravenscrofts, alone and in conjunction with other Europeans, had already taken away far too much from the original inhabitants of this continent. He did not want to add to that debt. Yet the stranger looked at Raven with death in his eyes, weakening Raven's resolve.

He was not ready to leave the life he had with Cassandra. He wanted to watch Ransley grow up, wanted to be the sort of father he himself had never had. Beyond any selfish reasons, he had to live to stop the darkness that spilled from the cave, for the sake of the world itself. A younger Raven would have done the math and found the choice obvious, if regrettable. The man Cassandra called husband didn't find the path nearly so clear.

The stranger shifted impatiently. Raven could see him gathering strength to fight. He remembered hearing that before the European invasion destroyed their culture, the indigenous peoples of this continent did not draw such a strong distinction between Art and

Craft. That the most powerful of their shaman had combat magic of their own. Raven focused to strengthen his personal shields, but he knew he would not survive this encounter on defensive magic alone.

What would Cassandra do? But Cassandra was not here. He had to make the choice on his own, and trust to the changes her presence in his life had wrought that he made the right one. He took a deep breath, feeling the slight weight of the silver raven pendant against his chest. He remembered that the thing that made the most sense was not always the right answer.

"I will not fight you."

The stranger snorted in disgust. "You think I will not kill you if you do not fight?"

"I hope that you will not. I understand why you might want to. I think that you and I are here for similar purposes, and I hope for that commonality, if for no other reason, you let me live."

Words were not enough. Europeans had lied to the indigenous inhabitants of this land far too many times for words to have any meaning. He had to give some surety of his faithfulness.

Cassandra, forgive me if this does not work. Tell Ransley that his father loved him.

Raven fell to his knees, dropped his shield entirely, and spread his arms open exposing his chest in a gesture of ultimate surrender. "I know something of how many of your tribes think, and I know you do not revel in unnecessary killing, be it deer or be it a fellow man. I do not think that my blood on your hands will help your quest, but that is your choice to make. I will not fight you."

His life was in the stranger's hands, and yet he felt oddly unafraid. Strong even. Not like fire that consumes, not even like stone that withstands, but like water, which flows and turns course but ultimately finds its way to the sea, water that quenches fire and wears away stone. It felt peaceful, and freeing. He watched the stranger patiently, moments that lasted years, waited without impatience for his decision. "Believe me or not. I lay my life in your hands. I will not fight you." He made himself meet the man's eyes with a steady gaze, although he could not stop the small shudder that ran through his body.

The stranger's dark eyes were hard as flint, and Raven held his breath, sure he would be blasted to perdition. But then the man took a deep, shaky breath and laughed.

"My teacher has often told me winning is not always about defeating the enemy. That sometimes the victory is knowing when not to fight. That advice always troubled me before. I thought he counseled cowardice, surrender. I think I understand better now. Go in peace, brother."

The man walked past Raven, turned a corner, and was gone.

Shortly past the intersection of the two tunnels, the tunnel Raven followed widened into a half-round dead end. A broad form hunched over against the farthest wall. Raven froze, unable to tell in the dim light if it was a person or an animal. Given the confusing time stream, it could even be one of the cave bears or dire wolves that once roamed the continent.

He studied the form more closely, and nearly laughed when he realized it was nothing but an old woman wrapped in animal hides and sitting on a large, flat-topped rock.

"Make yourself useful, child." The woman's voice was weak and raspy with age. "Light the fire."

He swore that neither the logs nor the stones of the fire circle had been there before. He laid the wood with practiced ease born of many fireside nights with Cassandra and set the kindling alight with a controlled flick of magefire. Soon the bigger logs caught, and he sighed as the warmth reached him. The old woman smiled as he studied her in the orange-gold of the firelight. The pale gray of her hair gave no hint as to its original color, and the play of light and shadow made it seem as though her skin tone and facial structure were different from minute to minute.

"I am the mother to all," she said. "And I was old before the first humans walked the earth. You will not easily place me in any nation, in any time period."

He didn't bother to wonder how she had known his thoughts. "Forgive me, my lady, if I gave offence."

"No offence taken," she said warmly. "Curiosity is a good quality in the young."

He was scarcely a youth in age or experience, but he dared not say so. He sensed her power now; and only, he felt sure, because she allowed it. He realized that he stood before the most powerful being he had ever encountered. Without conscious decision, he knelt before her.

"Oh, none of that nonsense, now. Humility ill becomes you. Sit by the fire, child, and tell me why you are here." Her voice carried amusement, but also annoyance.

He sat facing her from the other side of the fire, mimicking her cross-legged pose. "My lady, I—"

"What did I tell you about humility? And you can call me Grandmother."

"Yes, Grandmother."

"Now answer my question."

It took him a moment to remember what question had been posed. "Grandmother, a –darkness, for lack of a better word, has come into our world. It kills, and it takes over people's minds and drives them to kill, as well. Those that sent me to the labyrinth have told me that it comes from another plane, like soul-stealers do. They say that it will end all life in our world if it is not stopped. It is nothing I understand, and I don't know how to combat it."

"Just as the scientists of your time talk about antimatter, some of those other planes carry what might be called antilife."

So his sense of the thing on that first day at the cave had been more accurate than he knew.

"And just as life is driven to find sustenance," she said, "to grow, and to reproduce itself in this universe and this plane, on other planes the anti-life replicates itself, seeks sustenance from other worlds, other universes. We do not know what drives it, any more than we know what caused that first spark of life to arise out of the primordial soup of amino acids warmed in the sun. But the planes are not always discrete unto themselves, as you who have called forth and banished soul-stealers know. There are things darker and more dangerous than soul-stealers. Things that will come on their own, seeking any leak in the fabric of the universe. Anti-life. Death that feeds on death as life feeds on life."

Raven shook his head in confusion. "But life feeds on death. Even vegetarians feed off the death of a plant. Even vegans that live on seeds and berries feed off the life that could be and is not."

The woman shook her head. "No, life feeds off of life, even if death results. But it is not the death itself that feeds us."

"I don't understand."

"This shadow you seek to stop is a thing from another plane. Perhaps it does not understand us either. Perhaps it is only seeking to survive, and we perceive it as evil because what it needs to survive is our pain, our fear, our death. But your alliance is to life, as it was for those that went before, those that sent you to the labyrinth. As should be the natural alliance of every people born under this sun and on this world. Your job then, is not to understand it but to stop it."

"I don't know how." Raven's voice, raised in frustration, echoed in the cave.

He looked up at her, daring to meet her eyes for the first time. "Grandmother, please. I can sense the immensity of your power. Surely you can save us."

She sat up straighter, and her eyes flashed dangerously. Still an old woman in form, yes, but all the grandmotherly kindness had gone, and he realized in that moment that the power she had let him sense earlier was only a fraction of her true strength. Bits of an old adage rose in his mind, something about the capriciousness of the gods. His mouth went dry.

"You dare to call the Old Powers back into the world?" In the shifting shadows, he saw the suggestion of spider legs spreading behind her.

Raven trembled where he was, unable to move, waiting for his soul to be devoured as if he were a hapless insect. Would Tony be the one to find the body? Would Cassandra? Would anyone know how he died? Would it even matter, if he could not stop the darkness?

And then the Grandmother laughed, a warm, kind laugh, an old woman once more. "Yes, child, they call me Grandmother Spider, though the webs I weave are not traps, but the fabric of the universes. You see me here as an old woman because I choose to take a form you can understand. They call me many things, in many times and places." She smiled. "In Ireland I was the Morrigan, the raven goddess that trained the heroes who protected the people. Yet I am not a goddess nor an old woman nor anything I could explain to your human mind. I can interfere in the universe that you know in small ways. But for any of the Old Powers to fully manifest into your world would destroy it more swiftly and more surely than this thing you call the darkness."

Raven's heart had not yet slowed to its normal rate, and yet he dared to ask. "Pardon my boldness, but I do not understand."

"The Old Powers are the powers of Making and Unmaking both. We can stir into being a universe where there is nothing but a void, but if we step fully into a universe already running its natural course, the disturbance will end that course."

Raven closed his eyes. "So you cannot help."

He slumped in exhaustion, hoping the Grandmother did not take it as disrespect. But to have come so far, overcome the challenges he had overcome, only to find that he was no closer to saving the world and the people he loved. . .

"Oh, child, usually you are smarter than this. I think you are not paying attention."

Raven bit back a protest; one did not argue with a goddess, or an elemental force of Making and Unmaking, or whatever sat before him. But he had been paying attention. The information all swirled around in his brain, making very little sense. He needed time to sort it, and yet once again, he had a feeling that time was running out.

"I said I cannot manifest in your world. I also said that I can interfere in small ways."

She had said that, yes. And something about training Irish heroes. He dimly remembered a rainy day in the library near his uncle's home and a children's book of folklore. A mighty warrior trained by a goddess. The Hound of Culainn. But the foe Raven faced could not be defeated by a sword, and Raven did not have the years to dedicate to training.

Grandmother's voice interrupted his thoughts. "Not every hero has the same tale."

Raven's jaw tightened momentarily. He would never get used to not having the privacy of his thoughts.

Grandmother chuckled, because of course she sensed that thought as well. "Will you take the hero's path, and find out for yourself how this tale ends?"

"Wouldn't someone from the Craft be better for this?"

She shook her head. "The type of Craft that drove back the darkness long centuries past has been lost to the world. Your world, your time, has split Art from Craft. There are benefits to this, the expertise that comes with specialization. But it means that neither Art nor Craft has the entirety of what it needs to re-seal the gap that was opened by the destruction of the land. Unlike most other mages, you have experience in wielding strength beyond your own."

"Are you speaking of the Ravensblood? It has been destroyed, and I will not make another."

Of that one thing he was sure. If there was a way to stop this, to save the world from being devoured by this darkness, that way did not lie in the dark magic that created the Ravensblood.

"The Ravensblood is gone, but your body's memory of wielding it is not. The memory of channeling more strength than it was meant to channel, the memory of yielding to the will, even to the point of death."

The cold chill of knowing came over him. "To the point of death, and beyond?"

"This is not dark magic, it does not specifically require your death as a sacrifice."

Raven heard the unspoken part of that statement. *It does not require death, but it may very well lead to death.*

"You have been chosen for this task. Who knows why? It could be as simple as you being in the right place at the right time. But you have been cast as the champion of the story."

"I will walk the path, then, if you can tell me the way."

She pulled from her pocket a small, rounded object and handed it to him. It fit into the palm of his hand, a heavy clay thing decorated with the stylized likeness of a crow or raven. He looked back to her, puzzled.

"Use this at the beginning of your path. It will call to you your guide and ally."

He looked more closely at the clay bird. It had a hole at one end and more holes at the top. A memory sprang up. Cassandra had dragged him out to the Saturday Market very much against his will, and there had been a booth selling small clay flutes that hung on a cord like a pendant. It stuck in his mind for the persistence of the craftsperson who tried to insist he try one, despite his insistence that he played the piano, not the winds, thank you very much. Those flutes could have been more garishly colored versions of this one.

He was about to ask more questions, but the fire suddenly flared, blindingly bright. He scrambled to his feet and stumbled backward. The fire went out like a snuffed candle, leaving him alone in the darkness.

Sitting up with a start, Raven opened his eyes. The screen-saver on the television provided dim light to the parlor and his back reminded him that maybe he was getting too old to fall asleep on the couch. In his hand lay the stone flute.

He dropped it as though it burned him. He knew little enough of dream journeys and vision quests; they were the purview of Craft, not Art. His one previous encounter with such things, though it had saved his life, left him with little desire to get better acquainted. But everything he did know said that it was impossible to bring back a physical object from the dream world. Magic simply didn't work that way. And yet here was the clay flute, mocking him from the cushion of the couch where he had dropped it.

TWENTY-TWO

Raven took himself to bed and quickly fell back to sleep, only to be startled awake, on his feet before he even realized where he was or what had awoken him. In the nursery, Ransley was screaming.

He dashed down the hall to the nursery. The door stood open, and in the soft illumination from the light globe he saw Tony, back to the door, unruly hair even more mussed than usual. Tony turned at the sound of his approach, and Raven took in the details. The nanny wore a faded tie-dye T-shirt over multicolored striped sleep pants. He cradled the wailing Ransley to him, bouncing him gently.

"He's not wet," Tony said. "And he shouldn't be hungry."

Raven concentrated on slowing his breathing. His pulse pounded in his ear as though he were in the midst of a duel for his life. Babies cried in the night. It's what babies did. Except. . .

"He usually sleeps through the night," Tony said. "I hope the little guy isn't coming down with something. It could be a nightmare. Babies get them, you know. Or so the specialists say, I'm not sure how they can tell. But I read up on baby sleep patterns, and a lot of other baby stuff, when you gave me this job."

Raven smiled, pulse returning to normal. Of course Tony had done his research. Despite the nanny's rather Bohemian exterior, he and Raven had more in common than most people would guess. Beyond even a past that they struggled to live down. Faced with an unfamiliar set of circumstances, their first instinct was to read up on the subject.

Ransley's wails quieted to hiccupping sobs. He stirred restlessly in Tony's arms, and caught sight of Raven. Instantly he held his arms out. "Da," he cried. And then, more insistently, "Dad!"

It was the first time he managed *dad* instead of *da*. Despite the unsettling thought of something so small and defenseless as his son experiencing a nightmare, Raven still felt warmth bubbling up inside him. He was a dad, against all odds and counter to everything he'd thought he wanted only a few years ago.

He reached out "Here," he said. "I'll take him for a little bit."

"Are you sure?" Tony said. "You can't have gotten much sleep. I don't mind."

"I'm sure."

Now that he was fully awake and certain of the safety of his son, the content of his dream returned to him in every detail. Only it wasn't just a dream, not in the conventional sense, any more than what happened to him in the cave in Australia had been a dream for all that he had wanted to believe it so. He had known enough Craft practitioners to respect that their magic was as real as his own. And just as a Mundane or a Craft practitioner could be burnt by magefire, apparently an Art practitioner could be subject to the dreams and visions of Craft, even if they had not trained for it and had really no idea what to do with it.

No. He was lying to himself. *Use this at the beginning of your path. It will call to you your guide and ally.* He could pretend to believe that the *path* was metaphorical, but he knew with a deep unshakable knowing that it was not. Knew it, and knew what he had to do. But right now, he would sit a little longer with his son and hope that Cassandra came home soon.

In the end, Cassandra didn't return home before he left. In the pale hours before true dawn, Sherlock messaged him on the crystal. Sherlock had returned back to headquarters; there were too many active situations for her to stay away. Cassandra and Rafe had remained at the logging road, grabbing some sleep in vehicles borrowed from the K-9 officers while the search went on. Waiting on the scene so they would be there if they were needed.

Raven felt it in his bones; he could wait no longer. He sat down in the library with a sheet of creamy white stationary and the fountain pen that he preferred for such things. Slowly, thoughtfully, he wrote out a letter to Cassandra. It wasn't a long letter. The first paragraph explained where he was going and why. The rest of the letter contained nothing that she didn't know already, and yet he wanted it said one last time. How he loved her and Ransley more than life itself. How he would always return to them if it was within his power to do so. That if he had not returned, it meant that he could not.

He folded the letter and placed it in the locked drawer with the Ravenscroft journal, where it would only be found if he did not return.

Raven faded back into existence at the spot on the trail where the sheriff's deputy had taken him that first day in Devil's Crossing, and where the sheriff had shot him. Gods, could that be just two days ago? Given the exponential growth of the darkness, he would not risk teleporting directly into the cave and possibly into a situation he wasn't ready to handle.

The high desert was broad and empty as ever, a landscape that could swallow him whole and never even notice. He could only hope that he had correctly interpreted Grandmother's instructions. He looked around as he slid his hand into his pocket, felt the cool smoothness of the clay flute. There was no one else in the area, and no wonder. The sky was oppressive, a horrid dark yellowish color that boded ill; he couldn't imagine anyone deciding that this would be a good day for a hike. Raven had only seen a sky change like that once before. It had preceded the worst storm he'd ever seen, one that had come a hair's breadth of becoming a tornado. He would almost welcome the lightning stabbing at the trees, the thunder that shook houses and the storm winds that made windows rattle, if only he did not have to face what lay before him in that cave. He could practically taste the darkness in the air, even from here, thick enough that even a Mundane must feel it on some level.

He took the flute out to his mouth and blew. He succeeded only in achieving a breathy sound like a child might make blowing through a drinking straw. Damn. He trained on the piano, not the flute, and certainly not a rudimentary instrument such as this one. He should have asked Grandmother for a lesson.

He refused to accept the end of the world rested on his lack of skill with wind instruments.

He tried again, and produced a soft, low almost-whistle. Again, and produced a mournful, warbling sound like the cry of a lonely bird calling for its lost flock. He waited. Nothing. The desert was still as death. Not even a wind stirring the long, sparse grasses.

He blew again, then slid the clay flute back into his pocket. Still nothing.

Maybe he needed to be closer to the cave. Maybe this was all useless. If it were not for the solid presence of the flute, he would think he was losing his mind. He walked a little further before blowing the flute one last time.

Silence.

Then he heard the rustling of wings behind him, the almost mocking *craik-craik* of a raven, as it settled on a boulder not far from where he stood. The bird looked up at him, cocking its head.

Oh gods, no. Not another enigmatic raven guide. He'd had enough of that in Australia. If the powers that be were going to send him a guide, could it not be—

"Hello."

He turned at the soft voice behind him. The woman had not been there a moment before. There was no cover, no trees, no shelter from which she could have come. No ripple of magic that indicated a teleport. And yet there she was.

Raven looked the woman up and down, taking in hair streaked in silver and white, hanging in two long braids down her white deerskin dress. Her coppery red skin indicated Native American heritage, but her eyes when she turned to look at him were so pale a gray that they appeared nearly white. He would have wondered about her vision, except that her gaze clearly focused on him, taking his measure and seeming somewhat disappointed with what she saw.

"Well, you're not what I expected in a champion. But Grandmother would not have given the flute to just anyone, so I guess you'll have to do."

Raven took a moment to summon every scrap of diplomacy he had; the stakes were more important than his pride. "You must be my guide, then,"

"Must I?" She sighed. "I suppose I am, for what it's worth. I am Winter Snowraven. You may call me Winter."

It must be a translation of her real name. But then this whole conversation must be translated. Who or whatever she was, she was not from this time. Probably not from any tribe still extant.

"I am—"

"Another Raven," she finished for him. "Yes, I know. Who else would come to mend the raven in the cave that protects us all?"

That hazy sense of unreality had increased. The colors, never very bright in this locale, had grown even more muted. Surreptitiously, he drove his thumbnail into his pointer finger to be certain that he could still feel his own body.

"Are we still in the real world?" He asked her.

She sighed impatiently. "Your kind. Always wanting to label things, always wanting to divide this thing from that thing."

He wasn't certain if your kind meant people of European descent or practitioners of Art. He suspected that in her eyes it was the same either way. Her enigmatic answer reminded him all too much of Bran Tarrant who had saved his life when he had been in hiding in Australia. Bran had been real, though. Or perhaps he should say that Bran had been flesh and blood, moving in the same time and space and more or less by the same physical laws as Raven himself.

"Grandmother told me to use the whistle to summon a guide. But a guide to what? I still don't know what's needed to stop this darkness."

"I was the one who stopped it last time," Winter said. "I and my wife, who wrought the petroglyphs. The warrior petroglyph at the cave entrance was a stopgap, a way of containing the darkness while we worked to bring the raven petroglyph into being, and later to protect people from coming too close to the raven. Though a creature of light, it is powerful enough to be dangerous in its own right. And of course, to protect the raven itself. We knew it had to stand for centuries upon centuries, long after anyone living remembered its purpose. We never imagined the time when men would create great metal beasts that could rumble upon the surface of the earth and destroy things deep within."

"The vibration from the earthmoving equipment that caused the crack in the petroglyph. Is that what brought the darkness across?"

He thought about the odd sound that Morgan had heard, the one that shook the earth. Could that have been the darkness shoving the crack wider? Or maybe the darkness shoving its way into their dimension?

"Say rather that it allowed it to come across. The darkness is a thing with long memory. It remembers how well it fed the last time it was loose in this world. It sensed, I am sure, that the feeding would be even better this time."

Because there are so many more people alive in the world today.

Without another word, she started up the trail to the cave. He fell in behind her. She had a surprisingly brisk stride for one of her short stature and apparent age.

"Wait," he called after her. "I still don't know why we are here, or what we are supposed to do to stop this thing."

"I died in stopping it, though I had the whole power of my tribe behind me. Our magic was different in those days. Not Art or Craft, but the melding of the two. So much was lost when the Europeans came and massacred the people. But that is another evil, long after we drove away this darkness that has come again.

My wife survived the ritual to drive the darkness back to its own plane, but her part of it was done with the creation of the art that became the petroglyphs. I believe she married a man from the new tribe, and had many children. It's hard to see things clearly, hard to keep track of the living from where I've been, but I think she was happy. I hope she was." Winter smiled a little wistfully. "I'd like to think that somewhere her blood runs through the veins of someone who walks the earth today."

TWENTY-THREE

Raven froze on the trail. "One moment. If you died stopping the darkness the first time—."

"Don't tell me you're going to start going on about the divisions between the dead and the living," Winter said.

"Wouldn't dream of it," Raven lied smoothly. "But I'm hoping you can answer some of my questions about the darkness since you have experience with it."

"I will answer your questions if you *keep moving.* It took you long enough to get to this point. There is very little time now left to waste."

"The first death that we had," Raven said. "In our time, that is. It seems like the darkness itself may have killed the victim. We certainly haven't been able to place anyone at the scene. The sheriff had one suspect, but I was never convinced. And from what we've seen, people who fall under the influence of the darkness don't simply get over it on their own, which eliminates all our persons of interest."

"In my time, too, it seemed like the darkness was more able to act on its own when it first came out, and more independent, as though it was boiling with pent-up energy. There were a few deaths that seemed to come directly from the darkness. Then as it moved out and disbursed, it seemed to work more through people, rather than on its own. Maybe it grew less able to act without an agent the longer that it moved through our world. Or maybe it was clever enough to think that the subtlety would allow it to spread further. Maybe it needed the power from the first direct death to move on and spread."

"The pattern of the spread doesn't make sense," Raven said. "If it were just going from place to place there would be a lot of places in between here and Bend, or here and Portland, that would have also seen a sharp spike in violent crime. And yet outside of Devil's Crossing, it seems mostly to be hitting the bigger cities."

"In the time I walked on earth," Winter began, "we did not have nearly the large groupings of people that your time has. But the darkness did seem to move to the places where the largest groups of people were congregated. It feeds on death, remember, and so life attracts it."

They walked on a little further in silence while he contemplated her answer. "So what do we do to defeat it?" he asked. "If it's simply a matter of repairing the crack, well, I'm happy to lend myself to the cause, but architectural magic has never been my strong point."

"Now that the crack has let the darkness through, it will not be enough to merely mend the physical damage to the raven. The darkness itself must be conquered and pushed back to where it belongs."

"How can we do that?"

"I cannot say for certain whether the darkness comes from the same plane as soul stealers. As you have no doubt guessed, they are similar, but not identical. The darkness definitely seems to be more autonomous, for one thing. And it has the ability to spread on its own, making it far more dangerous. Much like soul stealers, the darkness, once it has crossed, can only be countered with magic that is the opposite of its nature. In other words, healing magic. The petroglyphs are essential to keeping it out once it's been driven back, but they are already in place. If we are able to push the darkness back where it came from, then we only need to repair the raven, not make it anew."

Raven's step faltered as he took in the implication of what she was saying. "My background in dark magic means I am poor at healing magic. If that's what we need, there are other mages that might be better suited. Healers." Two sprang to mind immediately, although he was loath to name them, loath to bring them in to a mission that might well end in their deaths. Cassandra. Ana. He would gladly give his own life if it meant that they were safe. But was he willing to lay down his life in a futile battle that he could not win?

"I've battled soul stealers successfully, yes," he said. "But what we are facing seems far, far more powerful than any soul stealer."

"Indeed. Fortunately, healing magic has always been my strongest calling. But in this form, and without the power of the tribe to draw on, I need an alternate supply of raw magic. When I faced the darkness last time, my entire tribe gathered the night before in a ceremony that raised energy and fed it to me, so that what I went in the morning to confront the enemy, I did it with the tribe's strength as well as my own. Only a ghost of that energy raised still remains."

Only a ghost. Interesting choice of terms. Raven did not point this out.

"In the absence of my tribe," Winter continued, "you will need to feed energy to me."

"I'm no witch," Raven said. "I've never worked with a coven. I have no experience in sharing power."

"But you were a dark mage once," Winter said. "If I am not mistaken, you have more than once taken power given to you by another mage. And you have let your power be wielded by another."

Raven stopped walking altogether. He'd already noticed that she seemed to know more about him than she logically should, but this depth of knowledge startled him. Yes, he'd accepted power from Cassandra, once, and only with her consent. It technically fell within the realm of dark magic, taking another's power to wield as his own, but the circumstances had justified it. And yes, when he served under William, he'd surrendered his will to William and allowed him to wield his power. Not that William really needed it. It had been a test of his loyalty and his willingness to submit; he knew and accepted that. But at the time, William had been his master. Raven had given over his life and his power to him in every other way, so in the moment it seemed like a logical step, something he was glad to do to prove his fealty.

But back then Raven had been young and naïve, for all that he had imagined himself to be worldly. He was less trusting now. He did not really know this—person? Ghost? Spirit? He couldn't even say for sure what she was, and yet she was expecting him to make himself completely vulnerable to her.

Raven thought of how the darkness had taken over Harvey's thoughts. Could it be that Winter was merely an illusion meant to trick him into dropping his shield and letting the darkness inside? But he'd felt those delusions in Harvey's mind. They were full of pain and rage. Surely the darkness couldn't conjure up the image of a long-ago healer who sacrificed her life to save the world.

On the other hand, how well did he know this darkness?

"The choice is yours," Winter said. "I would not force you, even could I. But with my skill and our combined powers, we have at least a small chance of defeating the darkness. It's the only chance you have of facing the darkness and surviving to return to your wife and your son and the world that you defend. Otherwise—," she shrugged.

"So, you will not help me unless I hand myself over to you entirely?"

"I never said that." Her voice remained calm despite the implied accusation. "I will do what I can to support and guide you regardless. Though I have not walked this earth as a living woman for millennia, I still have an attachment to it. I still side with the life over, well, not death, death is part of life. But let us say I side with life over this thing that is the opposite of life. I am fairly certain, however, that if we do not combine your strength to my skill, we will not be able to defeat this thing. Even if you do as I say, we have only the slimmest of chances for success. I can promise you that if we join together we will be stronger. Maybe, just maybe strong enough to defeat the darkness."

"What are our chances of success? You said last time you had the magic of the whole tribe behind you, magic more compatible to yours."

"In my tradition, there is power in the unity of opposites. The object and its reflection; the bird in the air and the shadow it casts upon the earth; male and female; the light raven and the dark. The two styles of magic which in your time you have divided into Art and Craft."

"I thought you said you did not believe in divisions?"

She laughed, and despite this direness of the situation it was a merry sound, like the music of water dancing over the stones. "I never said I didn't believe in divisions, only that your people make entirely too many of them where there are none needed. So the question remains, my brother raven. When the time comes, will you yield your strength to me so that we may stand together against the darkness?"

Was it his ego that held him back? Or was it a natural instinct for self-preservation that should be obeyed? He had one chance to get this right, and not nearly enough information on which to base his decision. Not only his life, not only the Three Communities, but quite possibly all of life as they knew it all across this planet was dependent on him making the right choice.

Winter began to walk again; he followed in silence. It was his nature to stand on his own, to fight on his own. It was what he knew, even if he did not know how to fight this particular enemy.

The air became oppressive, thick. It pooled in his lungs, weighing them down. The heaviness in the air had nothing to do with the heat, nor with any dust in the air, nor with any natural phenomenon. The eerie yellow of the sky had turned to a deep blood-red, the sort of color that might herald the end of the world. Though he did not know much about Mundane meteorology, he doubted that any natural phenomenon had caused the change.

"So, how fast will the darkness grow if it's not stopped?" *Is there a chance that somewhere else in the world, some group will have time to band together and stop it if we fail?*

"No one can say for certain. It has always been defeated before. The darkness only came across once in this part of the world, but I know that my brave brothers and sisters in tribes of faraway lands have had to face it in earlier times, and later."

"Why then could I find nothing about it in any of the historical records?" Raven asked.

"Remember that long ago for you is still recent for the human race. There was a long, long history with culture and art and song, and, yes, magic, long before humans made written records. But from what I know, this thing grows massively more powerful the longer it is loose in the world. It is likely that if we do not stop it here and now, no one will be able to stop it later."

Even if William had won, even if he had managed a reign of dark magic that swept over the Three Communities, or even beyond to other nations. . .It might've taken decades or centuries and a river of spilled blood, but in the end, the light had always overthrown darkness. Even Nazi Germany had fallen in its time. But this darkness was not of this world, and it threatened all of humanity forever.

"When the time comes," Raven said at last, "I will yield my power to you." He could only hope that he made the right decision.

Raven felt as though icy waters churned in the core of his being, something he hadn't felt since his first magic duel outside of Guardian Academy, the first duel where there were no teachers to monitor and no safety rules to make sure that both parties survived the encounter. Only the stakes now were much, much higher. Higher than any stakes he had encountered before. Even on that first duel, his confidence in his own abilities had been firm. His nerves then had come from the knowledge that a duel does not always go to the strongest mage, and a lucky strike can give the weaker opponent the victory. When he went up against William the first time, Raven was so fueled by rage and grief that he cared less than he should have for his own survival. He'd had little else to lose beyond his life. Now though, now he had everything to lose, so much more than he ever dreamed of having.

As he came closer to the cave, he realized that what he had taken merely to be a strange shadow was something else entirely. Darkness streamed out of the cave into the light in the same way that light would stream out of a lamp into a dark room. He stopped, frozen, unable to make any sense of what he was seeing. He turned to Winter.

She merely nodded once. "Yes, I see it. It has grown stronger. It has been allowed to grow longer, and therefore is even stronger than it was in my time. I fear we have very little time left before it will be unstoppable."

Raven took a deep breath. "Lead on then."

Raven nearly blasted the figure teleporting in on his right before he recognized him. "Morgan, it's not the time right now for gathering potshards." Did the boy not sense the darkness all around?

Had Raven somehow been wrong all along? Was this boy somehow involved with the darkness? True cases of possession were rare, and usually it involved a mage rather than any kind of demon. But he'd heard of apocryphal tales of the possessed having the power of the entity or mage to control them. Was that what was going on?

"I'm not here for potshards and I think we both know that. I had a dream last night. The white raven woman was in it."

"Hello, Morgan." Winter said from Raven's other side.

"Don't encourage him," Raven said.

"You have Blue Deer's blood in you," Winter said to Morgan. "On both sides, as it happens. Her blood runs strong. No wonder I was drawn to you in your in your dreams."

Raven wasn't used to being ignored. He really wasn't used to feeling out of his depth. He looked from Winter to Morgan, now completely at a loss as to what might be going on.

"What we are doing is dangerous. This whole area is dangerous right now," Raven said. "It is no place for a boy."

"I'm a legal adult," Morgan said, jaw set defiantly.

"The law might say so," Raven said. "But no one your age is really ready to make this sort of choice."

"From what I understand, you were close to my age when you swore to William."

"You're not exactly helping your cause." Raven growled. "Not to mention, what experience do you have in combat magic?"

"What we will be doing is not combat magic in any traditional sense of the word," Winter said.

"Whose side are you on, anyway?" Raven said.

Winter frowned at him, a frown that reminded him of Ana when she was disappointed at him. "We are not enemies at war, but friends taking council together."

Her words left him feeling oddly abashed. Must be her resemblance to Ana. He pushed the feelings aside. "Wait a minute. He said that you appeared to him in a dream?"

"I can't recall. Perhaps I did. Or perhaps I will at some time in the future. Time means even less in the dream world than it does in our world."

Raven didn't know what to say. Time always seemed very relevant to him, especially now. The clock was ticking; the darkness spreading. He let the topic of the dream go. "The point is that he is barely more than a boy. I refuse to take someone yet so young into a life-threatening situation."

"Isn't that for him to say?" Winter asked. "You're not bringing him anywhere, just as I'm not bringing you. He came of his own volition, just as you have. And, whether he had a true dream or not, the fact that he is descended from my beloved Blue Deer, the fact that he turned up at the same time we did, all this tells me that he is meant to be here in some way."

"I came to Devil's Crossing because I was supposed to save him. I refuse to get him killed."

"I'm not just your pet project. I'm my own person and I want to do this. I *need* to do this," Morgan said, and then more softly, "You're not the only one who had done things in his life that he needs to atone for."

Raven knew that feeling all too well. But Morgan had made one mistake, and he was so young. He had so much of his life still ahead of him.

"You already paid the dues chosen for you by the system. What we're about to do, it could be a death sentence. You don't deserve that." He turned to Winter. "Can't you see he's just a boy?"

She shook her head. "He's old enough to make his decision. In the tribes, boys his age were already warriors."

"This isn't your world. Children grow up more slowly here. They're given time to be children."

"I am not a child." Morgan said. "And you can't stop me."

"He has a point," Winter said. "What will you do? Tie him up?"

"You need me," Raven said to Winter. "You need me more than you need him. If you let him come, I will back out. I have more power to lend to the fight than he does. Can you really afford to lose that?"

"Why does this matter so much to you?" Winter asked. Her pale eyes looked for the truth, his truth, would be satisfied nothing less than the purest essence of truth.

"I have seen too many young people die. Some by my betrayal. One by my hubris and lack of perceptiveness. Please, let me save just one. If I go to my death this day, let me go with the knowledge that I saved at least one."

He saw Winter exchange a look with Morgan and for a long moment he thought that they would continue to defy him. Then the two of them exchanged small but definite nods.

"All right then. The boy will wait here where he will be safe while we proceed to the cave mouth."

Raven would prefer for Morgan to be far, far away, but he suspected that this was all the concession that he would get. He could only trust that Winter knew what the danger zone would be. Used to being confident in his knowledge, he now had no choice but to put his faith in another. *If we fail, nowhere will be safe.* The darkness grew heavier, pressed harder with every step. They had traveled only a few yards further when suddenly the pressure was gone.

He turned to Winter, looking for an explanation of this sudden grace. . .and then the darkness returned, slamming into him with the force of a hundred Hammerhand spells, driving him to his knees.

TWENTY-FOUR

Winter was beside him instantly, hand on his shoulder. He wasn't sure if he was hearing her voice with his ears, or if the voice was in his head, but the words were clear. *We make our stand here. Give over your power to me.*

Now that the moment had come, he wasn't sure he wanted to yield control. No, he corrected himself, he knew that he definitely didn't want to yield control. He wasn't sure he could if he wanted to, wasn't sure his instincts of self-preservation would allow it. If he gave her full access to his power, she could easily drain him to the point where he could no longer maintain his shield, and the darkness would devour him.

Brother Raven, do you trust me?

He didn't allow himself time to think, time to second-guess. He knew what his answer must be. "Yes. Yes I do."

Then lend me your strength.

He felt her power reach out to him like a questing hand. He wanted to shove that hand back, to strike back with spell lightning and magefire. Instead, he let her take hold of his power, hold his very life and soul in her hands. Light flared out from her, beautiful in its purity, and settled to a steady, warming glow.

Her shield was his shield now, an unbroken wall before them that pressed back the darkness. Winter's magic was something Raven had never seen before, a kind of combination of ward magic and healing magic, weaving a wall between the darkness and them. She pulled power from him, spun it with her own, incorporated it into the weaving. The woven wall turned a silvery gray from the combination of power. No longer white, but still beautiful. He wondered, briefly, what it looked like to her. Magic looked different for each mage, something seen with the mind's eye, rather than with normal vision. The darkness battered against the weaving looking for holes, looking for weak spots. The weaving grew taller and wider and thicker, still stunning in its beauty as it shone against the darkness. She pulled more and more energy from him; he gave it all willingly. This working contained the essence of life, building with it, creating from it, not devouring for fuel as death magic did. If the creation cost him his life he would pay the price and feel privileged to do so.

The darkness wavered, started to fade. Could it be this simple? Could Winter's weaving push the darkness back, keep it away as curtains at the window kept out the cold of night?

But then the weaving bulged in as though a strong wind had hit it. The darkness pushed against it, sliding along its edges even as Winter made it longer and taller. The darkness sought a way around the barrier, a way through. Winter pulled more power from him, and then more. Raven started deliberately pushing power out to her. He felt the darkness waver, give way. . .

And then it shoved back, stronger than ever. Winter staggered against the impact, and a bolt of fear shot through him. Winter took more strength from him; he yielded it willingly. The light held steady. The darkness shoved against them with more and more force. Minutes ticked by. They were at a stalemate. But he and Winter had merely human strength and this thing — Gods only knew. It showed no signs of tiring. With the Ravensblood, they might have had a chance. But the Ravensblood had been destroyed.

Raven delved down deeper into the core of himself, pulled every scrap of strength and will, and shoved all he had at Winter, giving her more than she would ever take on her own. He could sense that she had held back, trying to spare his life, but that would only end in death for everyone. He thought words to her, not sure if she could hear them, but trusting that she could at least feel his intent. *Do it. Take it all. Don't concern yourself with me. Just take whatever you need to stop this thing.*

The darkness battered at them, battered at them. He had given all his strength, and it still would not be enough. The darkness like a storm pushed harder and harder against the weaving until he could feel the whisper of its breath through the places where the threads had tattered.

Raven started hearing voices in the shadows, voices of those he had wronged, had killed. Voices of William's victims from the years Raven had served at his side. *Just my imagination.* His imagination, fueled by the darkness that somehow took his every regret and horror, turning it and twisting it against him. If the past haunted him, the best way to atone was to hold fast, and keep pushing more and more power toward Winter. The voices warned him that he was too trusting, that Winter took his power for her own purposes, would drain the last of his life in revenge for what his family had done. He pushed away doubt. He would not let the voices drive him to the same madness that had taken poor Harvey Heilman. He had come knowing what the price might be, come willing to pay it.

His chest burned, his heart pounded, irregularly and too fast. Still he pushed on, though his lungs hurt. His body screamed in pain as he tore from it the living energy needed to sustain it, feeding it all towards Winter.

The threads tightened, closing the holes, and the weaving held firm. The darkness receded and was gone. He felt Winter tie off the weaving. It was done, they had won. He breathed deeply, trying to catch his breath, joy and disbelief warring in him. It was over, and he was still alive. He could go back to Cassandra and put this whole nightmare behind him.

The darkness hit the woven wall with twice the power and three times the focus, like a flash flood down a narrow ravine, like wind carving out the sandstone of a canyon. It tore a hole through the weaving. What had been a barrier of magic became a tattered rag. Winter snatched at his magic. He shoved it toward her, as fast as she could take it. All of his reserves were gone; he was working on will alone, the magic consuming his own tissues like a marathon runner who had burned through his fat reserves and whose body was using the last of the fuel the muscles themselves had stored.

Winter was gathering the torn threads, reweaving them, but not fast enough. Not fast enough, not strong enough.

Raven screamed in anger and in agony. Every inch of his body burned; it should be impossible for the magic to draw so much from his physical self by will alone and yet he could only demand more of himself, and more.

Winter started closing the hole, threads of magic a blur of movement as she worked, but he had to keep feeding her the power. His heart banged an irregular beat against his ribs; his breath came in tearing gasps that hurt his lungs. And still, still, it was not enough. He had given his all, and it was not enough. They were going to lose.

Gods, they were going to lose. And then there would be nothing between this darkness and the people that Raven loved. This world that he loved. How far would the darkness extend in its devouring rampage? Would there be anything of humanity left?

He felt another presence behind him and a little to the side. Had the darkness made it through the weaving? Was the struggle lost? But no, he felt no darkness in his presence. And yet, something about this presence felt familiar.

Morgan?

Oh, gods, no! Morgan had promised, Winter had promised. They had lied to him.

Not a lie came the combined thoughts of Winter and Morgan. *We promised you that Morgan would wait someplace safe and he did.*

I waited until it was clear you will not win without the extra help, came Morgan's thoughts, twining through the magic.

You lied! Your life, your survival was to be the last balm to my conscience, my last gift to this world.

And yet how long would the boy survive if the shadow wins? Winter thought at him. *Your conscience still has its prize. You did not allow Morgan to come. Morgan came himself against your wishes.* Already she was weaving Morgan's strength into the spell. The weaving turned a warmer color, a pale gold like the first rays of sunrise, like wheat beneath the summer sun. Morgan's strength helped the weaving grew strong again. The tears mended, the woven wall grew thicker and taller and wider.

Then the darkness came back at them, came like a gust of wind, like a gale-force blast. The voices in that wind howled like the souls of the damned. Not just Raven's crimes now, but the crimes of every Ravenscroft that had ever cast dark magic. It wasn't real; the darkness was playing with his memories, his guilt. It was using himself against himself as it had done with Heilman. The wailing terror and rage built until it became a reminder of every death, every scrap of pain caused by humanity through the eons across the world. And more, adding all of the death and terror that had occurred even before human ancestors began to walk upright. Every death, a cacophony of suffering.

This was all that would remain of the world if the darkness were not stopped. They had done everything that they could, given every scrap of strength.

There is one thing left. The voice in his head was one he had never heard before, and yet he knew it. The raven on the cave wall. Images flashed through his head, too fast for words.

Morgan had seen/heard it, too. Raven felt it in the connection of their magic a half-second too late. Raven was exhausted, and Morgan had the reflexes of the very young. Morgan pulled out the blade that every farm boy carried.

In that moment, Raven's mind threw him back to Zack and death magic and the cells beneath William's sanctuary.

But Morgan slashed the knife across his palm rather than driving it into his heart. His blood spilled onto the earth. Earth and blood called out to the raven on the cave wall, joining its power to the theirs. Morgan shoved his life force out in a flash of gold streaked with blood red, creating a sloppy patch that tied directly to the protections put in place originally by the petroglyphs. Blood magic. Dark magic.

Winter had talked about the power of mirror images, of the thing and its shadow. The wall had been woven of light and life. Death was part of life, and dark magic had touched Morgan once before, and now he had given that part of himself up to the weaving.

But Morgan had given too much. There was no way the boy could survive the loss of that much energy; he had not the strength that came with years of working.

Winter took the patch and without hesitation worked it into the greater weaving. Stretched and twined it until it ran like a gleaming-bright ribbon through the subtler work. The wail of the darkness raised in volume and pitch, until he felt that the shriek would drive him mad.

The weaving, the weaving had to hold. He could not let Morgan's sacrifice be in vain. Winter was working faster now, trying to finish the weaving before the darkness could push through again. She wasn't going to make it.

Raven remembered the cave in Australia, remembered what Bran Tarrant had tried to teach him about not rejecting his heritage entirely. Remembered a spell in the Ravenscroft journal he had never thought that he would use. He snatched up the knife that Morgan had dropped and drew the blade across the old scar on his wrist, letting his blood spill over Morgan's. Murmuring the words to call on the strength of his own ancestors, a thread of black to run through the weaving.

And the darkness disappeared. Raven gasped in the suddenly clear air like a drowning man breaking the water's surface.

Raven crumpled to the hard earth, unable to even keep to his knees. Uncontrollable tremors ran through his muscles, and he could hear his own pulse pounding in his ears, unsteady and too fast. Sweat soaked his clothes, and he closed his eyes against the spinning of the world around him. The surface he lay on seemed to rise and dip though his mind told him he lay on solid ground.

Morgan. The thought made him grab hold of his slipping consciousness, made him force his eyes open, raise his heavy head enough to look around.

Morgan lay still on the ground, unmoving, his coppery-tan complexion gone a grayish-pale. *No. Gods, no.*

Fear for the boy impelled him to hands and knees, and Raven crawled the few feet to the inert form. He felt for a pulse. Nothing. *No, please, no.*

And then, there, so weak he might have imagined it against his fingers. A pause, then another weak beat.

Raven looked over his shoulder to Winter, who sat cross-legged on the ground, shoulders slumped, head drooping. She seemed almost translucent around the edges. Was that an effect of his own fading strength?

"You're a Healer. Save him!"

"He is beyond my help." Winter said in a raspy whisper that sounded too far away. "He is beyond our help."

"No. I can't accept that!" Not another young person dead from Raven's failures.

"He has linked himself to the petroglyphs," Winter said gravely. "The darkness has been driven away, but the raven on the wall must still be healed in order for the world to be safe. It will pull from his life force to heal itself. We can only pray that it will be enough."

"What? Why is it not taking from me, then? I also spilled my blood."

"Yes, but your blood is not tied to the land, to the petroglyphs," Winter said, voice calm and gentle in the face of his panicked rage.

Winter had said something about Morgan having been descended from Blue Deer, who fashioned the petroglyphs which Winter had brought fully into being.

"You brought him here to be sacrificed." And Raven had helped. In his own way, unknowing, Raven had helped. "You are no better than any dark mage."

"Your divisions and your morals are not mine. If you choose to judge me such, then so be it. Morgan came here willingly, gave himself willingly, even as you were willing to lay down your own life in the fight. He was not coerced, as your Daniel was coerced."

Her tone said her words had not been meant as an attack, and yet he flinched under them. "So we should, what? Just sit here and watch him die slowly, and you don't even know for certain if it will work? There has to be some other way."

"I already gave my earthly life force to stop the darkness the first time it came," Winter said. "Remember that I am not truly alive in the same sense that you are."

"There has to be some other way. You said my blood will not do, because I am not related—"

"There is one other way. In some ways our magics are not so different. The technique that you taught your apprentice Daniel to charge the Ravensblood would work as well to charge the raven petroglyph and seal the rift once more. It would be a more certain way of repairing the crack that allowed the darkness to come through and the raven would no longer draw from Morgan to heal itself. If you are in time, Morgan may yet live."

He no longer even bothered to wonder how this returned spirit of a shaman knew about the man who had been Raven's apprentice back when Raven was a dark mage. Daniel had died charging the Ravensblood. Raven was stronger in magic than Daniel, but he had also exhausted the last of his reserves.

"If I do this, I will die as you did," Raven said. "As Daniel did." He would never see Cassandra again. They had thought they had all the time in the world to be together.

"I cannot say for certain," Winter said. "Our situations do not exactly parallel. The petroglyph only needs to be healed this time, not brought into being. And yet I was not as exhausted as you are now when I worked the magic. You might survive still."

"But it is not likely."

"No."

Another thought came to him then, one that scared him worse than death. "If I replicate the method used to charge the Ravensblood, even if I do not die, I will have burned out my magic. I will be functionally a Mundane."

"Nothing is certain," Winter said.

But most likely, yes. His thoughts finished what he did not say. It would be dark magic, as all death magic was, even if the ritual was an act of self-sacrifice. That was nothing he could worry about now. Cassandra would understand. If it mattered to anyone else, they could prosecute his damned corpse.

"You knew it would come to this," Raven accused Winter. "And yet you said nothing."

"I knew it might. Would it have changed any of your decisions had you known earlier?"

He had come already knowing he might well die battling the darkness, and he had been prepared to pay that cost. But to deliberately give his own life in an act of sacrificial magic. . .worse, to risk living a half-life without the magic that defined him. . .He'd like to say that in the end he'd have made the same choices. But he could not swear to it.

At best, it would have been a distraction he could not afford when he had needed all his focus on fighting the darkness.

He hated that Winter was right.

Would there never be an end to the payment owed for his past? But even as he finished the thought, he knew the task he faced had nothing to do with what he did and did not deserve. What mattered was that it had to be done, and he was the only one who could do it.

There was no other choice now, not really. He could not let Morgan die, even if it were certain that Morgan's sacrifice was enough to seal the rift. He did not want to leave Cassandra, leave their son, but he would not be the man that Cassandra had married if he could let another die in his stead.

"I will need to be in physical proximity with the petroglyph to make this work."

"Go, then." Winter said. "I will stay with Morgan. I will feel when the petroglyph has been charged, and I will make sure that the connection separates cleanly so that he can recover without complication."

They were not very far from the cave, but he'd barely made it a few feet to Morgan. A thousand feet might as well be a thousand miles. He made it to his hands and knees. Tried to stand, failed, and fell. And so he crawled forward, cramping muscles screaming at every movement. The jagged rocks bruised his knees and tore at the skin of his hands as he dragged himself forward. Spikes of pain at least kept him conscious as the sun beat down, baking his fevered skin. Now and then a strong spasm ripped through his body, freezing him in place and stealing his breath.

Though magic was a thing of will and spirit, the will and spirit were housed in the body, and one could not abuse one's endurance as he had without physical repercussions. By all rights his mind should not have let him push himself to this extreme, and the tunnel vision that shadowed the edge of his sight told him that he still might faint.

No. He could not allow himself that luxury. Too much depended on this last push. When he no longer could keep to his hands and knees he crept on his belly until he gathered enough strength to push up again.

He couldn't say how long the journey took. The sun was not moving in the sky. It felt like eternity, like if he somehow made it back home everything would be changed, as though he were Thomas Rhymer returning from fairyland. He pushed the thought from his mind. He didn't think he'd be making it home. He'd have to make his peace with that.

He reached the mouth of the cave. Crawled further, reached the spear-carrying warrior and collapsed, panting. The cave floor was cold and it leached the heat from his body. He felt nauseous, and he shivered so hard it *hurt*. Spots swam before his eyes, and he felt momentarily disoriented, as though he were about to fall even though he already lay on the ground.

Shock, he registered distantly, as though the diagnosis was for someone who had nothing to do with him. *Shock from the temperature difference and. . .and. . .*

He was losing focus, and fought to pull his mind together. He was too close to give up now, but his limbs had become too heavy to move and his head ached as though someone had driven an iron spike through it and he *could not move*.

Despair crept over him. Strength of will had its limits, even for the most determined. At some point, the body reached the end of its endurance and failed. He couldn't even crawl. How was he supposed to channel magic?

Almost without volition his hand closed around the silver raven Bran Tarrant had given him. Remembering another cave in which he had nearly died. Only this time there was no dark-skinned, blue-eyed enigma to force-feed him questionable potions.

But then he could feel a warmth, a tingling, as though magic not his own swirled around him. Disconcerting to face unknown magic when he lacked strength to defend if needed, but nothing about this felt dark. It felt like soft desert wind and sun-warmed sand-stone, sounded in his head like a distant, half-heard chant. Something about it tickled his memory. Tarrant? No, that just popped into his head because he had been thinking of the man. It was almost like the signature he'd felt from the warrior petroglyph, yet simultaneously more powerful and less focused. It was as though the earth itself had absorbed the energies of a shamanic people long gone and radiated it back now that it was needed most.

He lay for a few more moments, soaking up power as a rock soaks up heat from the sun. Then he dragged himself to his feet and staggered forward, one hand finding support from the cool, smooth wall of the cave. When the way was no longer lit from the sun outside, he continued on in darkness, not wanting to spare even the tiny flicker of will it would cost him to waken a light globe.

It seemed like a lifetime later before he reached the place where the cracked raven was illuminated by the light that filtered through the hole in the cave ceiling. He knelt before it, palms against the stone. His heart beat slower now, still irregular. A tremor ran through his body as he centered himself, preparing the ritual words in his mind. The words that would act as a focus as he gave the last of himself to the carved bird on the wall.

He didn't feel ready to die. Did anyone feel ready to die, when the end came? Would he rather live on without his magic?

He was glad that the choice ultimately was not his.

Was this how Daniel had felt, that horrible night when his apprentice had charged the Ravensblood? *Daniel, I'm so sorry.*

Raven forced his ragged breaths to steady, just for a moment, just long enough that he could still his mind.

You are not alone. We are with you to the end and beyond.

Winter? But Winter was with Morgan.

The petroglyphs themselves.

Calmness came over him, peace came over him. His sluggish magic surged one last time, he shaped it with words and will and gave it over to the raven on the wall.

A distant rumble started, then grew louder. Thunder? No, it was the rocks of the wall moving, healing the crack in the raven, sealing the place in the ceiling of the cave where it had broken open. Dust drifted down over him, then pebbles and small rocks. Would the cave collapse on him? Cassandra would be sad if they were unable to recover his body.

He was tired, too tired to worry about it. There was nothing but darkness now, but it was the honest darkness of the cave, cool and comforting. It was a good place to sleep at last.

TWENTY-FIVE

Disjointed moments passed through his awareness. Were they dreams? Did the dead dream?

Cassandra's voice talking right beside him. But wasn't she in Portland? It had to be a dream. Unless more time had passed that he realized? Other voices that he recognized. Ana. Mother Crone. Even Rafe once. Was this that thing they talked about where your life passed before your eyes? He'd expected it to happen a lot quicker. But maybe the afterlife was akin to the ceremonial time of trance and minutes, days and hours passed by, backwards, forwards and around. Faster, slower, faster again, and things came and went in ways that made no sense in the real world.

He heard many voices chanting in a language he did not know. Apparently whatever automatic translation that had happened before had gone. He regretted its loss.

At one point, he opened his eyes to glaring white walls and bright light. If this was the afterlife that he was never to too terribly sure about, he didn't think he wanted to spend an eternity here. Maybe the chanting would come back if he closed his eyes? He slipped back into the welcoming darkness before he could manage any further thoughts.

The next time he surfaced, he was awake long enough to hear the muted PA system calling staff to various rooms using medical abbreviations that were their own secret code. So. He was alive, and he was in the hospital. Too tired to formulate an opinion on either of these facts, he slipped away back into sleep.

When he woke again, still alone in the white room, it was to dimmed lights and the steady quiet of the hospital at night that he was all too familiar with from his previous visits. Absolute peaceful silence, broken only by the occasional squeaking of the nurses' rubber soled shoes, loud only by the contrast. His whole body ached as though he had hiked the entire butte and then fallen off the top. Twice.

Cautiously, he reached for his magic. He wasn't strong enough to do anything with it just now, but he needed to feel it, to know it was still there even if he was not strong enough to wield it. This wasn't the first time he'd driven himself to the state of exhaustion, not even the first time he'd pushed to the point of risking his life. When he'd woken on those occasions, his magic had been weak, trickling through him like water sinking through sand, but it was there.

This time he could feel nothing. It wasn't like being behind an anti-magic ward, where he could sense his magic but not touch or shape it. His magic was gone. The magic that since his earliest memories had been as much a part of him as his hearing, his sight, his heartbeat, was gone.

He jerked upright in the bed, tubes and wires tugging on him in protest, muscles screaming at the sudden movement. His chest felt tight, and he realized he was breathing far too fast.

Nurses rushed through the door and clustered about him in a flurry of activity.

"Mr. Ravenscroft, sir, what's wrong?" a slender, dark-skinned young man asked him.

A short, blond woman pressed on his shoulders, urging him to lay down, while a taller brunette confirmed to her colleagues that the all the monitors were going wild.

Raven consciously forced his breathing to slow. Panic helped nothing, even if his magic—no, he couldn't think it, not if he wanted to get himself under control.

"Sorry, I woke up and I—didn't know how I got here."

True enough, if not the reason for his reaction. Senseless, to avoid talking about his loss of magic, when any mage near him who cared to focus on him could feel it, but saying the words would make it more real. Would make him feel as vulnerable as—

As vulnerable as he truly was at the moment.

Short Blond looked over at the brunette. "Call his wife. They finally got her to go back to the bed and breakfast for some sleep a few hours ago."

He should tell them to let Cassandra sleep, but selfishly he wanted, needed to see her.

The man introduced himself as Raj. "I'm an R.N.. We're going to take care of you. You're safe, everything's fine. Your wife and some other Guardians brought you here from the cave. They said to tell you that whatever you did worked. You just need to rest now. Can you just lie back and breathe slowly for me?"

He could. Indeed, he didn't think he could do much else at the moment. The short burst of adrenalin had left him, and his body felt as heavy as if it had been encased in lead. But he couldn't rest until he knew. . .

"Morgan." His voice came out raspy, weak. "Is he—"

"He'll be fine," Raj reassured him. "With some rest, he'll be as good as new. We were able to discharge him yesterday."

"Yesterday? How long have I been out?"

"It's been three days. We weren't sure you were going to make it. We nearly lost you. Probably would have, if we hadn't been able to bring in Ana Greensdowne to work with our staff healers and doctors. You are lucky in your in-laws."

"Very true." Cassandra's aunt had saved his life more than once, in different ways.

"You are very lucky to be alive."

Am I? Every muscle in his body ached. It hurt to move; it hurt to even breathe too deeply. That part was temporary. He'd lived through worse. But to live without his magic was worse than any nightmare forged of his darkest memories. Except to say that he preferred death over a life without magic was to say he would willingly give up the rest of his years ahead with Cassandra, give up watching Ransley grow to adulthood.

It might not be permanent.

It was rare for a mage to lose their powers, as rare as someone surviving a bullet to the brain. Rare enough that not enough evidence existed for a reliable prognosis. There'd been a tale or two of a mage regaining magic, but without any documentation and long enough ago to be more legend than case study.

Who was he without his magic? Once he had been Raven, the feared dark mage, William's right hand. And then Raven the spy,

Raven the reformed dark mage. Raven, Guardian International Investigation's ace in the hole. That last thing, he still could do. Although a mage to his core, he had always been a scholar as well. Much of what he did for GII he could do without magic. He still had the knowledge, the experience, the research instincts. He would just be handing off the information to people who still had magic. Staying home, safe, out of the field, while others went out to face the danger.

Could he live like that?

He would have to. If his magic did not come back, he would have to. The man he had once been would rather have died than lived without magic. Now, he had too much else he could not bear to leave behind without a fight.

Raven slipped back into unconsciousness before Cassandra arrived. When he awoke again, she was in the chair beside him, head pillowed on crossed arms on the edge of his bed. Her brow furrowed, even in sleep.

He tried calling her name, but his throat was dry and his voice weak and all he managed was a groan.

It was enough to wake her, though. Her face erupted in joy, and in that moment he knew that, whatever may or may not have happened leading up to this moment, this was real. No dream could recreate the beauty and the wonder that was Cassandra's smile.

"We found your letter," she said. "I swear, if I weren't so happy to see you alive, I'd kill you myself for going off like that."

He tried to find words to defend himself, but his thoughts were still fuzzy with sleep, and it seemed like too much effort to voice them. Besides, he suspected that, when he could think clearly again, he'd have to admit that she had a point. She usually did.

"When Rafe and I found you in the cave, you were barely breathing. I used healing magic to the last of my strength just to keep your heart beating."

Her eyes were red and puffy, and the dark circles underneath spoke of how little she'd slept in the last three days. He knew she understood why he'd had to do what he did. Just as he understood why she had to put her own life on the line as part of her job. Understanding never made it easier for either of them.

Cassandra filled in the rest of what happened between when he lost consciousness in the cave and when he woke in the hospital. Rafe had had his cell phone with him, though Cassandra had forgotten hers in her panic, and so they'd been able to contact the Sheriff's office. Sheriff Schmidt sent paramedics out with an ambulance so they didn't have to risk a two-person teleport to an unfamiliar hospital. Raven admitted to himself that maybe, just maybe, it was a good idea that GII started insisting their agents started carrying cell phones, though he'd never say as much out loud.

The paramedics had found Morgan, unconscious but stable, on the way to the cave and so he was brought to the hospital as well. He recovered consciousness in less than twelve hours. He was able to give enough details of what happened for GII's PR people. PR could spin the press a palatable story of what happened that skipped over unnecessary details about what was technically dark magic.

As it turned out, he had neither imagined, nor dreamed, Mother Crone, or Ana, nor a circle of chanting shaman. Cassandra's aunt Ana, the most powerful healer he knew, had probably saved Raven's life, but even she was not strong enough to do more than delay the inevitable. Since they had thought the circumstances of his injury had more to do with Craft than with Art, Ana in desperation had contacted Mother Crone. They had worked together until they were nearly exhausted and still it seemed that it would not be enough.

And then a group of Native American craft practitioners showed up, filtered into the room with the barely an introduction, and stood in a circle, chanting. Though it was magic that neither Ana nor Mother Crone recognized, they could feel the strength of it. Feel the intent. Feel it flow into them as electricity flowed from the battery.

They found themselves shaping healing energy in ways that they had never done before, probably would never remember how to do again. It had been enough to stabilize Raven.

The Native Americans filed out with barely a word to any of them. Not only was there no one that Mother Crone recognized, but no one anyone in the hospital had ever seen or heard of before. Perhaps one of them had been drawn by a vision, and called the others. Perhaps it was nothing more otherworldly than that. Or maybe they had come from all times and all places, pulled from across ceremonial time. The hospital had security cameras. They considered passing the film around the local Native American communities, to see if anyone could tell them who to thank. But in the end they didn't. They told themselves it was because they didn't want to intrude, didn't want to identify people who clearly had not wanted to volunteer their identities. More likely it was because the answer would be a little too strange for even a renowned healer and Mother Crone herself to accept.

Raven's hand crept to the silver raven on its chain. As Bran Tarrant had showed him, there were parts of magic that he still did not understand, might never understand. He was beginning to be more at peace with that knowledge.

Cassandra confirmed that the darkness was gone. The spike in violent crime has dropped as suddenly as it started. Devil's Crossing, Bend, Portland, and Seattle, Eugene, everywhere.

Neither of them spoke of the fact that his magic had gone.

It was another day before he could manage to stand and shower by himself, and two days before the healers and doctors agreed to let him at least return to the B&B. He tried, several times, to find even the slightest trace of his magic thrumming somewhere within him. Each time he felt nothing, and each time he felt the weight in his chest grow heavier. He worried about what he would feel when the initial numbness of the loss wore off. Cassandra stayed with him in the cottage, and he had to ask her to trigger the light globe if he did not want to flick the switch for the electric lights Jasmine had installed for Mundane guests.

Eventually he would have to face a decision about putting electric lights and other Mundane conveniences in the house in Portland. Soon he would have to arrange for a car to take him home if he could not teleport. But not yet. He wasn't ready to face that yet.

Raven's physical strength returned a little more each day. One day he was able to walk out and sit on the porch. That night, he thought he felt a stirring of magic, so faint that he might have imagined it. With Cassandra beside him, breathing softly in her sleep, he tried to trigger the light globe on the nightstand beside the bed. It stayed stubbornly dark. The next day he crossed the lawn to visit the pony at the fence. He spent a lot of time talking to the pony about the fears that he would not express to Cassandra.

He had told himself that he was all right, that he would be all right without his magic. Back at the cave, he'd be willing to die if need be to stop the darkness. Willing to live without magic, if that's what the fates decided for him. Faced with the reality, it was much harder to be so brave. Magic was as intrinsic a part of him as his eye color, or his love of opera. Was he even the same man without it?

Would Cassandra, a powerful mage in her own right, want to live the rest of her life bound to a Mundane? He pushed the thought aside as unworthy of him and unfair to Cassandra. After all they had been through together, how could he so doubt their love? Still, a sliver of doubt remained, whispering that he might lose all that he had left, and all of his logic and all of his faith could not quite silence that whisper.

TWENTY-SIX

Rafe came by one night after a dinner date with Scott, bringing a bottle of quite respectable cabernet. "I had brought it with me for after dinner, but we never got to it."

Cassandra looked up from arranging wildflowers in a jar of water on the table. "Hadn't expected to see you until sometime tomorrow."

"Yeah, we cut dinner short and decided not to go back to his place," Rafe said.

Raven bit down on his *good riddance*. Best let Cassandra handle the conversation.

Cassandra managed a neutral "Oh?"

"We, uh, had a discussion about how some things were handled. An argument really." His gaze flicked to Raven and away, and Raven suspected that the argument had something to do with Morgan.

Cassandra handed Rafe the glass of wine she had just poured. He took a generous swallow before continuing.

"Scott started going off about how Sheriff Schmidt had endangered Morgan in the hostage situation—"

"Is the man mad?" Raven said. "There is no way that whole scenario could have been anticipated. Craig went above and beyond by bringing me in. Were it not for his flexibility and dedication, we would have never gotten out of that standoff without a dead hostage, and maybe dead officers as well."

"Unfortunately Scott doesn't see it that way. He thought if Schmidt's men hadn't pursued Heilman, he wouldn't have felt the need to take a hostage."

"Heilman was a loose cannon," Raven said. "He'd already killed his family. And probably Morgan's parents as well, forensics haven't finished with that one yet. Craig and his deputies couldn't just let him going around with a loaded gun. Who knows who would be next on his list?"

"Hey, I'm not arguing," Rafe said. "Anyway, he thought it was irresponsible of the sheriff to bring in an *amateur*—his word, not mine, trust me—and thought that Heilman needed mental health help, not police involvement. So, yeah, we had words. And then he was blaming you for endangering a minor civilian up by the butte—"

Raven snorted. "I did everything in my power to keep Morgan out of it. I think your Scott needs to decide whether I'm an *amateur* or part of the evil establishment."

"He's not my Scott," Rafe said. "And after tonight, he's really not my Scott."

Raven raised his glass in Rafe's direction. "Here's to better luck next time. You really do deserve better."

Now he would never have to admit that he had worried about Rafe's association with Scott.

He tried the light globe again that night. He tried it again the next morning while Cassandra was in the shower, and again in the afternoon when she teleported into town to pick up some meat and cheese from the deli. His efforts resulted in a fierce headache and a still-dark light globe. Raven's first memories were of turning on the light globe in the nursery from his crib. He wasn't sure he was even walking then. Literally a lifetime of magic, studying, practicing, training, now gone.

The headache lasted into the night. The next morning, he resolved to try one last time. Swore to himself that he would leave it alone after that and resign himself to life as a Mundane. Pain sliced through his skull, ruining his focus, but he thought he saw the globe flicker just a bit. Had he imagined it, as he had perhaps imagined feeling his magic return?

He didn't try the globe again immediately for fear of exhausting what little strength he had remaining. But that night, with Cassandra asleep, he tried again. The light globe flickered, went dark, and then came to life, shedding soft light over Cassandra's sleeping form. She made a face in her sleep and snuggled closer to him, hiding her eyes against the light.

Just a light globe, nothing like the power he used to wield. No reason to get too excited. Or so he tried to tell himself, as he lay awake, heart pounding in joy despite the headache pressing against his skull from the inside.

The sheriff stopped in to visit the following afternoon. He brought the news that the Jansens' family lawyer, with the aid of some interns Alexander Chen had loaned her, was well on the way to getting the parents' estate settled, and in the meantime had managed to free up enough capital for Morgan to meet the day-to-day needs of the farm. One of the neighbors had loaned Morgan an RV to live in until the house could be rebuilt.

"After word went out about what he did on the butte," Craig said, "a lot more folks are feeling like he really did deserve that much, and more. Thinking about a fundraising night at the Devil's Pitchfork for whatever insurance doesn't cover on the rebuild."

LansingCorp had declared bankruptcy and abandoned any plans for a golf resort. However, there was a coalition made up of archeologists, the local tribes, and the Devil's Crossing Chamber of Commerce working on plans for a museum and interpretive center that would bring in both research grants and tourist dollars in a way that did not threaten the local environment, the character of the town, or any nearby sites of cultural or historical significance.

"They've started planning a powwow next summer to draw publicity and maybe attract donors," Craig said. "The powwow alone will be good for the town. Bring in tourist dollars, and bring some life to the place."

Raven imagined the dry, empty land echoing with drums and songs, and brightened by the vivid feathers and beads of the fancy dancers. Perhaps they should come back then with the entire household. He wanted Ransley to grow up exposed to broader and more varied cultural experiences than he had been. While he never expected to be the type of parent who had to bring a nanny on vacation, it seemed like something Tony would enjoy, so why not?

Raven and Cassandra were sitting on the porch swing, enjoying the sunset, when Morgan came to visit. He carried a basket containing jars of homemade blackberry and raspberry jams and some flowers from the garden. His mother had taught him well. Raven invited him to sit down, and Cassandra made some excuse to go inside so that they could talk privately.

Morgan sat on the artfully-distressed wooden chair in the corner of the porch, facing the swing. "Just stopping by to see how you're doing."

"I feel like I should be asking you that." Raven said.

"Hey, I got out of the hospital in just under two days. You were there for a week."

That wasn't what Raven meant, and surely Morgan knew that. But if he wished to avoid the topic of his parents; that was his choice to make and Raven would respect that.

"Whatever Winter did up by the butte more than saved my life," Morgan added. "She sped up the healing somehow. I felt her give up the last of her ghost, her spirit-self. Whatever you call it. She will never return to this plane in any form." He took a deep breath. "At least it appears to have not been in vain. The healers and the Mundane doctors both were amazed at what she had accomplished."

"I'm glad," Raven said. "I'm not sure you realize how close you came to dying."

"Believe me, I realize," Morgan said in all seriousness. Then he smirked. "You still mad at me?"

"If nearly killing yourself didn't teach you anything, then my disapproval would surely do nothing." Raven said. "To be honest, we might not be here to have this conversation without your assistance at the butte, and so I'm not certain I would have the right to disapprove."

Morgan gave a boyish grin, reminding Raven of just how young he really was. "So you're saying I was right."

Raven hid a smile at the cocksure tone. "I didn't use those words."

"You didn't have to."

"So how are things going otherwise?" Raven kept the question deliberately vague, not certain how comfortable Morgan felt talking about the traumatic events that preceded that day on the butte.

He had to ask, though. Had to let Morgan know that if he wanted to talk, Raven was there to listen. If Morgan was struggling, if he needed any kind of help, Raven would make sure that he got it.

Morgan took a deep breath before answering. "It's rough," he admitted. "No point in pretending otherwise. They say the pain fades in time, until only the good memories are left. I'm not sure I believe that, but I'm holding onto it anyway. Not sure I could get through day by day if I didn't. But the neighbors have been great. The Armstrongs down the road, they stepped in and took care of the horses until I could pull myself together enough to manage. Even now Mrs. Armstrong finds an excuse to call every day, or send one of her kids around, just to make sure I'm okay. Sheriff Schmidt put me in touch with a Unitarian minister from down the road in Barnett. I mean, I'm not religious. Mom and Dad weren't, either. But they did believe that there was something out there, beyond what we can see and feel, beyond our own magic. And, well, having met Winter, I could hardly deny that there's something after death."

Raven's own experiences with necromancy had brought him to the same conclusion at about the same age. He was glad that Morgan was coming to it in a better way.

"Anyway, Mr. Wojinsky, that's the minister, has met with me a couple times for counseling. He's not trying to push any of that God stuff on me. Well I guess he wouldn't. Not the Unitarian thing. He said sometimes it helps to talk and it has."

"I'm glad," Raven said. He was glad that Morgan had someone to talk to, and even more glad he didn't have to try to be that person, for both their sakes. "Any thoughts for the future? It's not too late to think about college."

"I know that. I'm looking into some online courses. Going away to college isn't really in the cards right now, what with being the only one to take care of the farm now."

"Couldn't you sell it?"

"Oh, I could. It would more than pay for college, even after the mortgages are paid. But the breeding program, that was Mom's dream. Producing old-style working horses with real solid temperaments. And I, I guess I'd miss the horses anyway. I mean it was different when I planned to go to college knowing the horses were back here when I came back on breaks, but to have them completely out of my life. . ." Morgan shook his head.

Raven had heard that horses were for some people like the magic was to him. Could never understand it, but it wasn't his to understand.

"Maybe someday, when I start getting older. If I find someone who believes in the bloodlines to take over. But not now. Not for a long time. And that's okay."

Raven wasn't enthusiastic about the idea of Morgan putting off a serious focus on his education, but it was understandable after all that he had been through. More than understandable. Still, it couldn't hurt to keep the boy focused on his future.

"Have you thought at all about areas of study?"

Morgan's eyes lit up. "I have, as a matter of fact. After everything that's happened, well the good stuff that's happened. . .The cave, the petroglyphs, Winter, it's all made me think I want to learn more about anthropology."

"Not the magic? You were quite impressive out on the Butte. You have aptitude, and I don't say that to everyone."

Morgan shook his head. "Oh, I'll always be a mage. Art is in my soul. But to practice seriously, like I would have to if it were my profession, that started to lose it shine after I made my mistake with Matthew Brock. And maybe it makes me a coward, but I just as soon not face dying again anytime soon."

Raven smiled. "It doesn't make you a coward. It probably means you're wiser than I. So. Anthropology?"

"Yeah." Morgan blushed a little, like he was confessing an ambition to become a rock star. "After what Winter sacrificed to save my life, I want to make it count for something. I've even talked to the people organizing the interpretive center. They said that that they'd be proud to have one of the heroes of the butte on board with the project. I don't know, I don't feel particularly heroic, but it's a nice change from everyone thinking of me as a murderer. They seem to think a part-time internship is impossible. I either have to work around the hours I need to spend at the ranch, or else do something remote online, but we can work all that out in the future."

It was the first time in their short acquaintance that Raven had heard Morgan speak of the future with enthusiasm. It might even be the first time he heard Morgan speak of the future as if he believed he had any future at all.

"You know anthropology and magic aren't mutually exclusive," Raven said. "And you don't have to be a professional—or risk your life—to further your studies in the Art. There's a mage I've read about. Her father is Nez Perce, and she's been studying the way pre-European shamanism actually overlapped with both Art as well as Craft." Raven had come across articles by Laura Hawkweed while researching petroglyphs. "I understand she's looking for apprentices, and her cousin is PA to Cassandra's aunt. Let me know if you want her to put in a good word."

"I'll think about it," Morgan said.

Whether Morgan followed up or not, Raven was going to look into whether Ms. Hawkweed needed any financial assistance for her research. Raven found the loss of magical techniques morally offensive, but recent experiences led to a practical interest in seeing the revival of lost Native magical knowledge in particular.

"And Morgan, if you ever need anything, and I do mean *anything*, let me know."

Morgan met his eyes. "I will."

And Raven felt confident that he would. Confident that Morgan understood. It would not be a stranger's charity. After what they went through at the butte, there was a bond between them stronger than blood.

A week after that, he had enough strength to teleport to the sheriff's bar, where he was hailed as a hero by the staff and the patrons alike. He still got headaches when he used magic, but they were getting better. It was a price he was more than willing to pay.

Craig insisted on treating him to prime rib on the house, and Raven ordered a side of those seasoned curly potato things that he grudgingly admitted having developed a fondness for. By the time he finished the meal, the sheriff had brought out a celebratory slice of chocolate decadence torte. He had to have sent one of the waitresses down to the bakery to get it, as it was not on the menu.

His dinner at the Devil's Pitchfork was the most he had eaten at one sitting in a long time, way more than he eaten since waking up from the cave. He'd split the dessert with Cassandra and Rafe. He hadn't asked why the latter was still hanging out in Devil's Crossing. Had he stayed to support Cassandra, or was he really that worried about Raven?

A partial answer came when the sheriff walked out from behind the bar to speak with them. Rafe slung an arm over the sheriff's shoulders, and before returning to the bar, the sheriff gave Rafe a kiss that bordered on inappropriate for a public space. When Raven raised an eyebrow at his wife's work partner, Rafe merely gave him a cocky grin in return.

"Someone works fast," Raven said.

Rafe chuckled. "Well, I had to do something to keep myself occupied while you were sleeping. I came in here for dinner on my own a few times after Scott and I broke things off. Craig came over to keep me company. It turned out I got along a lot better with him."

"I see that," Raven said.

How Rafe was going to make things work with the sheriff, given the distance, was not any of Raven's business. Although he imagined there was going to be a lot of teleporting in Rafe's future, and he would be seeing the sheriff hanging about Portland as well. He couldn't say he was sorry.

Thank you for reading Raven's Shade. If you liked this book, please consider leaving a review on Amazon and/or Goodreads. Not only will you be helping an author with sales, you will be helping your fellow readers in finding books they might enjoy.

More books by this author in the Ravensblood series:

Ravensblood

Raven's Song (novella)

Raven's Wing

Raven's Heart

Raven's Vow

Books by this author in the Werewolves and Gaslight Mysteries:

A Hunt by Moonlight

Moon over London

Other books by this author:

Brother to the Wolf

Where Light Meets Shadow

The Stolen Luck

Made in the USA
Middletown, DE
10 March 2021